# WATCH ME GO

# WATCH ME GO

## Mark Wisniewski

G.P. PUTNAM'S SONS
NEW YORK

G. P. PUTNAM'S SONS
*Publishers Since 1838*
Published by the Penguin Group
Penguin Group (USA) LLC
375 Hudson Street
New York, New York 10014

USA · Canada · UK · Ireland · Australia
New Zealand · India · South Africa · China

penguin.com
A Penguin Random House Company

Portions of this novel have appeared, in slightly different form, in *The Antioch Review, The Best
American Short Stories 2008, The Virginia Quarterly Review,* and *The Idaho Review.*

Library of Congress Cataloging-in-Publication Data

Wisniewski, Mark S., date.
Watch me go / Mark Wisniewski.
p.    cm.
ISBN 978-0-399-17212-0
1. False imprisonment—Fiction.  2. Jockeys—Fiction.  3.  Murder—Investigation—
Fiction.  4. Organized crime—Fiction.  I. Title.
PS3573.I8773W38    2015                2014026895
813'.54—dc23

Printed in the United States of America
1   3   5   7   9   10   8   6   4   2

BOOK DESIGN BY STEPHANIE HUNTWORK

For Elizabeth

# WATCH ME GO

# Prologue

AMONG DOUGLAS "DEESH" SHARP'S well-guarded thoughts was the idea that his public defender, Lawrence Gerelli, might win more often if he'd now and then iron a shirt. Worse, Gerelli had a tendency to show his hand by letting himself go sour-faced, and here Gerelli was, doing that again as he sat across the table in the small white room and said, "Mostly, Mr. Sharp? You have a belief problem."

"As in you don't believe me?" Deesh asked.

"As in we need twelve jurors to believe you, and they're going to be hard to find."

"So you're saying plea bargain."

"The plea bargaining's already begun, Mr. Sharp. The prosecution here in the Bronx is talking about sending you back to Pennsylvania—where, unlike here, people are still relatively comfortable with the death penalty."

And there was that sour face again, and Deesh found himself leaning back in his folding chair to say, "Man, *nobody* gets to twelve without first having two in this room."

Gerelli began gathering his notes and electronics. "I'm late for an arraignment," he said. He snapped closed and yanked up his briefcase. "You want life here in New York, Mr. Sharp, just say the word and I'll bust my ass to get that for you." He glared at Deesh, who glared back. "You still want to go for broke, we'll talk about building cases next time." He walked out, and the door swung closed.

And right away, Deesh felt less alone. He flattened his hands beside the bolted steel ring his wrists were cuffed to. He appreciated this small white room, its cleanliness and brightness, the safety implied by its particular silence.

Then, from behind the room's white door, there was a cough. And a knock. The door opened, and just behind the guard stood someone short, so this wasn't who Deesh had hoped—it wasn't his son—and the guard stepped aside and Deesh saw the face, a woman's face, a way-too-fine, almost dollish face on a very short, white, deeply suntanned young woman whose curves struck Deesh as impossibly sweet, too.

"Who the hell is this?" he asked the guard.

"She signed in," the guard said.

The cop's wife? Deesh thought, but the woman eyed the handcuffs so intently there was no way she hung with cops. Deesh felt himself holding his breath while she stood behind the chair Gerelli had left, braced as if she were set to run off if need be.

"So you're the infamous Deesh," she said, in her own kind of sadness.

"All day."

"I'm Jan Price."

"Means nothing to me."

"I knew Tom Corcoran personally," she said, as if this explained everything. "The jockey," she added. "And there are things about his gambling I can testify about."

Bullshit, Deesh wanted to say, but she looked away quickly, at one of the bright white walls, brow knitted, maybe about to cry, maybe not.

She said, "But I need to know you didn't kill those other two guys."

She kept on looking at that wall.

"I didn't kill anyone," Deesh said, and he knew, given his experience with whites this beautiful, that right about now was when the ugliness in her would show.

"Then why are you in here?" she asked.

Her eyes met his, but he was already shaking his head, as if to suggest that, no, he would not have this conversation, though now here he was, also asking, "Isn't that obvious?"

And she said, "No."

He raised a cuffed forearm, pointed at it best he could.

"But Deesh," she said, "you're not the only black guy out there. I mean, for some reason, they arrested *you*. And what's eating me up is that I happen to know that, when it comes to Tom Corcoran, you're as innocent as a colt learning to walk. But if you're a killer anyway, why should I help you?"

And it was only now that Deesh realized he could actually care about this woman—in that same solid way he'd once cared about his state champion teammates—because here he was, saying to her, "Ms. Price, you're asking me to tell you a very long story."

And she said, "Not necessarily, Deesh. I'm asking you to tell me the truth."

# 1

# DEESH

NINE TIMES OUT OF TEN it's a woman who calls Bark to answer his classified ad in the Westchester *Pennysaver*, and sometimes when we pull up to her yard in his pickup, she's outside waiting for us. Sometimes she even has something inside for us to eat, which, besides needing money, is why James and I never ask Bark if he wants our help. We just get in his truck and hope he lets us go.

But the truth, Jan, is that on the morning he drives us north of Poughkeepsie, no woman, or anyone, is waiting outside. Maybe this has to do with the five hundred dollars this woman offered—she doesn't feel the need to be friendly beyond that. Or maybe she's with the junk that needs to be hauled. Anyway Bark pulls off the country road into her driveway, which drops through her uncut lawn toward her shabby yellow house, and we all get out, Bark headed to knock on her front door.

"Hey," I hear from the left-hand side of the house, and I turn but see no one. "Down here," the voice calls, and there, crouched near an open crawl space hole, is a woman about as dark as me, maybe five years older.

"Over here, Bark," I shout, and Bark makes his way down the porch, then over to her, James and I lagging behind to let her know he's boss.

"I took care of the rest myself," she says, and Bark kneels beside her, then pokes his head and a good half of him into the crawl space. He stays in there for a while, making sure, I figure, that we can do what needs doing. Then he's back out, and he stands, slapping dirt off his knees.

"Just that oil drum?" he says.

"Yeah," she says.

"I thought you said there was a bunch of stuff," he says.

"No," she says. "Just that."

"What's in it?" he asks.

"I have no idea," she says, but she's scratching her arm and keeps scratching it; if she's not flat-out lying, she's more than a little nervous.

"Because the thing is," Bark says, "I can't just take a drum like that to a dump without them asking what's inside."

"Then don't take it to a dump," she says. "Just, you know, get rid of it."

Bark grabs his unshaven jaw, considering. Probably he's stumped by why a sister is living more than an hour north of the city; plus it doesn't make much sense that *any* woman living in a house this shabby could have five hundred dollars, let alone give it to us to haul off a drum with nothing bad in it. It crosses my mind this woman loves some guy who's given her five hundred to get rid of the drum, some dude, maybe a white one, that she has it bad for and cheated with—and that inside the drum is this man's wife. But all kinds of things are crossing my mind, including how I could use five hundred dollars divided by three.

"How 'bout a thousand?" the woman says.

Here's where all of us, including her, gaze off at her uncut lawn, the dandelions and weeds in it, some of them pretty enough to call flowers. We gaze our separate ways for a long time, letting whatever truth of what's going on sink into us while we play as if it isn't, and I feel my guts work their way higher toward my lungs, threatening to stay there if Bark agrees. But there's a lot I could do with my share of a thousand, especially since I'm used to walking away from these jobs with fifty at most. I could eat more than apples and white bread and ham. I could start saving for a truck of my own—to haul things for pay myself.

Then, to the woman, Bark says, "In cash?"

"As soon as that drum's in your truck," she says.

Bark glances at James, who nods.

"Deesh?" Bark asks me, and I know he's working me over with his eyes, using them to try to convince me in their I-don't-care-either-way manner, but what I'm watching is the woman's feet, which are the tiniest bit pigeon-toed. They are also perfectly still, which could mean she's no longer nervous, but my eyes, I know, are avoiding her fingers and arms. Still, the sight of those pigeon-toed feet has me giving her the benefit of the doubt, maybe because I once had it bad—really bad—for someone who stood like that.

"Why not?" I answer. I haven't, I tell myself, actually said yes, but when I look up, James is following Bark into the crawl space, the woman checking me out.

"Sure appreciate it," she says, in the flat way of someone who's been with enough men to deal with us no problem. But now she's scratching her collarbone—over and over she's scratching it, without one bug bite on her. There's death in that drum, I think, but with her pigeon-toed feet aimed at me, I fall even more in love.

Then she walks off, toward a creek behind her house, and it hits me that if I want my share of the thousand, I should get my ass in that crawl space, since the actual removal of the drum might take but five minutes—and the last thing I need is Bark and James saying I don't deserve a cent. Then I realize that if I don't take a cent I might not be guilty of any crime that's going on here. But wisdom like that helps only if you're not desperate for cash, plus I need to be in Bark's truck to get home, and even before I'm done thinking all this I'm on my hands and knees, my head brushing morning glory vines, then on its way through the square opening in the foundation of the woman's house.

It's quiet in there, and it stinks. James and Bark are on their bellies, snaking their way over damp dirt and rocks toward the drum, which lies on its side in the far corner. With the thousand in mind, I work myself toward them, trying to get a hand on the drum when they do—but Bark yells, "We got it, Deesh."

"What are you saying?" I ask.

"I'm saying this is a two-man job, so back off."

"You trying to cut me out of my share."

"No. It's just there ain't enough room for all three of us if we want to get this thing past us."

"So what do you want me to do?"

Bark humps up his backside, reaches into a front pocket, pulls out his keys, tosses them toward me. "Pull the truck down the driveway," he says. His hands dig dirt away from the drum. "As close to the house as you can," he says.

"Bark," I say. "I haven't driven in fifteen years."

"You'll remember," he says. "Just start it, put it in gear, and steer so you don't hit nothing."

"Okay," I say, though Bark's confidence in me has taken away the little I have in myself. I used to have confidence—gold confidence—but the older I get, I have less. Still, I back myself out of the crawl space, pretend the woman isn't watching as I jog up the driveway to Bark's truck, hop inside it, start it, put it in drive and let it roll down there. Steering is easy, but when I put on the brake, I about fly through the windshield. The woman, still near the creek, has her arms folded now, and again she's checking me out. There's that kind of thing between us, that curiosity about each other we'd ruin with conversation, and I want to make love to her bad.

Now Bark and James are yanking the drum top first through the hole in her foundation; the drum is too wide to roll out. They struggle like hungry playground kids—whatever's in that thing is dumb heavy. Wind blows past my face, the woman now picking a weed's blue flower from between pebbles beside the creek. It's her husband in the drum, I think. She got carried away in an argument over nothing and the thousand is all they ever saved.

"Deesh," Bark calls to me. "Gonna help us or not?"

I nod, toss him his keys, which he catches like it's the old days. I walk toward him and James, and all three of us roll the drum to the driveway, flattening a strip of knee-high grass, acting like we haul mystery drums every day. This one is the rusted old orange you'd expect, but its new yellow lid has barely a scratch or a smudge on it, and as we team up near Bark's tailgate and lift on the count of three, we take extra care to keep the lid on. Dead weight, I think as we lower the works onto the bed. If this isn't a corpse, she would have said so.

# 2

# JAN

**WHAT I WOULD TELL A JURY** from the get-go, Deesh, is that pretty much all of the horse folk you find at the Finger Lakes racetrack, not just the Corcorans, have long lived and breathed horseracing. For instance for pretty much all of my twenty-two years, certainly ever since I was the gossiped-about, shabbily dressed girl born to the reticent single mother in Pine Bluff, Arkansas, my dream had been to ride the fastest of thoroughbreds in upstate New York, seeing as that's what my father did when he was still alive.

A jury would also need to know that thoroughbred racing often comes down to the keeping and telling of secrets. Matter of fact, for my entire life—until just a few months ago—all my mother had ever told me about my father's death was that it happened three weeks before I was born, and that he had drowned well upstate from here, in a tangle of sun-bleached weeds near a shoreline owned by Tom Corcoran and his wife, Colleen. And that because of all this we were poor to the point that we should be grateful for her job working the counter at the Rexall on Main in Pine Bluff.

See, it wasn't until the night before my mother and I left Arkansas to head for that lake—because the Rexall was forced to close thanks to a Walmart Supercenter two miles up Main—that she let me in on details beyond those. Like how when the search party of sheriffs and wardens and divers gaffed my father's corpse, one of his legs was wrapped twice with thick black fish line leading to a huge prehistoric-looking fish. Like how this fish was a muskellunge— or, as people upstate would put it, a "muskie." How this particular muskie was a monster, easily six feet long. How this muskie then lay in a sheriff's outboard like guilt in the guts of a killer, and then, after the sheriff took photos, was dropped into the lake for dead by my mother, who, as soon as she headed off toward the Corcorans' house, heard a splash and turned—only to see the muskie's tail propel it back into those sun-bleached weeds.

"It was like that fish was death itself saying *'See y'all later'*" was how my mother put it, her point, I figured, being that I should remember that I, too, will die, that therefore I should follow her footsteps when it comes to things like religion and sticking to the straight and narrow.

But that's getting more into me and my mother rather than Tom Corcoran's death.

What I'm trying to say is that people out there need to know that tragic death and gruesome injuries and need of all sorts (not just financial) and gambling and welshing and debt and vengeful violence have long, long been a way of life around the Finger Lakes racetrack.

People out there should also know that my father's death left my mother so depressed and anxious she will never board an airplane. And that, as she and I plunked our butts down in a nasty coachline bus for the thirty-four hours of drudgery between Arkansas and upstate New York, I was under the false impression that I'd stay with her in the Corcorans' house for a few weeks to better understand my father's life and death and legacy, but that, after I'd proven my fearlessness about all that, I'd move someplace where my own life could flourish, maybe someplace west or overseas.

I actually believed that then. I believed New York State would be only a place to visit. Somewhere in Kentucky, though, my mother began talking bluntly. And telling me things as though I were a normal adult rather than the daughter of a sex-deprived widow enamored of preachers. Things like how my father had gotten tangled up in those sun-bleached weeds in the middle of the day—not long at all after he'd sipped wine to relax himself to sleep. Things like how for a month or so just before he drowned, he tried to sleep as much as he could, to fight the impatience he felt while fishing, a pastime he'd adopted because owners weren't letting him ride mounts on account of his recent failures to win.

Things like how these failures to win were thanks to a spill he'd taken on the homestretch just before the finish line, a spill that caused a yelp from him to reach the grandstand when his left hand was trampled, so that now the bones inside were just tiny pieces floating in an ugly swollen-up mush; like how his last day was a Tuesday covered by clouds shaped like toadfrogs, and how Tom Corcoran was the last person to see my father alive.

Tom Corcoran—or so my mother said on that bus ride—had jocked more than his share of horses that lost, and back then he was past the middle of his career and putting on weight, so he'd jog twelve miles every Tuesday, the dark day at the Finger Lakes track.

And on my father's last morning, Tom woke and put on his sweats and looked out his bedroom window toward the lake and saw my father sitting near the shoreline, leaning against a young crab apple tree. Resting against the other side of that tree was a bottle of port wine, which Tom thought odd, since my father had always told apprentices never to drink before sunset. Tom then headed down to that shoreline to say hello, but as it turned out didn't say boo because my father was fast asleep, with one-hundred-pound-test black nylon fish line not only cast out into the lake but also wrapped around his ankle.

And see, Tom *knew* why that ankle was wrapped with that fish line: My father had already tried tying cast fish line to the trunk of the crab apple tree—so as to leave a baited hook out in the lake overnight—only to return the following morning to find the line snapped by what had to have been a huge muskie.

Tom considered tapping my father's shoulder, to wake him and ask if he wanted to study the *Form*'s freshest charts, but he didn't touch my father at all, because my father hadn't done a single thing right at the track since that cavalry charge of hoofs had mangled his hand.

But all these details about my father's death, as well as any lessons they held about the effects of drinking, were *not*, my mother told me, as important as my future, and my future, she promised, would *not* require that I live in upstate New York forever. I'd need to stay there merely as long as it took to get our feet on the ground moneywise, which the Corcorans, who my mother had kept in touch with on and off, had been generous enough to offer to help us do. And let me just say something that I think every public defender should mention to just about any jury: If you ever wonder why people do twisted things, just remember that, more often than not, it comes down to someone losing or needing or otherwise wanting money.

Anyway wouldn't you know that, right then, my mother added her "little" kicker detail about the Corcorans. About the fact that they had a son named Tug, who'd recently turned twenty-two just like me, and who now managed a horse farm on their acreage while he saved for college tuition.

A spoiled smarty-pants, I thought, but to be polite given all those stuck-on-a-bus miles ahead of us, I took enough interest to ask, "This farm is for racehorses?"

"Can't say I know for sure," she said. "When it comes to race-horses, Tom Corcoran tends to hold his cards pretty close to his vest."

# 3

# DEESH

**BARK SLAMS THE TAILGATE CLOSED**, works his toolbox and
scrap wood to make sure the drum won't move. No way are we taking it to the dumps we sometimes hit, even the unguarded one that
isn't supposed to be a dump. The woman has her back to us, facing
the creek. I'll never see her again, but I need to. Finally she walks
toward the crawl-space hole, hooks its screen window back onto
it, and heads into the house. While she's inside, James flicks a
horsefly off his neck. She returns and walks toward us with her lips
pursed. She's even finer-looking with sunshine on her face. She
gives Bark a handful of cash folded in half. He counts it, mostly
twenties, then nods, slips it into his shirt pocket, and says, "Anything else?"

"Nope," she says.

"Any ideas about where we should take it?" he says.

"That's your business," she says. "Anyone asks me, I never seen that drum in my life."

"Right," Bark says, and the way he gets in his truck—without a handshake or a good-bye or even a nod—tells me he wishes we could just roll the drum back down the lawn and give back the cash. But he starts the engine, lets it eat gas while James and I get in beside him, me in the middle. After we back up and ease out onto the road, I notice the woman's gone—inside her house, I guess. And we're not backtracking to return to the Bronx. Instead we're headed north. Farther upstate. Two miles an hour under the speed limit, none of us making a sound. The radio's off.

I think to ask Bark where we're going, but it's like the three of us have made a side deal not to talk. And if anyone's going to break that deal, I'm guessing, it'll be James, but James doesn't say jack, and neither do Bark and I the whole time we cruise over tar-striped highways zigzagging us toward tree-covered hills. I imagine it'll take hours to reach those trees, and maybe it does, but maybe it doesn't because my gazing at them helps me remember Madalynn, this tall, willowy woman from my past and Bark's, that one and only woman I ever had it bad for, and when we're finally alongside the shadows of those trees, I'm all worked up about lovemaking with her. Behind us in Bark's truck bed is, as far as I know, only one shovel, and damn if I'll be the one to use it. We pass a farmhouse, a line of crammed-together mailboxes, a boarded-up gas station where a rusted sign reminds us of when unleaded was $1.44. Bark is scanning the bushy fields on either side of us, trying, I can tell by his grimace, to be more smart than scared.

We pass a state park with no one in the guard station. Then Bark is speeding down a straightaway. There's no one around us, from what I can tell, but no place for the drum. Then Bark brakes and pulls over. There's a hill to our right, but it's a football field away. "How 'bout here?" he asks.

"Where?" James says.

"Yeah," I say. "Where?"

"Right next to the road."

"Are you high?" I say.

"Got any better ideas?" Bark says.

"Someplace more hidden," I say, and for the first time ever, I wish New York was one of those middle-of-nowhere states. "With trees."

"*You're* high," Bark says. "The last thing we need is someone up here seeing three brothers walking out of some woods. They'll follow the truck. They'll read my license plate. We get out now—without any cars passing us—and roll it out quick and take off, there's no way anyone can trace anything to us."

"Then let's do it," James says. "Fast," he says, and he's out his door. And Bark is out his. And again I tell myself I'm with them anyway, so I might as well make sure I get paid. James can't lower the tailgate so Bark slaps away his hand and lowers it himself, and they roll out the drum, and I do what I can to help, though all I manage is to get my fingers on the thing two seconds before they drop it on the weedy emergency lane. I roll it farther still from the road, over a small rise and into a shallow gulley. It gets stuck against a rock surrounded by mud, and that new yellow lid now feels slightly loose, but Bark and James are back in the truck—and behind me, on the highway, a car is coming. I think to run, then undo my fly as if I'm about to piss, using this as an excuse to turn my face as the car passes, honking its horn.

It doesn't stop, though. It's two white women in a Prius, speeding to wherever. When I get back in the truck, Bark says, "What you do that for?"

"To take their eyes off the drum," I say.

"That was *stupid*," James says.

"I don't think so," I say.

"He might be right," Bark tells James. Bark waits until the speeding car, shrinking ahead of us down that straightaway, is out of sight, and I decide not to mention that the lid felt loose—they'd blame *me* for it. Bark glances behind us, U-turns, and takes off in the direction we came from. Now, with the drum gone, James starts talking as if he has to make up for everything we all three didn't say since we left the woman's house, asking why we did it, asking why *he* did it, saying we should have thought it over, should have discussed it in the privacy we had to ourselves in the crawl space—one of us, he says, should have put a foot down to keep all of us from losing our heads.

"We could have said no!" he shouts. "But we had to be greedy. We got all stupid for bad money!"

# 4

# JAN

THERE ARE PLENTY OF OTHER THINGS about Tom Corcoran
any jury you face should know, things I learned in confidence because, for a stretch of some very intense days just a few weeks ago,
Tug Corcoran opened up to me like a man possibly falling in love.

Things like how, on the very same morning my mother and I
were on that crowded bus headed upstate to spend this summer
with the Corcorans, Tug walked through his parents' woods to his
horse farm, then saw that Silent Sky, the only horse boarded in his
care then, was gone.

Things like how he also then noticed a hole in his horse farm's
fence wide enough to roll a tank through.

And like how Silent Sky herself had never been a bolter, never
as much as glanced whenever Tug had opened the gate to tend to
her, so the question that not only appeared in Tug's mind but then

seemed destined to stay was: What—or who—had prompted Silent Sky to leave?

And see, Tug first tried to convince himself that Silent Sky's owner, Jack Silverton, had taken her on the sly so he could euthanize her to cut expenses. But Jack Silverton had money—old, endlessly flowing money—as well as a soft spot for thoroughbreds, a soft spot that competed with Tug's own.

So even before Tug finished jogging across the meadow toward the hole, he suspected Tom Corcoran of having something to do with this. He hated suspecting his own father, but if his father had taken Silent Sky to sell her for cash to gamble with? Well, he damned sure hated that, too.

And see, there was no denying the fence had been vandalized. Two birch-log planks had been cracked clear through, another yanked out toward the woods. Leading away from Tug were barshoe hoofprints, wide enough to assure him they'd been made by Silent Sky's flat, spread-out turf hoof, and just before the hole the hoofprints were all crowded up, meaning she'd stopped to resist whoever had haltered her and led her out.

Then Tug heard "What the hell?"—and there, across the meadow near the path through the woods, stood his father, the same Tom Corcoran known to local gamblers as the retired jock who still hung around the track and couldn't, for the life of him, contain his will to win big. Since Tom had retired from riding, there'd been plenty of moments like that moment right then: when the sight of Tom, a man who struggled to care for his family because his first love was to gamble, would irk the hell out of Tug. But there'd been plenty of worse moments, too, moments when Tom's presence had made Tug want to strangle the man, like when Tug's mother would ask Tom a favor and Tom wouldn't pay her any mind, or when Tom would second-guess a bet he'd lost, or when Tug had gotten all charged up talking about his dreams about breeding champions on his horse farm and Tom would interrupt to say how proud he'd feel when Tug would finally leave the house for law school.

But like the good son he'd always tried to be, all Tug did now was calm himself. Though then there he was, saying directly to Tom, "Whoever kicked those logs was either large or fairly strong. Or, I guess, pretty pissed off."

"Why would they be pissed?"

"No clue, Dad. You mind telling me?"

Tom raised his lucky blue coffee mug just past his chin, then held it there, inches from his unshaven face. "What's *that* supposed to mean?"

"All I'm saying is that, of the two of us, you're the one spending time and cash with grandstanders."

Which was as bold as Tug had the balls to be back in June— about how tired he was of acting like Tom and Tom's track pals hadn't gone too far with gambling, fixing races, bookmaking, and whatever else they were up to.

"Tug, those guys don't care about jinxed mares," Tom said. "I mean, she had no real upside, right?"

"Yes, but why—I mean, what are you saying?"

"Just that I can't imagine why anyone I know would've wanted her."

"You can't?"

"No."

"Well, *I* can," Tug said, not so much because he'd imagined reasons *specifically*. Though he still did suspect that any of the regulars in the Finger Lakes grandstand—including Tom himself—might have stolen Silent Sky to sell her to a rendering plant for gambling cash.

"Maybe it's better," Tom said, facing the hole. "Since a couple new boarders are headed here anyway."

He went all still then, as if considering something most crucial, and Tug went still, too, remembering Silent Sky's fondness for being scratched between her ears.

"Thoroughbreds?" Tug asked.

"No."

"Standardbreds."

"No."

"Then I don't get it, Dad. What, exactly, are we talking about?"

Tom gazed at an oak trunk beyond the cracked logs, sipped coffee from his lucky blue mug. He squinted as if he'd just swallowed something bitter, faced Tug squarely, then used an obviously put-on upbeat tone to say, "People."

# 5

# DEESH

**JAMES GOES ON ABOUT HOW** he hates being poor, hates the *end-lessness* of it—it's like we were all born into these rubber bags we can't punch our way out of. There's no *light* in his life, he says. Not even in summer. Never was. He never should have hung with us, even in high school. He should have listened to his mother when, after we won state, she said we were bad influences, God rest her soul.

But that's as close as he gets to talking about the death in the drum, and his carefulness about that promises me there was death in there hands down, even though I've been waiting for him to zip it so I could say that, for all we know, we just dumped off a crammed bunch of laundry that got moldy after the creek rose and flooded the woman's house. There's a million things other than a person that could be in a drum was what I convinced myself while James went off like that, but now that he's done, that million feels like a million too many.

Then a single word won't leave my mind—*fingerprints*. Bark turns on the radio and presses SCAN, but it keeps coming back to this station that plays lite songs for white folks. He lets it play, though, and the news comes on, and I listen, expecting the dude to report a dead body found in a drum even though I know that's impossible this soon. After the news ends, Bark snaps off the radio, and I imagine he's thinking the same thing I am. For the rest of our lives, we won't-but-will want to hear any news on any radio or watch it on TV.

And I don't need to ask him if this thought is on his mind a mile or so later, because a glance from him, as we roll toward the city, tells me. He's remembering how, just a week ago, as he and I walked side by side to a hauling job in Brooklyn, we came upon that Madalynn from our past, willowy Madalynn—she looking even finer than she had when I was the lucky brother to spend nights with her. How she was now walking toward Bark and me without yet realizing he and I were who we were, she side by side with an all but grown-up kid who, from the looks of things, must have been her son, Jasir. How after we all four came upon one another, Bark stopped her by simply standing right in front of her, forcing her, with his closeness and stillness, to look up at him. How that left me smack in front of Jasir. How Jasir was obviously as sinewy as I'd been at his age. But, see, that's not what got me as the four of us stood there. What got me was how Jasir folded his arms over his chest a moment before I did. How, right then, as he and I stood there on that sidewalk, he was holding himself in the exact same way I always had and still do, palms flat against ribs, no telltale fists, just a wiry young man maybe protecting or hugging himself or both. And as Bark and Madalynn went on with their small talk, Jasir and I stood like that—arms folded to make each of us look far too much like the other—though we both played this off as if we cared only to listen to Bark and Madalynn. But, hell, if I heard anything right then, it was only Jasir's thoughts, and what he was thinking was: *This serious dude is your daddy no doubt. Looks too much like you not to be. Did it with your mama and good.*

And in Bark, too, on that sidewalk in Brooklyn, there was no doubt. One glance between me and Bark then made me sure that, when it came to being Jasir's father, he felt free and clear, and a quicker glance now confirms it. I mean, that's how things have been between Bark and me since our second championship season. All he and I needed back then was eye contact to know if I should lob the ball down to him or fake away and come back with a bounce pass or pull up with a jumper he was set to rebound. We'd never say a word, never even nod. We were tight like that, and now we're still tight, but I don't like where our tightness has taken us.

James never had that unspoken vibe with us; in fact, he was always yakking at us and everyone on the court, refs included, even at the families in the stands. I used to think this was because he had the least talent of our starting five, but anyway since then he's used talk as a weapon, keeping the threat of it to himself at times, letting the world have it when he's backed into a corner. In a way it was good he talked so much when we played ball—it hid that eye contact Bark and I used—but now he just sits. And what makes me worry even more is that it's Bark who finally speaks up, and, worse, what Bark says is: "I vote we go to Mississippi."

"Mississippi," I say.

"It's far and we'd blend in."

James says, "Bark, we don't know a damned soul in Mississippi."

"Exactly," Bark says. "So we ditch the truck in Virginia or something, take a bus the rest of the way, start all over down there."

"Hang on, man," I say. "For one thing, if we don't know anyone, where would we . . . live?"

"We'll rent. Like we do now."

"With a thousand dollars?"

"Deesh, it's not like anything's keeping us in New York," he says. "None of us has a woman. None of us has a job other than to haul junk. Maybe this never crossed your mind, but you can haul junk for cash just about anywhere."

None of us has a *woman*? I think, and again I remember Madalynn, then realize that, when you count up all the years that passed before we saw her and Jasir last week, Bark's right.

"But we'll go through the thousand like that," James says with a snap of his fingers. "We got gas to buy, bus tickets, food—and you don't just walk into a new town and start *living*, in an apartment and all, without a good pile of cash."

"True," Bark says.

Maybe ten miles pass while the three of us sit like strangers on an A train. Then, just by Bark's suddenly stiff posture, I know what he's got in mind. He's not just heading to the city; he's heading to his favorite place to hang out, Belmont Park, to try to bet our thousand into more.

"Bark, tell me we're not going to Belmont," I say.

"Why not?" he says, and I expect James to start lecturing, but he doesn't.

"Well, *I'm* not going," I say.

"Where you gonna go?" Bark says. "Back to your nasty apartment to wait for the cops?"

"They ain't gonna find me."

"Well, they ain't gonna find *me*," Bark says. "I'll be in Mississippi. With a helluva lot more cash than I have now."

"You saying I don't get my share unless you win?" I ask.

"No," Bark says. "You'll get yours."

But it hits me he's already planning to take a chunk from my third for gas and wear and tear on his truck, which he does now and then—and which is fair, even though it seems unfair because he does it only when he wants cash to bet on horses. So now I'm looking at $300, maybe even only $275, and as many groceries as $275 might buy me, it feels like it's already nothing no matter whose pocket it winds up in, or where. Plus if Bark does leave for Mississippi and I don't go along, I'll need to find a new job.

And what if he wins? I think. Bark usually doesn't win, but, almost always, he comes close. His problem isn't that he doesn't know horses; fact is, in just about every race I've seen when I've gone to the track with him, he pretty much knows which horse will finish first. His problem is he lives for the big payoff, so he bets trifectas—which means he has to pick first, second and third in the exact order—and it's usually third place, or sometimes only the exactness, that gets him.

"I'll take you home, Deesh," he says now. "But on the way there, just hear out my plan."

He turns on the radio, turns it off.

"We don't bet every race," he says. "We bet one. And before we do, we study all the races to see which one's best."

I flick drying mud off the inside of one of my sneakers. "For the thousand," I say.

"Right," he says.

"We put it *all* on one race?" James says.

Bark nods. "You guys are the ones saying we need more cash to move. *You* got any ideas about how we can make a pile in a hurry? I mean, legally?"

Here's where I most wish James would go off on another yak-king streak—about all sorts of moneymaking ideas that never entered my mind. But again he keeps still. And all I can think about when it comes to big, fast money is what would have happened if I hadn't messed up my knee in the semifinals the first year we won state. Yeah, we won state anyhow. Yeah, everyone on the team propped me over their heads as we left the court. And, yeah, the ligament healed in time for us to win state again our senior year. But everyone who scouted us that year saw my ugly-ass knee brace, saw how I'd lost half a second off my first step to the hoop, and even though I'd compensated by improving my jumper and passing game, everyone knew my burst of speed was why I'd gotten those thirty-four letters of interest from pro and college scouts. Knew that, for all the points and assists I'd racked up, my best bursts of speed were behind me.

So we sit like that, all three of us, I imagine, remembering those days, as Bark takes us farther down toward the city, then pulls left onto the Sprain Brook, then exits onto the Cross County Parkway. The green of the trees and bushes and fields around us is too soon replaced by faster traffic and concrete, reminding us we live in the Bronx. And it's not Mississippi or the death in the drum or the hope of winning a pile of cash that changes my mind about whether I'll go along with Bark's plan. It's this appearance of the Bronx that does it. That feeling of being squeezed in. That feeling of knowing you are one of thousands, if not millions, of brothers caged into a future in which you will finally do something no-holds-barred stupid. There's that stretch of moments, after we pay the toll for the Throgs Neck Bridge and stay just under the limit while we rise, when you see the blue water and yachts and think the good life could happen to at least a few brothers. But then the water is be-hind us and a Mercedes cuts us off as we exit the bridge, and then there's the construction and the slowdowns. And you sit, itching to move forward, knowing that Belmont is, after all, a park with burgers and picnic tables and tents that sell beer.

Quit worrying, you think. We're almost there.

# 6

# JAN

**I FIRST SAW TUG CORCORAN** as he dove off the far end of the pier to swim to where the lake grew all shimmery. He'd taken that dive, I figured, to avoid having to meet me, but then I told myself that he and I were long past having excuses not to act like adults: Coincidence, I was sure, was why he was swimming right then. Tom Corcoran had gone straight to my mother and kissed her hello flush on the lips, Colleen showing no sign of jealousy, though already I could tell, by just watching her uninvested glance away from that kiss, that she and Tom weren't getting along. There was this kind of coldness centered between them, and she hugged me then only because he did, it seemed, and he went off talking, in a hushed way that brought my mother in close, about how we should go easy on Tug because his horse farm wasn't about to earn praise in the *Daily Racing Form* anytime soon. I took this as my cue to walk down to the lake, which had its own way of drawing me to it; on that day, in soft sunlight, the kind that makes you feel like you're a child again, all that water out there reflected azure so peacefully you never would have thought it could've hurt a soul, let alone your own daddy if he were a champion jock.

And Tug, as I stepped onto the pier, was backstroking toward me. By the time I passed the second or third piling, he'd stopped to stand between the pier and a tangle of this year's weeds, ripples around him fading, a minnow nipping at the taut skin just above his navel. He had the kind of shoulders you wanted to drape your arms over while you made out and talked, and I stopped walking only to tilt my head slightly, my insides gone to pieces about how the tan I'd gotten in Arkansas without trying might overwhelm any upstate New York man with skin as pale as his. And I'll admit that, already, there was this tightness in my chest, though back then I wasn't sure this was a sign of love—as I saw things then, he'd just made me go shy.

But it turned out to be me who said hello first, even as I'd now have sworn our eyes were putting a charge in us both. Then there we were, this other jock's only child and I, carrying on like good sports, with me telling him about my life's dream to ride racehorses professionally, about how I was sure I'd never win as many races as my father had but believed I'd still try. And my mention of my father had Tug's eyes darting everywhere except those sunbleached weeds, and I wondered if, instead of desire, he was destined to merely feel sorry for me.

"But right now?" I said. "I'm looking for work that'll pay up front."

"Wish you could help on my farm," he said. "But business is slow."

I shrugged.

"Anyway," he said. "Sounds like you need per-hour work."

"Already have some," I said. "Fishin' for pay for some old guy."

"Here?" he said. "I mean—on the lake?"

I nodded.

"Anyone I know?"

"I think your father said . . . Jasper?"

Jasper, as it would turn out, was Tug's family's oldest friend from the Finger Lakes racetrack. Back when Tug had been the kid who'd press his face against the chain-link alongside the homestretch, Jasper had been the soul entrusted to place bets for Tom if Tom found himself on an entry that seemed doped or otherwise geared up to win. Jasper would stand in the crowd near that same chain-link and—if Tom petted his mount three times quickly—walk away from the crowd, then run. Jasper would always have at least a few hundred dollars of Tom's in his back pocket, but no bet made on behalf of the Corcorans was supposed to exceed fifty, because, back then, both of Tug's parents believed that greed led to losing—not to mention they didn't want to reduce a given wager's payoff by driving down the odds.

Jasper's payment for placing the Corcoran family bets was the information about the live horse itself, but Jasper always pushed his luck: He was wise enough to bet a juiced horse straight up to win, but then, throughout the rest of the day, he'd consider any rumor, from anyone, a stone-cold tip, and he'd lose.

So it made sense that fish for Jasper's meals came from the lake. What confused me back then—and would confound me for weeks—was how Jasper could afford to pay me to catch them.

And why had Jasper chosen me, a woman who'd never even cast a line, to be the person in charge of reeling his meals in?

# 7

# DEESH

THEN WE ARE THERE, on Belmont's grounds, me and Bark and James, both of them, in hazier sunshine than we came from, looking older than I thought we were. Bark buys a program, the thousand again dented as it was to pay our parking and entry fees. He sits on a painted green bench near where they bring the horses to saddle and pet them before they bust ass out on the track.

"They already ran the first four races," he says, a little pissed, probably because it's hours past noon and he's gotten no kick from gambling. He slouches and studies away while James and I sit on either side of him. All we need, I think, is for Bark to find that one, best race. And to concentrate enough to pick the three horses in the right order. The corpse in the drum means pressure, I know, but Bark, I remember, played his best under pressure. In fact, *lack* of pressure was why *he* never made the pros or a college team. In the high school games we knew we'd win, which was most of them, he could never get himself to try all that hard, and, if you believed our coach, word got out he was lazy. But in those few big games, the major-pressure ones, he always showed up to leave sweat on the court, and even if his shot was off or he dragged down fast breaks from being out of shape, he did the kinds of things that make championships, like elbowing the wind out of the other team's star when the refs weren't looking, or giving a soft high five just before I'd toe the line for a free throw.

Now he's walking us to another green bench—beside the home-stretch of the track. Again James and I sit up against his shoulders. He's flipping pages in his program, back and forth from race six to race eight. He's got it down to those two, he tells me. I want race six so we'll know sooner if we've won or not, but I don't want to mess with what all those numbers are teaching him. He holds race eight closer to his face. He sighs. I look off around us.

"We'll do it in the sixth," he says.

"You know which horses?" James asks.

"The three horse for sure. And the one. It's just a matter of whether we go with the four, seven, or nine after that."

"That don't exactly sound solid," James says.

"Just being straight with you," Bark says. "What's left of the races today are hard as shit to pick."

"Can we just go with the three and one to finish first and second?" I ask.

"That would be an exacta," Bark says. "And *everyone's* gonna box the three-one exacta. Which means it'll hardly pay."

"We can't take the three and the one with all three of those other ones you like?" I ask. "I mean, in trifectas?"

"That would be three different bets," Bark says. "Meaning we'd bet only three hundred–something on each. Which again means a lower payoff."

"But we'd be more likely to win."

Bark returns to studying, though I'd guess he's also considering what I've said. Then I'm sure he's trying to figure how much each of those three trifectas could pay, but then I'm not sure of anything.

"How much do we need?" he asks.

"Who knows?" James says. "But you'd have to think five or six grand would be cool."

And here's where I both believe we'll win but also wish we wouldn't. I wish we could just get in Bark's truck and go home. I want to start the day over. I want to go back in time even before that, and meet the pigeon-toed woman before whatever happened in her life that forced her to call Bark. I want to make love to her back then, night after night, so often and well the drum will stay empty, and mostly I want to go all the way back to Madalynn.

But today is not at all in that past. It's today, and now race five is running, without Bark betting a penny on it, which reminds me we're here for serious business despite the white college boys beside us celebrating their summertime freedom by drinking beer, all of them hooting as the seven horse pulls ahead.

Bark looks up as the seven wins easily. He glances at the odds board and says, "Twenty-five to one." He hunches over to reread the program.

"You know what?" James says.

"Shut up," I say. "Let the man think."

"You're right," James says.

Seagulls almost land on the lawn inside the track, then swoop off. They're headed north, toward the drum. That seven horse was headed north, toward the drum. Wind blows past the three of us—north, toward the drum.

"The more I look at this," Bark says, "the more I can see *any* horse finishing up with the one and the three. And the way the crooks here fix these races, any horse could *beat* the one and the three."

"So what do we do?" I ask.

"Key the one and the three with every other horse."

"Which means what?" James asks.

"If the one and the three finish first, second, or third, we collect."

"Sounds good," James says.

"But they both have to finish in the top three."

"Sounds tough," I say.

"It's as easy as I can make it," Bark says.

"How much would we win?" I ask.

Bark shrugs. "Anywhere from double our money to a ton."

"But like you say, what good is double our money?"

"Deesh," Bark says, "we gotta leave here with *something*."

Which tells me that, today, he's lost faith in horses. If it were yesterday, or any day before we moved that drum, he'd have enough faith for the three of us. But it's today. It doesn't matter that he's got more cash in his pocket than he's ever had at the track. Today is today is today.

We all three sit. The horses walk onto the track, a jockey on each. Then Bark stands and says, "Let's do it," and James and I follow him under the grandstand to the betting windows, where we wait in a short but slow line. Finally, Bark leans in close to our teller, an old white lady. He talks so quietly she needs to lean, too, and then he pulls out the cash and hands it over for a ticket he reads even after his feet begin to shuffle off.

"Gentlemen!" the teller shouts. "Your change?" She's holding three twenties, and James jogs back to her, takes them, gives one apiece to me and Bark, then stuffs the third in his pocket. We walk back out toward the homestretch, and it hits me I might have done something for a twenty I'd never do again for all the money in the world.

Bark veers left, toward the bench near the homestretch. "Shouldn't we watch closer to the finish line?" James asks, but Bark keeps on. James stands still, knees locked, yakking about how what we'd see from that bench won't matter. About how he wants to eyewitness the very end. About how, if all of us shout enough near the finish line, we could affect whether we win or lose.

"Go ahead and shout," Bark says. "I'm gonna watch from here."

James huffs off, leaving me to decide who to watch with. I don't follow him since the last thing I need is the sound of his voice. I don't sit beside Bark since I'm pissed he's the reason I went upstate. I stand where I am, partway between Bark and the finish line—in front of the odds board beyond the dirt where they'll run. It all of a sudden doesn't mean shit that the three of us won state twice together, hung together on countless nights since, might end up together in Mississippi for the rest of our lives. We're all strung out along that wire fence like cousins who never met, each of us as alone as the skinny drunk beside me, all of us as stuck inside ourselves as whoever's rotting in that drum.

And we stay like that until the horses are in the gate.

# 8

# JAN

THE WAY THE CORCORANS had it set up then was the three up-stairs bedrooms went one each to Tug and my mother and Tug's parents, whereas I'd sleep on the first-floor summer porch, a long narrow room surrounded by three walls of windows, the widest facing the lake. During the day, this room was the best because all around were thick oak trunks and shiny rhododendrons and white blooming wisteria, and there was a family of chipmunks who spied on you and redheaded woodpeckers who charmed you by working upside down, and at any time a metallic green hummingbird with a scarlet throat might zing past as fast as a falling star, sip from a purple clematis, then dart to a lily the color of a conch shell's throat, with the jade and aqua and shimmering lake behind everything.

But at night, if you couldn't sleep, you'd hear creaks in the narrow ceiling overhead, let alone voices up there, sometimes hissed words if not clearly angry phrases, always between Tom and Colleen, often about money. And on my first night beneath such creaks and those voices, I lay under a lent comforter on the cot alongside that porch's only privacy-assuring wall, and outdoors beyond that enchanted yard loomed that same body of water, waves on it throwing moonlight at me, reflected brightness lapping along plasterboard inches from me if even a meek breeze rose, telling me more directly than any voice above me that, yes, let's not deny it, girl: You lay within a furlong of the lake that took your daddy twice—first when he drowned, again when your mother scattered his ashes from that pier.

And the longer I got worked up about how much easier my life could have been if my father hadn't drowned, the more I wanted to leave that porch, though doing so would risk running into a Corcoran, which I did *not* want to do. What I wanted was to get away from both the lake and the Corcorans, maybe go out in the yard between the house and the road, maybe, if I could muster the spine, follow the path through the woods south of the house to Tug's horse farm. Horses had long, long been my means of escape; riding them helped me avoid people I didn't like, and on a saddled horse you also had more power than anyone who stood on human feet. Naturally, then, in the middle of that first night I spent in the Corcorans' house, I wanted to see a filly or a colt I might take a liking to. Gnawing at me still was Colleen's caginess during dinner at the kitchen table that evening, when I'd addressed no Corcoran in particular to ask how many horses Tug had in his care; she'd grown all at once interested in whether Tom believed muskies were biting, as if there'd been something about Tug's farm she wanted kept secret.

Anyway I might have been more curious than brave when I pulled on my jeans and sweatshirt and sandals and tiptoed from the summer porch through the musty living room into the kitchen, which was lit by a high-watt bulb in a frosted fixture. I took two McIntoshes from the cracked ceramic bowl on the cherrywood table and, feeling not only brave but also generous now that each of my hands could offer a horse a surefire gift, escaped through the roadside door.

The lawn out there was a long stretch of crabgrass split by a path of flagstones sunken by rain and time and the weight of an unknowable number of horse folk, and it struck me that my father himself had probably walked on those stones, his actual flesh-and-bone feet pressing each a microscopic bit deeper, and this realization saddened me. If he hadn't drowned and were still alive, I thought, he and I might be talking now, and I headed left, then into the woods south of the lawn.

And in those woods I kept to the path Tug had cleared, a trail just wide enough for thoroughbreds. I pressed on guided by the same moonlight that had haunted me on the summer porch, and between the crowns of the trees on either side of me were also stars strong enough to not only guide you but also to get you to thinking about eternity and family and afterlife and anyone you really cared about, and I wondered: Is it through one skinny ray—from the least visible star—that dead fathers communicate with daughters? Or is it through sunshine?

And I did choke up a little while wondering this, but then I told myself to focus on the future, on how I might be minutes from meeting horses, maybe one who'd prove as wild about being ridden as I was about riding. Filly, mare, colt, gelding, bay, roan, chestnut—no distinction would matter if this horse would love to run with me—and then things went black thanks to a huge boulder on my right, more of a cliff, really, a slice of the earth's guts forced out past its skin by a glacier, it seemed. And the darkness here was thick enough to bring to mind bears and wolves and overly aggressive mama raccoons, but it also made the stars directly above seem brighter—trying to connect with my father was only a matter of looking up—and I stopped walking, as if stillness might help me hear my father telling me, through the brightness of those stars, whatever he had to say, maybe, I imagined, something like: *I walked there, too. And, yes, I've long loved you.*

And I felt taller as I walked on, and then, to my right and just south of the boulder itself, there it was, a huge, brightly moonlit meadow with a creek angled across the middle of it and a birch-log fence all around.

And compared to the darkness in the shadow of the boulder, the brightness here, on top of the openness, made you downright joyful, not to mention that miraculous feeling you get when you stand witness to something as defiant of logic as a meadow dropped into the middle of woods thick as hell. But then I noticed an uninhabited, shabby lean-to near the southernmost run of fence, and out there near the creek, where horses might have been drinking, there were none.

And there were none anywhere.

And part of the fence was missing—that section of birch logs was down. Maybe, I thought then, a colt had felt too penned and took his best running start and leapt and failed? Or tore open his coat bolting straight through? Either way I now guessed why Colleen had been cagey: A horse had died and she hadn't had the heart to tell me.

Then I thought, No. Not *every*thing ends with death. But I was glaring at the apple in my left hand as if it, rather than some six-foot muskie, was death itself, and I chunked it, hard, at the hole in the fence. My throw fell short, though it did bounce once and roll close, and I headed back onto the path to the house, where, as soon as I stepped inside the roadside door, Tom Corcoran glanced up at me, sitting as he was at the kitchen table.

He took stock of me calmly, as though women always trekked into his house at this hour, then asked, "What's with the apple?"

"I thought there were horses."

Spread out in front of him, I noticed, was a *Daily Racing Form*.

"There were," he said.

"And?"

"Is it really your concern?"

"Well, I think I can say it *is*."

"Well, then, let's just put it this way: We had a small mishap."

"When horses get lost in a forest, I wouldn't call it small."

"Then call it big."

He turned the page of his *Form*, his way, I was sure, of saying he was done with this conversation, either because Tug's farm was indeed none of my business or because the numbers in the *Form* were all that should matter to anyone. I pulled the screen door behind me harder, trying for a click I never heard, then stepped cautiously toward him and set the apple back in the bowl, and as I headed for the living room to return to the summer porch, he said, very quietly, "You're just like your father."

I stopped, facing the living room, which of course meant facing the lake.

"I mean, he was always going out in the middle of the night."

I turned. "You mean for walks?"

"Sometimes the man would *run*."

"At night?"

"He'd be out there getting a complete workout while every other jock was asleep. I'm surprised your mother never told you."

"My mama would rather pray to a ceiling than tell me the truth about my father."

Tom's watery eyes, unblinking and hazel and magnified frightfully by his glasses, wandered from me to the sink. Then he returned to studying his *Form*, a script more important, it seemed, than every father and daughter and family in the world. He struck me, as he squinted to read, as a formerly handsome man who might feel expendable; a husband whose paunch had diminished some attraction to him; a father whose thinned, graying hair probably scared the hope out of his son; a jockey whose retirement hadn't exactly helped the prospects of that same son's horse farm.

"Come to think of it," he said. He starred an entry with a plastic pen. "Early in your dad's career, he used to ride at night."

"Thoroughbreds?" I asked.

"'Just trust and let 'em run,' he'd say."

"*Real*ly."

He nodded. "The guy would slip the track's night security a little cash, then go crazy out there, galloping in the dark. He believed horses were happiest when they ran at night. If you rode one through the dark, he'd say, you'd be forming a bond that would help you win together from then on."

What I was hearing right now, I figured, was Tom Corcoran being a plain old horse guy.

He said, "The thing was, I tried it once, riding in the dark. Horse I was on wouldn't budge."

And we were both studying each other's faces then, as earnest, it seemed, as two people could be, though I had no idea what he was trying to say—other than that he had his own big mess of regrets and nostalgia and resentment and desire stuck in him, trying to charge out.

# 9

# DEESH

**I GLANCE OVER AT BARK**, who nods. Then I see that the horses are running, already on their way down the backstretch. Because of their distance, I can't tell if we're winning, and then, because of the odds board, I can't see them at all. I hear names being called, but to us it's all about the one and the three. Then I see every horse out there bunched into a pack, and as they reach the far turn, what looks like a three is in second. Then they're in their best full sprints toward and past Bark. Then they're passing me, getting whipped, with the three for sure in front. But the rest of them are gaining— or maybe they're not. The three might be fading, and a woman in the grandstand screams. And then I watch the rear ends of ten horses, and I haven't seen the one at all.

# 10

## JAN

**WHENEVER TUG COULD**, he'd fish with me.

And I always insisted that I, rather than he, do the guy stuff. I'd be the one to hook the baitfish under its spine, and it was my eager fingers that adjusted the float, and I'd add a split shot by using my molars as pliers.

And, most splendidly, I hoped, I'd cast.

Then we'd sit in silence that would ratchet up Tug's insides, because, as I'd learn later, he always felt far too serious when he was with anyone quiet, especially anyone who knew horses. As a kid, Tug had rarely heard silence at the track, where either some trainer was gossiping workout splits or some hot-walker was cooing into a two-year-old's ear, or some barn hand's hose water hissed while the track announcer yelled *Who's gonna catch him?* during a stretch run. The silences Tug had grown up hearing, certainly the memorable silences now, had been between his parents, often just after his father had lost so much cash at the track he'd refer to the experience as a "gofak" (good old-fashioned ass-kicking). So, for Tug, silence now went hand in hand with a truce called between spouses after vicious arguments about unpaid bills; it implied a woman was scared because a man had violated her trust, or that a man was at his wit's end because a woman herself had agreed he should place some huge bet he'd then lost, not to mention his head was spinning because the last time he'd *won* on a long shot, they'd both agreed that he should have bet more than he had. Such silence had too often spilled out onto the yard and sometimes even past the first piling or two of the pier, and too often Tug would retreat to the far end of the pier, where, if waves or wind or geese didn't speak up, he would hear silence as a pronouncement that he was maturing into his parents' worst financial burden.

Often, during the silences between me and Tug while we'd wait for muskies to bite, I would think about my own father, and I'd picture the baitfish down near the sun-bleached weeds, or my father's breathlessness in the ancestors of those weeds, or both, and I'd wonder if my father's ashes had dissolved or joined the muck at the bottom.

And as Tug would admit later, he'd be thinking of my father's death, too, and he'd figure there was nothing he could say to fix any of that horror, so instead he'd just dangle his legs off the deep end of the pier, facing the far shore, reading the pathetically upbeat hardbound his mother had bought him at a tag sale, *So You Want to Practice Law.* He'd apply this book's advice to the man his parents wanted him to be, the man who might finally make something of himself now that his horse farm had failed. He would despise that man—a student and then parasite of law—and sometimes, while he'd read, he'd sense an unsteadiness beneath his thighs, a quivering that was sometimes his imagination but sometimes meant someone on the pier was walking toward him, sometimes me.

And on some days, the bright ones, I'd begin my time outdoors by sitting on the pier to read as well, though I'd sit only halfway toward the deep end, facing the tangled weeds, where we'd often cast the float. If Tug had left the *So You Want* book on the pier, I might give a sentence or two of it a try, but mostly I'd read one of the dozens of old *Racing Form*s I'd pilfered from Tom Corcoran's sacred stack beside the living room couch. I'd study the charts rather than what most gamblers read—past performances—and when Tug finally conjured the nerve, on an unseasonably hot day I endured in only flip-flops and shorts and a lavender bikini top, to ask why I preferred the charts, I said, "Because my daddy did."

Once, when we found ourselves both looking up from our reading at the same time, Tug was all set to ask if I'd learned a priceless nugget from those charts, some key to wisdom or gambling success, but I beat him to speaking up by saying, "Tug, you got me all confused."

"How's that," he said.

"I thought you were a . . . horse farmer."

"I am. I mean, I was."

I pushed a frizzed strand of hair away from an eye. "And?"

"And as you might have gathered, my farm isn't quite operating at full capacity."

I came close to smiling. I nodded and said, "I did gather that."

"So . . ." He pointed at his copy of *So You Want to Practice Law.*

"So . . . *what.*"

"So when money isn't flowing toward you at all, there's—reality to consider."

47

I perused the shallows for the float, which now sat deeper than the sun-bleached weeds.

"Fuck reality," I said. "You know?"

I studied his face, critically, he thought. Then I continued reading, and he did, too.

Or tried to.

"We're *young*, Tug," I called out, without looking up. "There *is* no reality. At least none that lasts very long."

And then I gave him a genuine smile.

"So you're suggesting," he said, "that I just . . . hang in there."

Again, I returned to my reading.

"I'm saying I want to be a jock," I said, "and I don't hear anyone telling me to do anything otherwise."

Because you're Jamie Price's daughter, he thought. But he didn't dare say that then.

"So why should *you* give up?" I asked.

And then there I was, grinning even as I faced my charts, but then I looked up and over at him seriously, and he shrugged, and, in a manner that I'd later learn struck him as aggressively flirtatious, I shrugged, too, mockingly, a coy smile on me now, aimed at him.

# 11

# DEESH

JAMES IS STILL BESIDE THE FINISH LINE, pointing but not yelling. Bark, with his arms at his sides, leans back against his bench. Then both of them are walking toward me, as if I'm in charge.

"Well?" Bark asks James.

"I couldn't tell," James says. "They were all bunched together."

Bark shrugs, his eyes aimed at the odds board, on the three boxes beside WIN, PLACE, and SHOW. A lit-up ten is in the WIN box, the other two boxes unlit.

"We were right to key them with every other horse," Bark says. "*Nobody* would have guessed the ten."

"Which means a big payoff?" I ask.

Bark nods. "If we win."

Then, in the PLACE box, I see the lit-up number one. "Here we go," James says, and the whole board goes dark, blinks twice, then lights up. The ten is still up over the one, the SHOW box still empty.

"The three was toward the front," I say. "Wasn't it?"

"It was when they passed me," Bark says. "And it was *supposed* to stay up there."

He won't look at James, so I do.

"Well, James?" I say. "Did the three hold on?"

"It might have," he says. "But I'm telling you, man—from where I was standing, I really couldn't see."

"Sonofabitch," Bark says, and I look at the board, where a clear-as-dawn number is now in the SHOW box:

3.

"It's not official," Bark says. "And when it is, pretend it isn't. The last thing we need is someone following us out to the parking lot."

"Let's get in line," I say. "Let's get our cash and get out of here."

"Just chill," Bark says, but then he's heading back under the grandstand, and James and I jog to catch up.

"The three held on," James says, and he clamps my shoulder like he did the first time we won state, but hoop and all those wins back then hit me now as pretty damned small. Because this win now, with its promise of the kind of cash a guy could really throw around, has me wishing I could get back with Madalynn.

But I don't dare mention Madalynn now.

Not around brothers like these.

I say, "You know it, men. And there was *no* doubt, right? Never any doubt we did it."

# 12

# JAN

**ONE-POUND MUSKIES**, I soon learned, were worthless because Jasper wouldn't pay a cent for anything that weighed under six pounds. Tom Corcoran said Jasper refused such small ones because possessing them could get you fined just as catching them could, but Colleen, in a *very* hushed conversation with me, said Jasper sold the muskies I caught to pros who'd use them to win fishing contests—and that no pro cared about a fish unless he couldn't collar its neck with two hands.

Anyhow, Jasper would drive his metallic green '62 Ford Galaxie down the road behind the Corcorans' house every morning just after sunup. If I'd caught any muskies the previous day, I'd have hung a red mechanic's rag on the hedge of milkweed bushes alongside the road to town, and he'd stop. He'd sometimes sit in his Galaxie for a curious while, maybe till the end of some song on his

AM dash radio, and finally he'd stroll, kicking dandelions, across the crabgrass.

Sometimes when he'd arrive I'd still be on the summer porch cot, not completely awake, wishing for things like the pride my father must have felt when his mounts won big, and Tug would already be out there on the far end of the pier, watching the sun rise or whatnot, and my first perception of Jasper would be a quiet but strong knock on the roadside screen door. Colleen would usually answer, my mother upstairs praying or reading or still asleep, and I, in only a T-shirt but wrapped in the Corcorans' quilt, would overhear Tom offer Jasper a coffee, a lemonade, or a Schaefer beer. Jasper would usually say no but he'd sure be obliged for a glass of water, and then, after the plumbing beneath me rattled and shook and squeaked, Jasper would pass the windows that made for the south wall of the porch, bearing down on the lake as he sipped from one of Colleen's unmatched crystal goblets.

And Tug would have any muskies I'd caught alive in the lake, on his stainless steel stringer near the shore, and Jasper would place the goblet on shale beside the half-dead crab apple tree that had been split by lightning a year earlier and appeared lifeless except for three green shoots near it—the same tree my father slept against on his last morning alive. I'd get all stuck on the fact that, staring me right in the face, was this same crab apple tree, and Tug would nod hello to Jasper, who'd crouch and pull up the stringer, wipe his palms against the worn-shiny thighs of his trousers, slide a finger under a gill of the largest muskie, then lift it. If you were close enough you'd see its teeth and hear Jasper say, "Nine and a half," or "Eight pounds, ten ounces," a proclamation that itself suggested his life of watching 1,200-pound horses run had somehow left him with the sensitivity of a post office scale, and I never, for the first part of that summer, doubted him about that, or about anything. Then he'd slide his cash-fattened wallet from his shirt pocket, undo the rubber bands around it, and pay me if I was there or Tug if I wasn't, Tug himself good as gold for making sure the money would, one way or another, wind up in my mother's purse.

Sometimes Jasper would pay fifty to sixty dollars a fish, making for sums that, to my way of thinking, seemed impossibly high. Then he'd bend a finger into the shape of one of the loops on the stringer, and, with a calmness that made you sure his experience at the track had somewhere along the line taught him the pointlessness of worry, he'd mosey back to his Galaxie.

# 13

# DEESH

**AS BARK ACCELERATES US** away from Belmont, it's those three words—*We did it*—that keep running through my mind. But I'm not thinking about Madalynn or the trifecta cash. Mostly it's about the drum. Now and then I glance out Bark's passenger-side window only to picture the pigeon-toed woman's yellow house, but already, without even a kiss between the pigeon-toed woman and me, I have left her forever. I mean, that's how it's always worked for me: I'm attracted to a woman and I run from her. You might say Madalynn first started me on this pattern of behavior, but if so you could also say Bark did, too. And now, here in this pickup truck, Bark merges onto the Grand Central Parkway, and I ask, "Where we going?"

"My place," he says.

"For what?" James says.

We cruise, each staring through the windshield. We come to a quick standstill.

James says, "I thought you wanted to go to Mississippi."

Bark nods, squeezes the steering wheel.

James asks, "Bark, you hear me?"

"Uh-huh," Bark says.

"You got an answer?"

Bark's glare misses James to land on me, as if to say, *Li'l help, Deesh?* No doubt he wants my agreement. Through a closing hole in the traffic to his left, he accelerates, and toward his right shoulder he says, "There's something at my place we should have."

Shit, I think. His gun.

"Bark," I say, "we really don't need that thing."

He's gazing now, out the window to his left. "Deesh. If ever there was a time."

James, studying my expression, asks: "What."

I hold up a finger, cock the thumb beside it, fire an imaginary bullet.

"*Oh* no," James says. "I was with you on the drum, Bark, and I was with you on the bet, and I'd be with you all the way to Mississippi. But not with no damned gun."

"Then I'll drop you," Bark says, his quickness underscoring that he holds the trifecta cash.

And his two buddies from way back, his glances at me and James probably tell him, are still prep-school-boy scared about the contents of that drum.

Still I say, "Bark, you're being stupid. I mean, a gun's bad enough. But the real thing is why, when hundreds of cops around here are already looking for you—and *peace* in Mississippi waits for you—why wouldn't you just head for that peace?"

He smirks. He's used this smirk before, to mess with me. If there's one person in the world he likes to mess with, it should be James in my opinion, but in reality it's me.

"Deesh," Bark is saying now. "Why you always running?"

Again, traffic has us stopped cold. My eyes pin his. "Meaning what?"

"You know," he says.

"Bark, I have no idea what you're talking about," I say, though I know he's talking about Madalynn, who I've on and off suspected he's slept with. I can't *prove* he's been with her in that way, but we have this running joke, he and I, about him comforting the women I run from. We've never talked seriously about this joke, but it's code, if you ask me, for admissions that we've both called Madalynn in the middle of the night more than once.

As for either of us admitting out loud that we both might still have it bad for her?

Now there's something I'd never bet a cent on.

# 14

# JAN

**AT FIRST TO HONOR MY FATHER**, I took to running every night, sometimes well past sundown, and if I hadn't gone with Tug and Tom to the track I'd run away a few afternoon hours, too. You might say my running was simply me doing what most jocks, wannabe or otherwise, did when they weren't riding. But for me, gliding away from that lake house and later cruising back was how I assured anyone who cared that I'd not only ride soon, I'd also someday mess with a track record or two set by the man himself.

Then one day, after an all-out sprint over the last hundred feet of a jog into town, I was opening the screen door to the feed store on Main when the talk inside went silent. I headed on in as if I hadn't interrupted a thing, and Jasper and Bill Treacy, the owner of the feed store, were both sitting behind the glass counter staring at me as if the other weren't there. Usually I loved the smell of that feed store—a sweet, magic mixture of cedar, dog chow, and caraway—but this time breathing it in made me about gag, so I nodded at Jasper's raised eyebrows, bought three strings of licorice to keep myself from fainting, and walked out. I stood on the plank wood porch with my back to the bug-eaten clapboard and my eyes closed against sunshine, nibbling a licorice string half an inch at a time, wishing all sorts of things, none of them involving my life remaining as it was.

Then I heard Bill Treacy say, "Why the silent treatment?"—and I chewed a little faster.

"Because that was Jamie Price's daughter," Jasper said.

"Oh, *was* it now."

I stopped chewing to hold a breath.

"And Jamie's spill didn't happen the way most people believe it happened. The way it happened was my son was supposed to be holding back Cold Cash."

"Ronny was already riding back then, huh," Bill Treacy said.

Jasper paused. I pictured him nodding. "And this Cold Cash he was on was the favorite," he said. "In the first race, the race they usually fixed. And it was Jamie's turn to win."

Now I knew I would listen. The only question was how not to be heard.

"They had it that organized back then?" Bill Treacy asked.

Again, Jasper paused. "And when they come around the last turn, the leader was tiring and the trailers were in a pack. And Ronny's horse Cold Cash was on the outside of the pack, looking to the grandstanders like he was set to fly wide and win. Then the colt Jamie was on—I believe he was called Red Sox—got daylight to leave the rail."

"He'd taken the rail by choice?"

"He'd been boxed in. When he saw an opening, he moved Red Sox off the rail and found himself behind Cold Cash and a bit to his left. And Cold Cash was full of run, so Ronny eased him slightly using the left side of his reins—so the crowd wouldn't see— and Cold Cash stepped left and *stopped*. I mean, that horse killed a full run in two strides, and he did so right as Jamie whipped Red Sox, so Red Sox shot ahead with nowhere to go except Cold Cash's behind."

"And Jamie didn't jump off?"

"He jumped," Jasper said. "Smack in front of eight stretch-running horses. He was lucky all he lost was the use of that hand. Though from then on he figured himself unlucky."

Something squeaked: Bill Treacy leaning back in his chair?

Bill himself then said, "Proves luck is all how you see things. A jock that good should've known that."

"Jamie wouldn't have believed that if he *did* know it," Jasper said. "I mean, after that spill, he was just not right. Because his days were all of a sudden too long for him. He was so used to traveling an eighth of a mile in twelve seconds, he now had no patience for anything. Fact it's lack of patience why he ain't around."

I shifted my weight and a porch plank creaked. I pictured Jasper and Bill Treacy raising their chins in my direction. I considered running off, but Bill Treacy said, "How do you mean?"

"I mean the man," Jasper said, "couldn't wait for *death*. I mean before they drug him up from the bottom of the lake, he tried to *bring it on* with painkillers and a jug of grain alcohol. Because, see, Cindy—who he still hadn't married—was with child. And he believed that Ronny had slept with her."

"He thought *Ronny* had?"

"Probably because he held Ronny accountable for that spill.

Told his bourbon pals that Ronny had stopped Cold Cash on purpose—in order to ultimately win over Cindy. Course, Ronny would never do that. Because, see, Ronny *respected* Jamie. Respected him as if he were the king of the world."

"Even after the spill?"

"'Cause of the way Jamie had with thoroughbreds. What Jamie *didn't* have was the patience to see if his jealousy made sense— couldn't wait to even see the color of that baby. He was so sure that baby wasn't his, he tied that caught muskie to his ankle and swam out into those weeds. With a belly full of hundred-proof hootch."

"You know this as fact?" Bill Treacy asked.

"Bill, that fish wasn't big enough to pull *any* man into those weeds. Not the smallest jock in racing, not the drunkest drunk you know, not the biggest fool on God's earth. That fish was only as long as my arm."

"Says who?"

"I was one boat over when they drug the man in. And I know he'd been drinking because I saw his jug laying on its side empty on the shore. A jug that, Lord forgive me, I funneled a quart of mash into the night before—for a lousy five-dollar bill."

Bill Treacy and Jasper fell silent. I worried about my breathing: I was sure they would hear it. Get on home, I thought. Run like hell as soon as one of them speaks. The porch creaked—by itself, it seemed—and Bill Treacy said, "Does Jamie's daughter know this?"

"I doubt it."

"How 'bout Tom Corcoran's son?"

"Doubt he knows either."

"Probably better," Bill Treacy said.

Jasper coughed. "You know, Jamie's daughter's maturing this summer. Having quite the womanly growth spurt, I mean."

No, I'm not, I thought. My growth, I'd believed until then, had always been late and slow—the opposite of a spurt—and, for the past year or two it had slowed to the point that I'd quit measuring.

"As I see it," Jasper continued, "she's grown both wider and curvier in the last few weeks."

"And I figured her a natural-born jock," Bill Treacy said.

"Maybe natural-born," Jasper said. "But she's more of a woman than a jock now. Could end up fleshier than your average grandstander."

Then he and Bill Treacy laughed, and then they laughed harder, in that obnoxious way old, know-it-all men like them could, and I spit out what licorice was still in my mouth and walked off without caring about planks creaking or anything. I didn't care because I knew why Jasper and Bill Treacy were laughing—because, among the truest horsemen, grandstanders were nothing but laughingstock.

I jogged toward the canopy of elms at the end of Main. *Grandstanders are losers* was how Tom Corcoran had put it at the track a few days earlier. *Because they're either gamblers or on their way to being gamblers, and in the long run, gamblers always lose.*

And after the elms, I ran so fast I was sure I'd fade to walking long before I reached the Corcorans' house.

*Grandstanders are behind before they even sit down,* Tom had said, with damned near resentment. *The suckers pay just to get in.*

And with those words in mind, on top of what Jasper had said about my father, I did not fade. Instead, fueled by rebellion against pretty much the whole world, I accelerated through the opening in the Corcorans' milkweed hedge and onto their driveway, then sprinted to where my mother was hanging sheets on a clothesline slung between pear trees. She glanced over her shoulder at me as I stayed all out toward the lake, a wooden clothespin between her teeth, her face more worn than usual, it seemed, her upper lip raised slightly. Since we'd moved in with the Corcorans, she had this faint way of crinkling the corners of her eyes, and I pulled up and stopped at the Corcorans' orange forty-gallon drum, which I touched, as I always did, before I cooled down: my own personal finish line.

"Hey, Jan," my mother called softly, facing the laundry.

I aimed my shoulders in her direction, hoping she'd say more than that, since I was winded enough to need to grab my knees.

"They all inside?" I finally asked, my scalp itchy against my cap.

She shook her head, grabbed up a pair of jeans. "Tom's at the track; Colleen's getting groceries, I think. And Tug just headed into the woods saying he'd work on his farm."

"He's got a boarder?" I asked, and the thought of a horse now out on that meadow, whether it proved to be a thoroughbred or a standardbred or just some aging mutt, recharged my insides.

"I don't think so. Just repairing it to make a horse more likely, I expect."

"You see it yet?" I asked.

"See what."

"The horse farm."

She brushed a ladybug off her forearm, shook her head no.

"Not much of one," I said.

"Is that right."

"Pretty small, to begin with."

"Then why don't you help make it bigger?"

"You trying to get rid of me, Mama?"

Here she held an old blouse of Colleen's by the hem, well below her own chest, both sleeves touching sprigs of crabgrass, one of the rare times since we'd moved, I then realized, that she was looking me in the eye.

"Baby," she said, "I just want you to be happy."

I smiled at her more than was honest, a sort of Tom Corcoran smile, I thought. "And you figure my talking to Tug is the straight path to happiness?"

She smirked, the clothespin possibly to blame for the absence of a full-fledged grin, and then she returned to hanging up clothes, so I headed off, past the Corcorans' royal blue hydrangea and into the south woods.

In sunlight, the maple trunks along the way appeared thicker than I remembered, and the huge boulder on the right seemed less unnatural during the day, the meadow less promising and lonelier, and there was Tug, kneeling near the gap in the fence. The lean-to, I noticed, had lumberyard spray paint still on it. I ducked under a birch log on my side, walked across the meadow, stopped just short of Tug.

"Hey."

"Jan?" he said, without a glance up. He was wearing rawhide gloves and an old button-down that sweat kept stuck to his back. He raised a sledgehammer above a loose fencepost, and it was clear to me now that, physically speaking, he was a far better natural candidate to jock than I was.

"Not to imply that I know horses more than you do," I said. "But if you ask me, you're spending good energy on the least important part of your farm."

"I'm sorry?" he said, and down came the sledgehammer, with no small amount of anger, it seemed, since the fencepost split in half.

"It's that lean-to over there," I said. "You should, you know, make it so it's got four walls and a roof and a door you could close when it rains or gets cold."

"Then it wouldn't be a lean-to," he said. "Then it would be a barn."

I let him enjoy that one for a while. Then I said, "Precisely my point, Tug Corcoran."

He kept working on, as if I weren't there. If this were some recommended legal-schmegal tactic he'd learned from one of his secondhand law books—tapping into your opponent's insecurities by ignoring her—well, it did get my goat a little, but it sure wouldn't get me in bed.

"It's like with *people*, Tug," I said. "If they feel cared for when they're around you, they'll never *think* about walking away."

He went on working, now and then studying the outskirts of his farm to address the question of which nearby birch might make for a new fencepost, but possibly, I suspected, just to ignore me. For a while there, I wondered if my desire for a barn with four walls was rooted in my lack of privacy on the summer porch, which did, like the lean-to, have only one solid wall. But Tug said nothing about that, and soon I felt stupid for the times I'd imagined sleeping with him when I couldn't sleep at all.

"Anyway," I said. "I'm not up for fishing this afternoon. Maybe I'll go this evening."

"What, you haven't heard?"

"About what."

"The secret sprint."

I had no idea what he meant. He kicked at an intact log as if bent on breaking it, too. "Jasper's driving us out past Geneseo tonight," he said. He stared at my face so unrelentingly I was sure licorice had stained my teeth. "Some rich contractor claimed a horse. And the guy wants to have his friend ride it in a match race against a horse Bill Treacy's buddy just claimed."

"Ridden by?"

"You."

I folded my arms to hide my hands. "I'm not so sure that's the best idea."

"Why not?"

I was tapping one foot repeatedly, an expression of defiance I'd despised seeing my mother use—until I'd adopted it myself. "I've never ridden in an actual race, Tug. Not to mention I think I'm getting a little too . . . you know . . . thick."

"Now don't go being that way," he said. "Guys around here don't race their horses for shits and giggles. In fact it was Jasper who set up the sprint, and Jasper's seen you most every day this summer, so why would he have you ride without confidence in you?"

"I don't know," I said, though already I was constructing theories.

"Well, think about that."

"Maybe he wants me to ride once for money," I said, "because he feels sorry for me."

"He doesn't feel sorry for you, Jan. No one does. You were *born* to be a jock—it's in your blood, and that's a fact."

"If you think so," I said, but only because he'd taken on a sort of lawyerly tone of voice, and the last thing I wanted to do with anyone right then was argue for the sake of argument.

Still, I was confused about why Jasper wanted me to ride when Jasper himself had just called me womanly.

"Anyway, what's this horse's name?" I asked. "I mean, the one I'd ride tonight if what you're saying is true."

Tug wiped his hairline with the back of his glove. In heat this humid, his cheekbones appeared sharp. One of his feet pressed down against a spindly birch log in a standing section of fence, and I was sure he could break it easily.

"Equis Mini," he said. He blinked away perspiration and sunshine. "Latin for 'extremely small horse.'"

# 15

# DEESH

"**TO ANSWER YOUR QUESTION,**" Bark says to me, "I'm going to my place so we can stop being scared."

"And you really think a gun'll help us with that?" James says.

"I do," Bark says. "And yes, *Jimmy*, that *is* just my opinion. But we are talking about a ride in *my* truck, so anytime you'd rather walk, I'll be glad to pull over."

"No need," James says as he reaches past me to try to open the passenger-side door—and I shove him back down, ticked off all the more since here I am again, playing peacekeeper.

Then Bark, too, gets all fatherly:

"Okay, James. My gun will be in that glove box in front of you, so you decide. Mississippi, or your apartment. Choose your apartment and I will take you there. Not all the way to your building, mind you, since your building will probably have *officers* in front of its entrance, but I will drop you within, say, four blocks of those officers. It's just that you need to let me know what you want now, so I can plan the best route through this traffic."

Then we all three sit as still as we had when we'd been screamed at by our hoops coach. It's like we've scrapped and lucked our way this far, but now we're all benched, losing our biggest game. Then it hits me that what Bark told James goes for me, too—head for Mississippi with an unregistered gun, or go home to wait for cops to knock.

"Then I'm out," James says. "But don't take me to my place, Bark."

"Then where?" Bark says.

"My grandma's."

Traffic lets us move maybe three or four feet.

"In Queens," James adds.

I roll down my window and look ahead and behind: cars as far as I can see.

"Fine," Bark says.

"You take me there?" James asks.

"I *said* I'd drop you."

And again, we all simply sit. This, I realize, might be our last conversation ever, and as scared as I am about the drum and the gun, my throat catches because of plain old sentiment.

Bark clears his throat. "Obviously the story we all stick with is that, today, none of us went upstate."

"Agree with you there," James says.

"Today was all about the horses," Bark says, "for all three of us."

"Right," I say, and now here's Bark, asking where James's grandma lives, up near Ditmars or down toward Queensboro Plaza, and here's James, telling Bark she's just off Steinway on about Thirty-fourth

Ave, and now here they go, talking restaurants and clubs in Astoria like Bark's a cabbie James just met. There's no mention of the trifecta cash, not once. But I know James has it in mind because *I* have it in mind.

Bark picks at an ingrown hair on his neck. James closes his eyes. I'm still deciding if I'll travel with Bark. My gut says play the same card James did—insist we go minus the gun—but I can't read Bark for whether, with one friend gone, he'll value his last more or prefer flying solo.

For a moment I want to say, James, you are *bailing*. Then we are whizzing ahead, and I can't remember having rolled out of traffic, which confirms that, for a stretch there, I lost myself in thought. Stress, I think. Or are you just aging? Or were you thinking about Madalynn?

Then there we are, pulling over on a street full of houses just off Steinway, and James's posture straightens as he points at an upstairs duplex with white trellises without vines. Bark brakes hard and James and I get out, and there, on that sidewalk, I wonder how it feels to know one of your grandmothers, and I figure Bark wonders this, too.

But Bark's counting the trifecta cash.

"Maybe you'll need it more than I will?" James says, though he's lingering right there, near Bark's open passenger door.

Bark hands James a folded share. He snaps off another few bills and gives those.

"For Grandmama," he says.

James nods, pockets his share, heads for the porch. Halfway up the stairs, he stops and turns and nods at Bark, then at me.

"Cool," he says.

"Right," I say, but he's already turned to ring his grandma's doorbell, so I get back in the truck, closing the door as we accelerate off.

Bark shakes his head and says, "Pussy."

He means James, though what I also hear is that Bark is not at all up for another request to travel unarmed.

Then he says, "You just know he'll tell Granny about that drum."

"Count on it," I say.

"The way I figure things? She takes those extra twenties and he tells her they're from me? Best investment I ever made."

And again there is more than words to Bark's words. There's the point that he still holds my share of our money, that money still talks, that I'd be smart to stay on the good side of power. And already I miss James, because James's verbal flow always gave logic a chance to be said out loud and considered. With Bark and Bark only, everything's glances and cash and manhood. There'll be fewer quibbles without James, but there'll be fewer laughs.

Still, as Bark and I and his truck roll out of Queens, instinct from somewhere, maybe the father I never saw, tells me that to abandon Bark now would be a loser's move. After all, Bark's been my man since high school. He's found me work when I've needed cash. His time spent with Madalynn, platonic or not, proves we're cut from the same cloth.

On the Triboro, all lanes become jammed. Silence up here grows thorns. There's no arguing about the truth that the Belmont win, by assuring we'd travel in this rush hour, cost us time.

Bark clicks on the radio. A truck jackknifed, the broadcaster says, and someone in it died. No one will budge until everything's chalked and photographed. I tell myself this means fewer cops looking for us. But then comes top-of-the-hour news about a murder in Putnam County.

"No way," I say out loud.

Bark's considered answer is, "You think?"

I don't dare say a word, sure my voice would crack. If James were here now, we'd be lectured. But now there's no doubt about one thing. Bark is headed for his gun.

# 16

# JAN

TOM CORCORAN HELD his secret sprints on an abandoned run-way six miles west of Varysburg, a flagging town on the shore of the Tonawanda River. Jasper owned a dirt-road-accessed acreage between two rolling hills there, and he and Tom ran the two-furlong races based on an understanding that results would never be leaked to the *Form*. One of the horses would be connected to some gambling pal of Tom's, the other to what Tom called a "rookie owner," a rich grandstander who knew nothing about training but had recently claimed his first racehorse for fun. Rookie owners came and went all the time—in fact Jasper's theory was that horseracing relied on them—and Tom would bump into them at the stables, try to take them under his wing, and give them tips on feed, hay prices, and so forth. After he'd won their confidence, Tom would tell them about secret workouts he knew of, two-horse sprints where owners could assure their horses were tight without having impressive workout times reported publicly. Without grandstanders knowing about the workout times, primed-to-win horses, when they did run at Finger Lakes, would presumably command higher odds, meaning, again presumably, that rookie owners could cash in on long-shot-priced tickets. And of course nothing was certain but rumor had it that, thanks to a run of luck that began with a secret sprint, one rookie owner quit his job laying concrete to live in a penthouse with a view of pretty much all of Central Park.

To keep the sprints secret, owners supplied surrogate jockeys such as sons, daughters, or neighbors. Rookie owners would agree to an evening, usually a Tuesday, the off day at the track, and, given the nature of the horse people present, wagers took care of themselves.

Tom and his gambling pals would arrive on Jasper's acreage a couple hours early, so they could slow down the rookie's lane with water tanked on the back of a pickup and rake the mud over, then double-check the rookie's gate to make sure it was rigged to open a half second slower.

A half second advantage is all you need in a sprint.

A half second puts you out in front by two and a half lengths.

# 17

# DEESH

"HAND ME YOUR CELL," Bark says, and now, seeing I've already caved in about the gun, I want to say, *Man, who do you think you are?*

But I know who Bark is. He's the one driving. So all I say is, "Why?"

"We're *disappearing*, man. I leave both our cells at my place, cops'll figure we're still in the Bronx."

I yank out my cell, hand it over, hiss out a sigh I keep mostly to myself. Then we are rolling again. We slow down, then glide. A block from Bark's building, he double-parks, gets out and jogs off, not a word over to me, which trips me about what he'll do in there. He has no woman to call is our current understanding, though I wouldn't put it past him to be speed-dialing Madalynn. I'd call her myself if I had my phone. I'd tell her a disguised good-bye.

Then Bark's back outside, across the street, walking toward the truck. His posture says he's armed. He ignores me as he gets behind the steering wheel.

"No need for it to be loaded," I say.

"Right," he says, without even a quick glance over.

Which, if you know Bark like I do, means his gun's not only loaded—it's begging him not to stay hidden.

# 18

# JAN

AS TOM AND COLLEEN CORCORAN and Jasper and my mother and I and Tug crammed into Jasper's Galaxie to head for the secret sprint, the Corcorans' yard struck Tug as emptier than usual, and he cringed when he realized why: The forty-gallon drum his family had burned leaves in was gone.

Had Tug not been Tom Corcoran's son, this drum's absence would have struck him as the result of petty thievery, but, of course, Tug would *always* be Tom's son, so now, as Jasper's Galaxie headed off, Tug considered a reality most every Finger Lakes horse person had taken to heart at least once, the absence of The *Form* Monger's wife.

That cautionary tale had played out semipublicly back when Tug was just the tongue-tied kid who followed Tom around the track, and the upshot of this tale, as Tom once explained it to Tug, was that she, The *Form* Monger's wife, disappeared because an odds-defying losing streak had compelled The *Form* Monger to double down and borrow from loan sharks. Only days before The *Form* Monger's wife disappeared, The *Form* Monger had bitched and moaned openly in the grandstand about how he was so jinxed he'd even lost one of his garbage cans. And ever since she went missing—that is, for the past fifteen-odd years—the conclusion of every grandstander has been that The *Form* Monger's once-super-fine-looking and now-long-gone-from-sight wife's remains are still out there somewhere, in that can.

And what a jury would need to know is that a week or so after The *Form* Monger's wife disappeared, The *Form* Monger himself showed up in the grandstand after the fifth race with his right arm wrapped expertly in gauze minus the hand he'd once assumed was as inseparable from him as his wife had been—the conclusion being that this hand had been sawed off at the wrist, drained of its blood (since blood leaves telltale stains) and hidden amid the contents of a Dumpster trailer-trucked to New Jersey.

And people would also need to know that The *Form* Monger then came to be called The *Form* Monger because, perhaps as a coping mechanism and certainly as a way of scrounging up cash to bet, he'd soon begun obsessively scalping used *Daily Racing Form*s. And this is no lie: Nearly every day since both his wife and his hand disappeared, the guy has been at the track, pretty much always on the move, cruising up and down the grandstand's concrete stairways to see if any *Form*s lay discarded, sometimes following bettors to the parking lot to beg for their "recyclables" (his word) if they appear to be leaving early, sometimes even rummaging through the track's trash cans. And ever since the spring his wife disappeared, he's struck track patrons as repugnant not only because his stump remains gruesomely purple, but also because, as soon as he sells enough scuzzy *Form*s to have scrounged two dollars, he bets using a system that eventually guarantees loss: He bets to win on the favorite.

Anyway, now, in Tug Corcoran's eyes at least, the Corcorans' missing forty-gallon drum meant a serious warning. It meant someone in the Corcoran household might disappear like The *Form* Monger's wife had. Maybe it also meant that if Tom Corcoran didn't then pay off his losing bets, a hand or a foot of his would go missing, too. But what bore through Tug's thoughts now, as Jasper drove to the first and only secret sprint my mother and I would attend with the Corcorans, was that it might have been *anyone* in the Corcoran house who was on the verge of disappearance.

Why, Tug wondered, would the victim necessarily be his mother?

If loan sharks did in fact abduct the person loved most by the losing gambler, the person now about to go missing—given Tom and Colleen's marital problems—could be my mother.

Or me.

Or hell, Tug probably realized then, those chumps might go after a guy's first and only son.

And true, Tug's concern about the missing drum now portending someone's early departure *was* speculation on Tug's part, or maybe just paranoia. But there was logic behind it, and it only knotted Tug up more to realize that this logic was not the bookish kind used by attorneys but instead the kind used by thugs.

Like everyone taking that ride in the Galaxie that evening, though, Tug said nothing of this. Instead he sat stoically in the backseat between his mother and mine, with me (oblivious as I was then to the fact that the drum was even missing, let alone what its disappearance meant) directly in front of him, between his father and Jasper. Whether Tug would mention to his father or to anyone at all his fear about the drum was a question Tug analyzed for miles—because, as Tom tended to see things, fear not only meant you were a pussy, it also, even worse, caused more loss. Don't Bet Scared Money was one of Tom Corcoran's mottos, but this had never meant any Corcoran should refrain from betting. It just meant they shouldn't be scared.

Because, when it came down to it, Tom Corcoran *was* going to bet.

And Tom's motto about not betting scared money did little to calm Tug now. All the motto did was run through Tug's mind and make his stomach queasy. Tug remembered a trick Tom had used to fight fear of odds-on favorites, glaring directly at one's opponent to remind oneself this opponent would perish like everything else, but it occurred to Tug that he himself didn't know who his father's opponent was. His father, for the record, now sat motionless in the front seat, and it occurred to Tug that, at this very moment, Tom might have been preparing to glare at his opponent as soon as the Galaxie arrived at the secret sprint. But what really got Tug right then, as Jasper sped on, was that he, Tug, was glaring intently at the back of his father's head, which maybe should have told Tug that his opponent was the very blood he and Tom shared.

Suffice to say the drum's disappearance had Tug all screwed up, to the point that he almost got emotional in that backseat, confused as he was by flared-up sentiment and shock on top of his long resentment of his shame for having been raised in a family prone to gamble, and he told himself not to mention the drum's disappearance to anyone, certainly not to me, since if he did, he might break down so pathetically I'd consider him *worse* than a pussy.

Which was to say (using Tom Corcoran's language) like a god-damned baby.

And after Tug promised himself to keep his mouth shut, he sat quietly for miles, glaring at the back of Tom's head.

And when Tug could finally breathe in the boggy smell of the Tonawanda River, it hit him that *this*—the smell of a body of water he'd never fished or swum in—probably embodied the sum total of the peace in him that night. And when Jasper finally turned down the puddle-strewn gravel road that unfurled onto the acreage, I had already put on the riding helmet Tug had treasured as a kid, and quite a few horsemen were already present, maybe thirty, standing near their muddied cars and pickups, wearing Stetsons and pressed jeans and new checked shirts. Tug recognized some of these men from when he was nothing but a toddler at the stables, but there were also horsemen younger than Tom: slimmer, meaner-looking men Tug had never seen, the kind of guys that struck one as criminals whether one wanted to be an attorney or not, all with poker faces that, to Tug now, suggested that Tom might have owed any of them a boatload.

Bill Treacy was unhitching a two-horse starting gate from a tractor, and Tom and Jasper opened their doors and stepped out and stood on either side of the Galaxie, apparently surveying the crowd. Tug envied me for this chance Tom had given me, renowned as Tug himself now was as a failure at his attempted horse farm—and Tug felt stuck between Colleen, who was gazing through the windshield at a new horse trailer behind a shiny truck, and my mother, who seemed glued to the Galaxie's backseat.

"Is the rookie owner already here?" Colleen asked. She said this as if only she and Tom knew about the gambling he and she both did, and Tug smelled the lemon juice she'd put in her hair to lighten it. She rolled down her window. "Tom?" she asked. "Is the rookie already here?"

Tom's navy blue T-shirt—all we could see of him—didn't move. "Tom?" Colleen said.

"Quiet," Tom said, and Tug knew why Tom wanted quiet: If the rookie owner had already arrived, it was possible *we* were being set up.

Tom took a step toward a group of horsemen, stopped, then walked quickly to Bill Treacy. He helped Bill Treacy unhitch the starting gate, lit a cigarette for him while they talked. Then he returned to the Galaxie.

"Come on," he said without looking in. "We're all right."

I adjusted the helmet's chinstrap, and Colleen stepped out and Tug stepped out, and Colleen grabbed Tom fiercely by the wrist.

"He rigged it before we got here," Tom said. "Because he was worried this particular owner would come early."

"So the rookie *is* here," Colleen said.

"Don't worry," Tom said. "We're all right." He still had fewer white hairs than brown. "We're all right as long as we get gate number two."

"But *Tom*," Colleen said.

"Colleen? I've known Bill Treacy for twenty-odd years. Yes, the man's dishonest, but I know how he sounds when he lies."

I stood beside Tug now, and Jasper headed off to the back of a trailer, then returned leading Equis Mini by the reins. Equis Mini was indeed a tiny chestnut, thirteen hands at most, but he had sheen without sweat and fine composure, too, and he wasn't soaped up at all.

Jasper saddled him, then settled him by ruffling up and patting down his mane. "Horse looks right, Tom," he said. "All he needs is a top-quality jock." He winked at me, and Tug studied his face, as candid a face as any nearby.

I turned to Tug. "Should I do this?"

"Of course," Tug said. "It's what you've always wanted, right?"

Tom squeezed my shoulder and said, "Riders up," and I took his leg up and mounted. I felt regal up there, in command of the world almost, my vision actually sharper, my worn jeans with holes in the knees apparently inviting the gaze of most every man there. By some instinct of their own, it seemed, my hips urged Equis Mini forward, and Equis Mini moseyed toward the gate. He looked tight enough for sure, ears pricked, Jasper and Tom flanking him, Colleen and Tug flanking them, my mother finally stepping out of the Galaxie.

Near the gate, Jasper handed me a whip, and Tom held my ankle. "Take him out to that barbed wire and back," Tom told me quietly. "You don't want him standing as long as it'll take to make the wagers and so forth."

"Sure," I said, and Equis Mini responded to my heels, trotting proudly toward the sun. He felt geared up and eager to run, and after we reached the fence and began heading back, I saw the rookie and glanced off quickly, because his way of looking at me assured me that, in his mind now, I was his to desire.

And now, as if Equis Mini were having misgivings of his own, he stopped trotting to stand. Maybe it's my weight, I thought. Maybe I will always be too heavy. He dropped his head and held it low. He stayed there, fifty feet from the gate, as the rookie jock was mounting his horse. I leaned down and whispered "Treat a lady right" into his ear, and he seemed to consider this, then raised his snout and blinked.

But as Tug would tell me later more than once, the rookie's

horse was all muscle no matter what angle you saw him from, the rookie jock easily smaller than me. And then my mother sidled up near Colleen and held hands with her as they stood on the number two lane side of the dirt track, and Tom climbed onto the outside of the number two stall.

"I guess," Tom said loudly, "we get this one."

I steered Equis Mini toward him. "They're entering their stalls!" a drunk on the rookie's side of the track shouted, and I pulled up Equis Mini, to let the rookie jock get in the gate first. He did, and after his people closed him in, I turned Equis Mini around and let him walk a big circle, to let the rookie's horse get fractious, and my glance over at Tug had me sure Tug was realizing I was a lot more experienced—with both horses and men—than Tug had thought when he'd met me.

Then, after the rookie's horse began rearing up and its jock flipped his whip under his armpit, I steered Equis Mini toward the correct stall, and Jasper loaded him quickly and Bill Treacy buzzed open the gate. Equis Mini broke cleanly and I whistled just once; we straightened course and I heard nothing beyond breaths and hoofs hitting dirt until we were well past the finish.

"Twenty-*one* flat!" some guy with a stopwatch yelled.

"That's blazing!" someone else yelled.

Everything around me seemed unsteady right then, with Colleen, beside my grinning mother, giving me a big thumbs-up.

"You won," Tom shouted in my direction, and I eased Equis Mini out of a gallop. Tug looked damned alone right then, waiting as he was, back there with his parents and my mother and all those horse folk, to feel privilege kick in: If Tom had bet enough to worry Tug as much as he had, Tug was now that much closer to affording law school.

But mostly Tug was thinking about that forty-gallon drum.

The rookie jock eased down his horse beside Equis Mini and me. Like one seasoned rider to another, we talked half standing in our stirrups. In Tug's mind then, there was no question this other jock was chatting me up—and I'm here to tell you that, yes, that's exactly what the guy was doing. And after the guy told me no one had bet on me, he was downright gross, saying things like how he himself didn't at all mind the meat on my bones, how my ass was making him hard right there in that saddle, how he wished I would ride him that night, how the women's restroom at the north end of the grandstand was always pretty much empty, so if he'd ever see me at the track, all I'd need to do was nod his way.

And as Tug would tell me weeks later, it was right about then, as this guy was being crude with me, that Tug, without hearing a word of it, breathed in the Tonawanda's smell and, for the first time in my presence, got tearful and hot-faced in a way that over-came him so quickly and powerfully he completely gave up on understanding himself. Tug's fears about the missing forty-gallon drum made sense to him, but what confused him was that there was this little piece of him that wished his father *would* disap-pear and never return, and Tug hated how this little piece of him-self had been there for a while now and seemed destined to last forever—and he turned away from me and everyone present as best he could, glaring at the tear-blurred tree line along the Tonawanda itself.

But that river's smell did sort of calm him. It reminded him of moss and turtles. Then he heard the peaceful sound of hoofs trot-ting willingly toward him, and he collected himself and turned to see Equis Mini and me pull up near Tom, Tom's face sporting a grin Tug knew well was impossible to read.

"You won," Tom told me again.

And I asked him, "Did you bet on me?"

"What?" he said.

"You didn't bet on me, did you, Tom," I said. My thumbnails dug into the rough side of the reins, and now here I was, getting all teary eyed, like Tug just had. "You backed *down*," I said. "You thought I was too big for the horse."

"None of us backed down, honey," Colleen called softly.

"Yes, you did," I said. "The rookie jock just told me. And he didn't have reason to lie."

"Sure, he did," Tom said. "He had pride. Pride and losing make any man lie."

"*You're* lying," I said. "You didn't bet on me, and we all know it."

"Jan?" Tom said. "That's no way to talk to me."

"I want to see the four thousand," I said.

"My money's my business," Tom said, and Tug kept his eyes fixed on Tom's face right then and glared at him hard, as if to say to him, *Four thousand?*—because, even for the Corcoran family, four grand was a hefty chunk to bet on a sprint.

Then again, Tug realized when Tom's eyes skipped from Tug's to mine to Colleen's, their forty-gallon drum was gone.

Tom loved one of us more than he loved the rest, and—if you believed gambling lore—that person's days were numbered.

# 19

# DEESH

**"SO YOU DIDN'T LOAD IT?"** I ask Bark.

"Why would I?" he says, and he pulls into traffic, turning up dashboard hip-hop I right away snap off. He speeds uptown, away from Mississippi unless we're using the Tappan Zee Bridge, hangs a right onto 216th, stops across from his favorite bodega.

No freaking way, I think, but he's already out his door and run off, so here I am, again double-parked, no flashers on, rush-hour traffic approaching behind, and this is 216th Street in the Bronx, remember, with dusk already thick—it's like I'm asking for trouble. What Bark's doing right now is buying a six, since, without beer, he won't be able to stay cool. He'll sip as he drives. He'll sip because winning big at the track makes him as nervous as he gets when he loses. He'll sip because he used to deal weed and smoke the profits—until cops fired eighteen rounds into the only nonmob supplier he knew. He'll sip because he then sold crack until a white dude in a GMC Yukon with thick-ass bulletproof windows told him to take his business elsewhere. Mostly, though, he'll sip because, on top of everything that's happened today, he can't handle the fact that last week, when he and I ran into Madalynn on that sidewalk in Brooklyn, she didn't care enough about him to ignore him as seductively as she ignored me.

# 20

# JAN

**WHEN EQUIS MINI BURST OUT** of the starting gate in that secret sprint, there was no need to whip him or urge him or jab him with my heels. There was just speed and our breathing and a feeling of flight, but none of that feeling was because of me or despite me. Instead there was only this sense of what you might call mutual shimmering, which I'm now quite sure has everything to do with the fact that there's an afterlife.

What I'm saying is that, yes, I got teary eyed just after the sprint because of what that rookie jock had said to me, but there was a lot more to it than that. Mostly I got that way because, during that sprint's twenty-one seconds, it hit me that my father's departed spirit was somehow inside that little horse; somehow, wherever my father's soul had gone after he'd drowned in those sun-bleached weeds, it was now back on earth with me; somehow he was, through Equis Mini's effort to run as fast as a shooting star, trying to say to me: *If you, young lady, truly want to keep on, know I am here, with you.*

And this got me all the more emotional right then because, for months before that sprint—years, really—I'd been trying never to think about my father because of something that happened when I was a junior in high school. See, I had this friend named Stephanie Campbell, one of those best friends you get stuck with because you're a dumbshit in your teens, and Stephanie invited me for a Saturday night sleepover, and beforehand her parents spoiled us by making us a steak dinner with champagne and au gratin potatoes and asparagus—in fact I'll always remember Mrs. Campbell as the adult who taught me to eat asparagus spears with my fingers.

And Stephanie and I ate our steaks and drank that champagne and stayed up till all hours talking in her room, mostly about the many vacations she and her parents had taken, and I fell asleep listening to her, then had this dream about riding a train over the Pacific Ocean. And the train made an unscheduled stop at a station crawling with vines, and I was about to drink water from a natural spring there when I ran into my father, who, in the dream, was a thoroughbred *owner* and even more handsome than my mother had always described him, but then I needed to get back on the train and he said he wanted to stay, so I hugged him harder and harder—and I woke up hugging Stephanie, who kept trying to shove me off her and shush me. And she was all flustered because she thought I was trying to hump her; she insisted I leave and never talk to her again, and then, within days, there came to be all sorts of rumors about me at school—I was a lesbian, I'd slept with half the girls' varsity lacrosse team, I had a large collection of dildos, I rode horses because straddling them brought me to orgasm, I regularly went down on the retired hot-walker who'd taught me to ride horses in the first place, and together this hot-walker and I had manually stimulated a stallion.

If these rumors strike you as outlandish, remember one thing: They *did* all take root in small-town America. And let me say for the record that none of these rumors were true. Not that I was a virgin, so might I add that there were also numerous false rumors about what I'd done with a good portion of the male population of Pine Bluff. I guess you could say I never did fit in there.

But what I want you to know I still haven't said. Which is that I got so despondent about the rumors I practically stopped going to school and spent as much time as I could hanging out with old horses at the retired hot-walker's trail-riding stable. And one day the retired hot-walker took a look at me and must have seen despondency all over my face, because she said, "There's a woman here needs to see something, and she ain't me," then drove me, in her dented sky blue Subaru, for miles and miles until, on a two-laner in country that was darned remote even for Arkansas, she stopped. And out my window was pretty much just a bright white post-and-board fence, and beyond the fence was land pitched gently upward so you almost couldn't see, on the horizon up there, a big old decrepit mansion. And between that mansion and us, near the white post-and-board, were a couple of silver thoroughbreds—two-year-old colts, it appeared, since they still had muscle to put on.

And the hot-walker nodded to assure me we were there to watch those colts, so that's what I did, already in love with how their coats shone, how they stood beside each other despite the smooth acres of emerald grass stretching out for them, and then one nudged the other's withers in play and headed off, away from the fence, and the other kicked up turf to follow, and soon they were side by side in a canter, and then they broke into a gallop, challenging each other for the pure and unquestioned fun of it, like two kids seeing who's fastest on some school's asphalt track in summertime.

This was joy I was seeing, gloriously contagious joy. Both of my arms had gooseflesh. And the hot-walker said, "Honey, *that*, right there, is why your daddy was a champion. The man made every horse he rode want to run with such joy." And I nodded, and she went on to say, "Those kids in Pine Bluff badmouthing you? They only *wish* they could have been born to a daddy like that."

And from then on, I would want badly to run in a race like I'd just seen: two souls moving ahead uncommonly fast, conjuring the words *I Am Here, With You.*

# 21

# DEESH

**SO, YEAH, HERE'S BARK LEAVING** the bodega across the street from where I sit in his truck, and I remember one of those thoughts I was sure Jasir had—*This serious dude is your daddy no doubt*—and Bark nods at me with a forced smile. And it's then that I see this cop, a white guy, maybe half a block east, walking toward me on 216th, Bark now jogging with his eyes like lasers on mine. And it hits me right then that any decent person can end up being trapped by friendship, because if you care, you care, and there's always that question of how much of your own lot you'll risk for your friend— versus how much you'll fend for yourself.

And here I am again, putting my ass on the line for the sake of friendship with Bark, because I'm sliding over onto the driver's seat of his truck, to keep the cop's attention off him and his damned concealed gun.

And just as Bark gets in the passenger side, the cop points at me. As in the cop wants me to stay put.

Take off, I think, though now here comes the cop, hustling ass toward us, all proudly uniformed and weight trained and clean shaven, motioning for me to roll down the driver's-side window.

Just drive, I think.

But I am Bark's friend.

I roll down the window, all the way, to keep the cop's focus on me and therefore off Bark and the gun. Bullshit the guy, I tell myself. Sometimes you're good at that.

Then the cop draws his gun. It's all of a sudden as if my insides are up to my throat, to the point that I can barely say, "Sir, what are you doing?"

"My job," the cop says. "Hands on the steering wheel, brother." He waves the gun at Bark and says, "Hey, *big* guy. Paws on the dash."

# 22

# JAN

**BEHIND THE WHEEL OF HIS PICKUP,** Tom Corcoran said, "Care to bet with me tomorrow?"—and Tug thought, Here we go, because Tug was sure Tom had yet again scared up a serious lock, some juiced-up sure thing supposedly set to get the Corcorans back to even with whoever had absconded with their drum.

But Tug shook his head no. Then he went all tongue-tied, like his mother sometimes would after a horse they'd piled on lost. And then there Tug was, promising himself he'd never bet a cent for the rest of his life, not even on a raffle ticket for the worthiest cause—since it was finally clear to him that the best thing gambling could do was distract a guy from what a guy wanted but couldn't have.

But then there was Tom, glancing back and forth, between the moonlit road and Tug.

"Why not," Tom asked.

Tug shrugged. You don't dislike the guy, he thought. You just hate being scared.

Their pickup's engine purred, and Tom leaned back. "Something wrong?"

"Not at all."

"It's about Jan, right?"

"Yeah, what happened last night anyway?" Tug said. "*Did* you cancel a bet because you thought she looked too heavy for the horse?"

In the blue glow of his dashboard, Tom went as still as a gut-hooked muskie floating dead in morning sunshine.

"You did, didn't you," Tug said. "You canceled your bet on her."

Tom sighed. "Tug, I didn't cancel a damned thing."

"Wait. No. *Dad.* Don't tell me. You actually bet *against* her?"

"Don't want to discuss it, son."

"You did! You bet against her!"

Tom kept shaking his head no.

Tug shook his, too, all but breathless. "And you *lost!*"

"That's enough out of you," Tom said. "That's enough."

And it was those last two words of Tom's that assured Tug that his father had lost far into the thousands. Plus he was betting against people he was supposed to care for. And it had been months, Tug realized, since Tom had mentioned their progress in saving for Tug's college tuition.

Milkweeds zipped past. Tug swallowed something like carsickness: disdain. Despite it, he eased his eyes toward his father, who handled a curve with the confidence of a man who'd never lost a cent, but then Tom's gaze at the road lost spirit, as it would after his quietest arguments with Tug's mother after a luckless day at the track. Tom was, as everyone needed to admit, an outsider, a guesser, a wonderer—in his own words, a goddamned grandstander.

So as a kind of compromise Tug said, "I guess you were just trying to help her."

Tom nodded, then drove on.

And Tug thought: Remember, you're this man's *son*.

And what's important is you're both still here.

And now they were picking up speed.

"I was sure she would lose," Tom said. "And I thought the experience of riding Equis Mini would be the best way to let her down easily."

Which was the most direct way Tom could muster, Tug figured, of admitting that, yes, Tom *had* bet against me when I'd won on Equis Mini.

Which assured Tug that, yes, Tom had also vandalized Tug's horse farm's fence and walked off with Silent Sky.

*Tom* had sold Silent Sky to a rendering plant for gambling cash.

And that was that.

And now here Tug was, grabbing the dash because Tom was hitting the brakes.

"What," Tug said.

"Someone," Tom said. They stopped completely and Tom clicked on the brights. "Someone's up there."

"Where."

"I think that's her. Off to the side. God, Tug, that is her. What in hell is she doing?"

And, see, I'd only been doing what Tom had more or less advised me to do, running in the dark. And when I'd do this and any headlights behind me brightened, I'd always veer onto the gravel shoulder and turn to see who it was, and this time the glare from the brights had me unsure, but their steadiness on me had me feeling, with butterflies pretty much gone crazy in my stomach, that I was facing the Corcorans' pickup, which might have meant Tug was there.

Then I heard Tom's voice call, "What're you doing?"

"Running," I shouted.

"From what."

"Just, you know, trying to get in shape."

"Want a lift back?"

"Got a ways to go but thanks," I said, and it was only then that I noticed someone else had gotten out, too, Tug, I sensed given the silhouette's angular torso, and I couldn't make out his eyes or face but saw him headed my way, and Tom got back in the pickup, then held on to his door.

"Son?" he called.

"I think I'll stay," Tug called, maybe a little peeved, maybe a little nervous, and I wondered what was on his mind while neither he nor I nor Tom spoke, and then I felt a finger touch the side of my neck, on that ticklish spot where your jawline begins, and a jolt shot through me. This jolt was like the electric feeling I'd had on Equis Mini but far shorter and much stronger, and it teased me with promise about kissing later in secret and making love, and I didn't know what got me more, the charge it put in me or how Tug had made sure it hadn't overpowered me. And then he, Tug, very quietly said, "You had a bug there," and if this was a lie, I didn't care: I just wanted another jolt.

And Tom, from beyond the glare from his brights, called, "Suit yourself," and then came the slam from his yanking closed the door Tug had left open.

And then the truck itself rolled toward us but went right on past. It stopped and made a U-turn, then passed us again, gone now except for the sound of its shifting gears, and I pretended to listen to that sound fade, to let Tug know I, too, cared about family, but also to offer that same place on my neck.

Because my loudest thought then was *Kiss me there.*

# 23

# DEESH

**YOU'RE NOT SCARED, I THINK.** And you've been cool around cops before. Still, I don't like the look in this one's eyes: too self-assured and enthused for a stranger planning to stay cool also. I grab the steering wheel and say, "C'mon, officer, you can't just shoot a guy."

"I can if I have reason," he says.

"Well, I think it's clear to everyone here that I haven't done anything."

He considers my expression, which I'd swear is blank. With his focus now off Bark, I feel the tiniest victory—for my friendship with Bark and my kinship with everyone born black and thin on love. The cop glances over the roof of the pickup, then to his right, then his left. He is young, easily five years younger than Bark and me. He says, "You double-parked, bro."

"That's not cause for arrest," I say. "That's just citation material."

His finger, I notice, is on the trigger. I say, "Anyway, officer, since when does a working brother's quick double-park threaten your life?"

He studies me hard now, tacks on a seriously slow once-over, fascinated, it seems, by my hairline, then my shoulders. He says, "Boy, why not just worry about *your* life?"

And all I can think to say is "Did you just call me *boy*?"

"Opie, you're like fifty years out of date with that boy shit!" Bark shouts, and he's facing the windshield, maybe looking for more cops.

"You guys saying you have a problem with me?" the cop asks.

"Just trying to clue you in, man," I say.

"Yeah," Bark shouts, louder this time. "Y'all need to open your ears and learn from us elders about how to be cool."

"Maybe you should show me how to be cool out here," the cop says. "Maybe you should get your lazy ass out of this truck and stand in front of me like a man and tell me why, in this country, any guy, of *any* age or color, can't *jokingly* call another guy whatever the hell he wants."

I clear my throat as an excuse not to swallow. He's blabbing on like this, I'm sure, because he's power tripping if not looking for probable cause, and I'm all the more sure that, by now, Bark's got a finger on his trigger, too.

I say, "Officer, you need to know this about my friend: He's had a history of unjustly being called lazy."

"I don't give a shit about anyone's history," the cop says. "All I know is I'm looking at an overweight black man being driven around with a six-pack on his lap. If that doesn't strike you as lazy, pal, you've got some serious self-respect issues."

"Just chill, man," I say.

"*Fuck* chill. I got a job to do, and I'm doing it." The cop swallows now, the nose of his gun rising. "So get out of the car," he says quietly. "I want to see nothing in your hands, no bottles, no phones, and I want both of your lazy asses standing still out here."

And being the let's-just-get-along guy I've long tried to be, I wish that all three of us—Bark, this cop, and I—could go back and start over, not back to five minutes ago, but to our grammar school days, when we all could have grown up more mellow.

And it's just after I wish this that Bark shoots the cop.

# 24

# JAN

"**WHERE'S YOUR FLASHLIGHT?**" Tug asked me.

"It's broken," I said.

"Let me try fixing it."

"You can't," I said, now directly beside him. "I mean, there isn't one. I just didn't want you to think I was weird."

"How could you be weird? That's simply not possible. All I wanted was to know what you were doing out here."

"I told you. Getting in shape."

"So you *are* running."

"Uh-huh."

"Why at night?"

"Because. My father did, to help him beat fear." I kicked at a pebble, more butterflies in my stomach, but somehow they felt smaller. And, really, that's what I loved about Tug Corcoran: Being around him excited me yet made me feel altogether solid. "Because when you're winning a lot and getting tight mounts," I explained, "jocks on long shots will box you in—because they're envious and they'll do what they can to beat you. And when you're boxed in, you might luck into seeing an opening, which could scare you because you know you could get bumped and go down. But you can't fear going down. Because if you do, the hole will close and you'll lose."

And it was obvious what Tug was thinking then. Everyone knows that, he thought. *Grandstanders* know that.

"Which means you have to trust," I said. "And running in the dark helps you trust. Because trusting means forgetting your fear, which running in the dark helps you do."

Now Tug was the one kicking at pebbles. "How do you know all this?"

"Your dad told me some. That last part—about trust and forgetting fear—I made up. But it makes sense, doesn't it?"

"I suppose," he said.

"Why wouldn't it?"

"I don't know. Because trust can mean fearing but going ahead anyway?"

I went silent right then, and despite myself I kept still. But Tug seemed to feel patient with me, all of me including my theories and habits whether they'd prove weird or not. And it hit me that no one had ever felt patience like this for me, not even my saintly mother.

And I asked, "Is that what it's like for you?"

"Let's put it this way: If I ran with you right now, I'd be afraid."

"Because you can't see the road?"

"Yes."

"You don't *look* at the road, silly. You look at the stars."

I grabbed the sides of Tug's head right then and aimed his face skyward, my fingers partway over his ears.

"In the gap," I said. "Between the trees on the sides of the road."

And stars did form an obvious lane, wider than Tug would have guessed, it seemed, and I wondered if I had him tempted.

"That's our path," I said, and I took his hand, and we began. We ran slowly at first, side by side, and, as he'd later tell me on the summer porch, he watched the center of the lane of stars and heard my footsteps beside his and allowed the asphalt's flat grade to assure him. He thought of potholes briefly and slowed down some, but then, ahead, the sound of my footfalls thinned, so he accelerated, hearing that false wind sound that had always suggested freedom to him, freedom his paths had never led to. Then he was beside me, paced evenly with me, worried less about what bothered him most—that damned missing drum—and soon, rather than worry, he simply thought.

It's just a drum, he thought. The fact that it's gone means nothing. You can't lose your mind every time he loses money. The guy loses but he wins and things generally stay the same.

But as Tug and I ran on, he thought more, now about his father's long-held theory that when you really want something and almost get it but then don't—like when you lose a bet on a long shot by a nose—you taste both success and failure at the same time, and as a result, you feel nothing. When Tom had explained this theory to Tug, Tug had wondered if Tom was trying to tell Tug, or maybe his own self, that he and Tug's mother had never quite been in love. But now, as Tug ran with me, he wondered if maybe instead Tom had been preparing him, in Tom's indirect manner, for a life in which Tug neither ran a horse farm nor practiced law, a life in which Tug's career chose Tug rather than the other way around.

And that career, Tug now thought, might not be impressive, lu-crative, or rewarding. It might be only a job, just a way to afford a mortgage or maybe only rent. After all, there were plenty of people in the world, many of whom were regulars in the Finger Lakes grandstand in fact, who were ecstatic about any grunt work tossed their way, and it *was* possible Tug would come very close but then miss out on becoming what he wanted to be, then instead become one of those people.

If this is your fate, Tug thought as he ran on with me, get used to it. But then he felt incapable of impressing me—because if he did end up being a grunt worker, he'd never be in my league. For a long stretch under those stars I had just shown him, he resented his parents for raising him as they had, but then he assured himself that they'd done their best, which was, of course, all a guy could ask for, and then I reached a crossroads brightened by street light and sprinted across it, and he followed me into this new darkness.

And this darkness felt denser yet safer until the sound of my footsteps stopped altogether. I'd quit to catch my breath, so he quit, too. He came to a stop and turned, then stepped toward me and stood maybe three feet from me, each of us with hands on hips, both of us breathing hard and loudly, our natural way, it seemed, of conceding that the nervousness we often felt in each other's company would never be the same, I closer to being a jock, he closer to being whatever he'd become, both of us closer to mar-riage and maybe children, and, regardless of all that, both of us now sharing a bond that could always be our secret, since right now, on this road, only we knew that we'd thrown ourselves into sprints in this darkness.

And it was then that I stepped toward him and stood smack in front of him like I was pretty much saying:

*Do it.*

*Kiss me.*

And after several consecutive moments that each could have been perfect, he took a step back. Later I'd learn he'd done this because he'd seen that jerk hitting on me at the secret sprint and figured I maybe needed a break from men, but just after he stepped back, I wondered if he'd just blown our chances for a best-in-a-lifetime first kiss. And then, the longer we stood, with no summer breeze or starlight between us, the more I felt disappointment and doubt and an irksome new nervousness.

And I should probably also admit that it was then, as we stood there, that Tug realized he'd always cherish me for telling him to let light from stars guide him, so he wanted to thank me—though he was wise enough to know that thanking me out loud right then might ruin whatever good moments we had left. So he decided to instead thank me with a gift as soon as possible, not with anything near as risky as an engagement ring, just something to let me know he cared for me, maybe even believed that, despite our weirdnesses as horse folk, love between us was possible.

The problem with gifts, though, diamonds or not, was that they cost money, of which Tug never had more in his pocket than the few dollars luck had spared him if Tom had just won big. Yes, Tug had saved cash for college thanks to the horse farm's best days, but that cash had long been untouchable, sitting as it did in his parents' savings account.

What Tug needed—and soon, he realized—was work, any kind of work, even a low-paying stint like mucking stalls for some trainer who'd recently won a few purses and could now afford an extra hand. Though for Tug, employment had never come easily. Just after high school, when he'd hunted for a job painstakingly—before his parents had relented and let him use their meadow for his horse farm—owners of the most lucrative horses and the thriving shops on Main had often asked him one question, a question whose unfriendly undertow now made him cringe:

"You're that Corcoran guy's son, aren't you?"

# 25

# DEESH

**THE COP LIES ON ASPHALT** less than five feet from me, and, from the sidewalk beyond him, a teenage brother eyes me. He is not Jasir, but he still makes me realize how I, Deesh, look sitting right here, in this pickup beside this fallen cop with a bullet-torn cheek.

*"Go!"* Bark screams, the barrel of his gun now up against my ear, so I drive off, freaked by death's quickness, by Bark's now undeniable bonds with violence, by the hundreds, hell, thousands of nights I've hung with him. Were we ever blood-brother tight, even when we won state? There has always been this tendency of his to end our conversations, to not even answer my most direct questions. There has always been this unvoted-on rule that, somehow, Bark is in charge.

Hell, right now, up against his gun, I am taking lefts and rights and swerving exactly as he tells me to. I am speeding all the way to the GW Bridge, where I accelerate onto the lower level, to hide us from the helicopters he fears. Maybe, I realize, he's played pals with me for those times when, against my better judgment, I'd accept UPS'd packages full of baby powder and crack for him at my address, or I'd answer his phone when common sense screamed it was stupid to help him lay low.

And now, on the dash radio, there's this white dude saying, "police activity in the Bronx," which means Bark and I aren't far from millions of people wanting our faces torn by bullets, too.

But the broadcast gave no descriptions, I tell myself, and to calm myself I try to picture Mississippi, but Mississippi, right now, means nothing to me, no fellow tenants sure to smile, no women I've slept with, certainly no Madalynn and definitely no Jasir, and now Bark and I roll from the GW into Jersey, approaching overhead signs for Fort Lee, I-95 South, the Palisades, Highway 1, Highway 9, I-80 West, something about the end of I-95, and Bark is screaming since I'm screaming since I'm clueless about where to steer. The lane-lines are all screwed up, some new, some faded, some crooked, some suddenly ending, a trucker in front of us veering as if to say *he's* the boss of this stretch, so when I see his flushed-pink face in his side mirror I scream at his move, at any racism in him, at the dead cop's racism, at all of the white hatred in the world.

# 26

# JAN

THE FIRST TIME TOM TOOK ME to the backside of the Finger Lakes racetrack, he drove up to the wooden arm keeping us from the parking lot, and the guard in the booth said, "Got your ID?"

"You serious?" Tom asked.

"Track policy, sir. Always has been. Just got a new boss is all."

Tom glared straight ahead. Tug sighed so hard his shoulders rose and fell.

"Your phone work?" Tom asked.

"Sir?" the guard said.

"Does your *phone* work."

"I think so."

"Call your new boss and ask him who Tom Corcoran is."

And the guard made that call, which took an embarrassing while, but then the wooden arm rose and he and Tom exchanged nods, and we parked and Tom strode toward the shedrows, Tug following, me following Tug while I tried to pretend I wasn't excited as a mutt pup to be on a real racetrack's backside. Near one barn, Tom lingered for no reason apparent to me, and then, as if to show someone what a fun guy he'd been when he'd jocked, he stole a carrot from a feed bin and told a couple of chatting owners there *was* such a thing as a free lunch, so there were chuckles then, even a few laughs.

And there were a few people he knew enough to say hi to, some of them owners, though mostly we gossiped with stable hands, and, for a while, Tug talked to one of them about his horse farm, but if you asked me, people on that track's backside soft-pedaled Tug kind of like folks in Pine Bluff had done with me.

Then it was just Tug and Tom and I standing with paper cups of coffee on a freshly hosed sidewalk, and Tug glanced past Tom and said, "Think you could lend me some cash?"

"For what?" Tom said. He stuffed his fingers into his front pockets.

"Thought I might join you in backing a horse today."

Tom glanced at the grandstand. He cleared his throat, maybe to make Tug wait. Then all he said was "Why?"

"Just to join you," Tug said. "And just for one race. I just want to bet *one* horse and cheer it in for you. You know, like when you rode."

Tom set his hands on his hips, a man wise enough to know a kissing-up son when he saw one.

Finally he said, "What if we lose?"

Tug forced a smile, and Tom frowned, as if to etch that question—*What if we lose?*—into Tug's soul.

"You guys won't lose," I said, and they both stared off.

And it was maybe a second or two later, as I remember it, that Tom Corcoran cussed—only one word, but the bull's-eye.

Then he said, "How much you want," and he pulled money from his pocket, an inch-plus wad of bills folded once. The sight of so much cash put a stir in me, and his finger and thumb gestured the cash toward Tug, who could, or so it seemed, have as much of it as he wanted.

"I don't know," Tug said. "Twenty?"

Take it all! I thought. Use it for your farm!

"Wanna start small, huh?" Tom said. He unfolded the bills and thumbed out four hundreds to expose a fifty, then thumbed fifty after fifty until a ten showed. "No twenties," he said. "Tell you what. Take one of these and owe me the rest." He held out a fifty like some magician. "Just don't get bet happy on me."

And with a small nod, Tug took the fifty.

"'Bet happy'?" I asked.

"That's when you *think* you know something about horses when in fact you're just lucky," Tom said. "Happens to young men who grow up around tracks."

Tug shook his head, barely but more than once, and rolled his eyes.

"Remember," Tom said. "The best smartness comes from your heart, so once you lose sight of your heart, you'll end up betting for betting's sake."

And here he again shot me the look he'd given me on my first night in his house, the look that suggested he was trying to tell me something, which now seemed to be *Don't mess with gambling—don't even start,* and, yes, I appreciated him for that, but mostly I wished it was well past dusk and I was out running with Tug.

"But here's my simplest and best piece of advice," Tom said. "And this goes for both of you."

I widened my eyes: *Yes?*

"Always remember there are only seven important words."

And Tug walked off in a huff, like any adult child fed up with his father's advice.

Though he did then call over his shoulder, "Go ahead. Let's hear the big seven."

And Tom said, mostly to me, *"All you have to do is win."*

Tug was again shaking his head, well on his way to the grandstand, and then I heard:

"Hey, loser."

And there, maybe sixty feet down the shedrow, in shade created by a warped plywood overhang, stood a man I would come to know as Arnie DeShields. The darkness between us barely dimmed his smile, which was white and thick and fake, and he, arms crossed, was also white and thick—and tall, six feet if he slouched. So I could have looked at him as a fount of insight about how I, a young wannabe jock already considered overweight, might succeed at this track; here was a person whose size had always meant he could never jock, yet he'd figured out how to be a player here.

"Watch his hands when I talk about Devilette," Tom whispered, and he led me toward Arnie while calling, "What's the word, Arn?"

Arnie was all eyes on me as he spoke: "Pietro let us down hard yesterday." He spat tobacco juice, an orange shot raising dirt in an empty stall, and I knew—by the way he kept his hands in his back pockets and rocked on the balls of his feet, along with his deft but searing inspection of my breasts—that I'd better play it tough around him.

"Pietro didn't force you to put money on it," Tom said.

"Who said I put money on it?" Arnie asked. And here he checked out the rest of me with no apparent shame, as if he'd heard those rumors spread about me in my high school, then said to Tom, "Alls I'm saying is that the man said he was going to send the horse— and then the thing don't even land in the money."

Tom kicked down dirt. "Can't control the jock once the gates open," he said. "Right, Jan?"

I nodded, and sunlight bore down through a hole in the roof.

"I suppose," Arnie said, "you're here to ask if I'm sending Devilette tomorrow."

"It's his third maiden race and he won't be favored," Tom said. He tucked in a side of his shirt. "If he's tight and you *don't* send him, you're insane."

"Maybe I was insane to begin with," Arnie said, and he folded his hands over his paunch and cracked his knuckles, then let his fingers settle on his fleshy hips.

"Maybe we *all* begin insane," Tom said, with a wink at me. "Anyway Jan wants to make her first bet ever tomorrow. You can't help her out with some information?"

He's using me to get a tip, I thought, and I held my breath, trying to play it all off.

"You want to jock and you're already telling strangers you back horses?" Arnie asked.

"You're not a stranger," I said. "And I ain't telling no one anything."

He smiled so eagerly I could have slapped him right there. "Just remember me down the line, girl," he said. "After you collect on your first win bet ever."

Then he gave Tom a quick, sheepish nod, as if it killed his male pride to even imply what he was clearly saying: *I've gifted you. Now keep this secret so it pays off well.*

And with that and nothing else, he walked off.

Tom followed for a step or two, stopped quickly and completely only to follow all the faster, and encouraged by his speed as well as my curiosity about how a winning horse looks the day before it wins, I followed Tom.

And the first part of Devilette I saw clearly was the white Texas-shaped blaze on his snout. Then, as we headed for his unlit stall, I saw more of his head, coal black and sturdy, the whole of him calm as a statue, mane braided too tightly. He didn't flinch when I petted his neck, but his eyes struck me as flat and mean, and he stood easily three hands higher than Equis Mini had.

"He's a monster all right," I said, and Arnie and Tom nodded as if I, little Janette Price, had out of nowhere been named resident expert on what it took to win.

"Filled out in the chest," Tom said.

"Tight as a drum in a freezer," Arnie said.

"You got his front ankles wrapped," I said, remembering the wraps the hot-walker had used on her gimpier trail horses.

"To keep Pietro guessing," Arnie said.

"Gonna miss the post parade and unwrap at the last minute?" Tom asked.

Arnie shook his head. "I'm leaving 'em on. They won't stop him from winning. I want to beat that bastard Pietro and keep him guessing at the same time."

# 27

# DEESH

"BARK," I SAY. "I'M PULLING OVER if you don't put that thing down."

"It's down," he says.

I glance. His finger is off the trigger, the gun aimed down, to his right. How long has this been? Am I now aiding and abetting? And in this truck still hangs the wisdom acted upon by James: Bail on a brother before he bails on you.

Still, I drive on. You are, I remind myself, helping a man who shot a cop in the face.

And this man might still love the mother of your son.

An exit approaches. I pass it. You are a friend, I think. You are Bark's friend, and you don't bail on a friend.

And now here goes Bark, gun still aimed at the floor, working folded cash from a front pocket.

He says, "We don't ditch this truck soon, we're screwed."

"Agreed."

"So take the next exit," he says. "Then we'll have a running start on whoever might look for us."

*Is looking* for us, I almost say. "You think we should hide in Jersey?" I ask, then, after his nod, add, "Jersey's not far enough, Bark. I say we run far. Remember, we do have that cash."

"So you're saying Newark Airport."

"Too risky," I say. "With all that security? I'm thinking a bus depot, a small one. And we find it fast so we buy our tickets before we're on every TV in America."

Bark says nothing.

"And no gun," I say. "Just talk. Just whatever we need to say to get tickets."

"Fine. I mean, right? They're not gonna pull over every bus in the country to hunt us down."

*Yeah* they will, I think, but I stay quiet. And for a good half a mile, the skinny scared kid in me wants to be caught and arrested and kept far from Bark for the rest of my life.

"I'm also thinking," I say. I try three quick glances to make my point, but Bark doesn't get it—or doesn't *want* to get it, so I say it: "I'm also thinking we go different directions."

"Uh-huh."

"We need to be smart, Bark. Someone saw two brothers drive away from that dead cop. So as much as people will think black, they'll also think two."

"So where for me then?"

"You wanted Mississippi, so I'd say south. North too damn soon means Canada, where they'll check any bus at the border, so that leaves me with east or west."

"And east means back home," Bark says.

I nod, then picture myself asking for a job on some ranch in Wyoming. I might never hoop again, in a future like that.

Bark says, "You should take the gun."

"I don't think so."

"You're gonna need it, man."

"Not as much as you will. You killed a cop, Bark. You kill a cop, you need to go down shooting."

And here Bark stares longingly out his window.

I think of Jasir and say, "Plus I can't be found with that gun."

"Well, I sure can't," Bark says. "So get in the right lane—I'll toss it."

"No-no-no, Bark," I say. "Do *not* open that window." This is the advice of ex-cons talking: No other street smarts in me want the gun near.

"But it's evidence!" Bark screams.

"Which is why you don't want it out there."

"So where, then?"

"I don't know," I say. Flustered by a sudden sea of brake lights ahead, I say, "Just, just—let me take it. I'll toss it when my bus stops someplace remote."

"Like where?"

"I don't *know*, Bark," I say, shaking my head in disgust of him, of the gun, of what has become of my once stardom-promising life. "Pennsylvania?" I say. "There's bound to be a stretch in Pennsylvania that's nothing but trees."

"Fine," he says, and we go quiet, and I change lanes.

Then he says, "Here's yours."

"My what."

"Profit share. For being my blood."

I glance over and see green. I realize that, yet again, Bronx-style poverty is forcing me to sell myself out. I've done this so often it feels almost natural, and this time it will tie me even tighter to a cop shooter, this acceptance of cash that looks to be less than a grand. Very stupid, the goody-two-shoes core of me warns in some teacher's high-pitched voice, but here goes Bark recounting Benjamins as if he's always been into fairness, folding them as he hands them over, and here I am taking them, maybe but maybe not such a stupid move since, yeah, yeah, this *does* strengthen my ties to at least one murder, but cash, I know damned well, can be lost easily. Plus: As Bark places the gun on the floor just behind my feet, I tell myself I'm no longer the fool I was minutes ago, when I was one pothole away from having a bullet whiz through my brain. And then here I am, cruising down an exit ramp into Passaic, no small town but no Newark either, and the main thing is that Bark is right: These wheels need to be ditched pronto.

We pass closed warehouses and bankrupt banks grayed by soot. I head in the direction of older buildings—wouldn't a bus depot be downtown? I would ask for directions but fear being seen, then remember Madalynn declaring, before she got pregnant, that I never asked her for anything and that the reason I never did was pride, and now here's Bark, after I brake for a red light, calling "Bus depot?" to a scraggly, strung-out white dude who nods in a direction I follow. And when Bark points at the depot, there's no need to ask if we should park at least five blocks away, no need for Bark to say *"on"* or *"off"* as he shows me how to work the safety. And after we leave the truck and he holsters the gun for me between my waistband and the small of my back, there's no need for him to even raise his chin to have me stand lookout as he yanks off his truck's plates, which he hides under his shirt, then slips into a trash can as we walk.

And our coolness stays strong all the way to the depot, where I hope we'll lie well enough. I don't believe I could *aim* a gun, but that's what every convict once thought. Mostly I'm worried, as we approach the depot, about who's inside—and who will be.

And now, in the depot's parking lot, sit three idling buses, signs on two announcing the destinations D.C. and Denver, the other sign blank.

"Looks like you're set," Bark says.

"You could go to D.C."

He nods, and I remember the sweetness of an alley-oop pass I fed into his dunk in our junior year state semifinals.

"Want the gun back?" I ask.

"We'll see," he says, and we walk in. A shiny-scalped brother works the ticket counter, no one in line. I head on over. Bark stops under a TV hung from the ceiling by chains.

"One to Denver," I say.

The teller glances up. "Round trip?"

"Yes, sir."

"That'll be four hundred sixteen," he says. "And I'll need some ID."

I reach for my pocket, pull out the Benjamins, let him see them as I thumb through them, letting him know, I hope, that I can tip big.

"You know?" I say. "My ID's in my wallet." I set seven fanned hundreds on the counter, slide them over. "Which I lost." I glance over at Bark, whose jaw is now clenched.

"Gonna need that ID sooner or later," the teller says, and I nod, and then he does nothing but type.

A message to the cops? I wonder. Or plain business?

A grungy printer prints, and the teller swipes up my cash, counts it, makes change he slides toward me—with the ticket.

"Tips get me in trouble," he says, and I grab the ticket and the change. "If I were you, I'd board now."

"Appreciate it, man," I say, and I head for the door certain he's set to call 911. I flash Bark the tiniest thumbs-up, then step outside, on my damned own, bound for Cleveland or Chicago or who knows.

In the bus, which is crowded, the air is hot. I sit directly behind the white driver. Across the aisle a black woman old enough to be a grandmother and the white woman beside her are on cell phones, talking quietly. The driver swigs from a plastic bottle. My hamstrings absorb revs. I want to turn around but no way. I try to make plans for when the inevitable happens:

Pull out the gun and shoot? Pull out the gun and aim?

Pull out the gun and aim to get the bus to stop, then run off of it?

Run off with someone to use as a hostage?

Maybe the old woman?

But the old woman can probably barely run.

Under me, brakes hiss. We are backing up onto the street. We stop. We ease ahead, make a left. We are rolling when a squad car speeds toward us and stops, facing me only, it seems, the bus squeaking to a halt, its driver standing and pointing at his chest as if to say *Me?*

A cop leaves the squad car, pistol drawn. He heads toward the bus and I stand and step into the aisle, beside the two women. The old woman glances at me, though she seems too focused on the cop's gun to notice the one that's now at my side. Outdoors, the armed cop is flanked by his partner. They walk toward the front of the bus, then pass it to head toward the parking lot, where Bark might or might not now be. I slide his gun back against my waistband. Has anyone seen? A white guy five rows back speaks into a phone.

The engine of the bus revs, and we accelerate. Just make it to D.C., Bark, I think as I sit, though I know Bark's odds are long.

Still, I can hope. Everything, I remind myself, needs to appear innocent. I close my eyes as if asleep, open them. No one near is checking me out, the white guy now off his cell, motionless, his own eyes shut. The driver looks to be busting ass to leave Jersey, and, yes, he could be headed to some cop shop, but after we merge onto I-80 West, I doubt it. Behind me might be true relaxation: newspapers being unfolded, chips bags being torn.

Then it strikes me that, if those two cops find Bark in the bus depot parking lot, they'll ask that teller about me.

But that teller's a brother, I think. He won't squeal.

I reconsider this, then decide there's no predicting who'll squeal when about anything. Plus I keep remembering the cop's open dead eyes. And the thud of that drum upstate when Bark, James, and I dropped it beside that straightaway. My thumb rubs mud from the zigzagging tread of one of my sneakers, mud maybe from that gulley itself.

Should've never touched the drum, I think. Should've never gotten involved with money that big.

# 28

# JAN

THAT FIFTY-DOLLAR BILL was by far the most money Tom Corcoran had ever given Tug to gamble with, and the next morning he and Tug hit the track without me, standing with horses and barn hands just outside shedrow stalls, often without speaking, just breathing the smells of hay and feed and sun-softened hose rubber. Then the beginnings of shadows said it was just past noon, and Tug felt the weight of another day's races come upon them, in a way, he then believed, only he, Tug, could, and Tom pulled an emerald blade of grass from between his teeth, elbowed Tug, and said, "Let's go."

They were beside the Capizzi barn then, Frank Capizzi and his brothers having never arrived, and they walked away knowing the Capizzis might have juiced a horse and were now keeping it secret, and the Ecuadorian hands watched them leave.

Devilette, the only tip horse Tom liked on that day's card, was running in race two. How Tom had gotten the tip was something he didn't want to discuss with Tug, which bothered Tug, though not enough for Tug to force questions about it, and anyway what bothered Tug most was he couldn't decide what gift to buy for me. It needed to be something serious enough to let me know he'd always cherish our running in the dark, yet he didn't want it to cause me to consider him sappy—and he didn't want it to remind me that he wasn't stinking rich.

Before race one, as Tom bought programs, greed urged Tug to bet Devilette as half of a daily double, but Tug knew what any grandstander knew—the double was a sucker bet—so he brushed off that temptation, then followed Tom across the upper grandstand toward the empty seats nearest the top of the homestretch. Tom had named this area The Crux because that turn is where jockeys most often affect races: where their whistling gets loud, where they flap whips dramatically to force oncoming horses to run wide, where they cuss to rattle the favorite or talk to fix results, where they kiss-kiss secretly game horses into finally making big moves.

"This is good here," Tom said now.

"Without the crowd," Tug said.

"Without anyone."

Tug wondered who else Tom was avoiding. Tug's mother? Some loan shark? Me?

And Tug eyed the odds board as Tom studied his program and chewed his fingernails, a habit recently revived from the days when he rode.

"Let the first race go," Tom said, as if to himself.

"I told you," Tug said. "I'm backing *one* horse. In one race."

"And you like Devilette."

"Shouldn't I?"

"Not with your life."

"I thought you said he was a lock. I mean, this was one of those man-to-man tips, wasn't it?"

Tom flipped to race two in his program.

"It was," he said.

Devilette was the three horse, which meant he didn't have to break against the rail, and he had Jorge Garcia on him and no workouts listed, his morning line six to one.

"His odds will go off lower than that," Tom said, and Tug slipped two fingers in his pocket and fished out the fifty Tom had lent him and wondered if their tip had long been common knowledge, and race one began and ended with the frontrunner stealing the win. That meant today's track might have been biased toward speed, and Tug realized, given what he knew about Arnie DeShields from Tom's riding days, that Devilette was probably trained to run from behind. So a speed-biased track, Tug told himself, would only make their wagering victory more impressive and heartfelt, and he remembered Tom's speech the previous day about winning and heart and luck, and he supposed the point of that speech was that if he, Tug, won this bet on Devilette—or any bet on any horse, really—he should temper all joy about making money so quickly and easily, and Tug resented such discipline and wished he could be elsewhere, but then he told himself he was about to make the cash necessary to buy the perfect gift for me, and sitting there, in that grandstand beside his father, felt right. Tug stared at the pond in the middle of the track during a silence that bothered him minimally, then remembered watching me reel in the last keeper muskie I'd hooked, then wished he'd kissed me after we'd run through the dark so his memory could now replay whatever would have happened after such a kiss, then wondered why his father and mother had kissed for the first time, touched each other, made love, married, taken vacations, cheered for horses, argued, retired, kissed for the thousandth time, ignored each other, spent days with him, lied to each other, stared at their aging nakedness, bet on strangers' horses, slept. He glanced at Tom and reminded himself that Tom would always be his one and only father, then noticed that Tom was now watching the pond. Tug wondered if Tom was picturing my dad—Tom's long-ago colleague, the renowned Jamie Price—groping for air in the sun-bleached weeds only to swallow water, and then the bugle announced the post parade, and Devilette appeared from beneath the grandstand and stepped onto the track, black and shiny as a showroom Maserati, all of its ankles wrapped with bright white tape, one hoof, then another, spoiling the freshly furrowed dirt.

And Tug had long known that Arnie DeShields didn't wrap ankles to keep them strong.

He wrapped them to make gamblers feel fear.

# 29

# DEESH

**NIGHT THIS FAR WEST IN JERSEY** is twice as thick as it gets in the Bronx, and trying to see through it out my window gets me thinking about Madalynn and her complaint, before she got pregnant, that I never asked for what I needed, her claim back then being that there was only one way couples in poverty stayed true: awareness of need nursed by constant mutual asking. Had my pride allowed me to *ask*, she'd say back then, we could have both known our needs and *been* something, and I now wonder if maybe, when you really get down to it, she was right, and after we pass a sign that says DELAWARE WATER GAP, another says ENTERING PENNSYL-VANIA, and I shiver.

Even if those cops in Passaic wanted my arrest to catch me by surprise, I tell myself, they would have pulled this bus over by now. Everything's cool.

But across the aisle from me the white woman, ponytailed, maybe college age, keeps glancing over, like she's ready to ask something—until I'm set to say what's up, when she sighs and faces the all but black night. And now, with her eyes off me like that, my mind won't stop seeing the cop down. Won't stop focusing on how blood filled the hole in his face. Won't stop thinking about how that was *it* I was looking at—death—and how it forever would be caused by a bullet fired from the gun now pressed against my hip bone so hard it hurt.

A mile marker says Pennsylvania will stretch three hundred miles. I watch darkness grow darker, thanks to more trees and monstrous hills. Only here and there are the lit yards of lone houses, but still I think:

*Keep going.*

*You need to be in pure nature.*

# 30

# JAN

DEVILETTE HELD HIS HEAD HIGHER than the rest of the field, trying to see beyond the odds board, and Jorge Garcia, in bumblebee-colored silks, sat on him comfortably, going with the bounce of the canter.

"Prepared to lose?" Tom asked.

"Why?" Tug said. "You don't think he looks right?"

"I think he'll be there. But a savvy handicapper never bets a penny he can't afford to lose."

"I can afford it," Tug said, and Tom stood, and Tug handed him the fifty. "Ten to win on Devilette," Tug said, and it wasn't lost on him that Tom was about to do for him the very kind of thing that had gotten Tom in trouble, and Tug considered asking for the money back, but Tom raised a thumb and walked off. Tug wondered how he'd pay Tom back if Devilette didn't win, then convinced himself that, if he lost, he'd find work, any kind of work. He imagined himself trying for jobs he'd never considered—truck driver, auto mechanic, gas station cashier—and his horse farm struck him as the kind of dream that makes you look foolish unless you're born with a silver spoon, and his face grew hot from shame and sentiment about certain horses he'd cared for and that god-awful feeling he sometimes got when certain he'd never know what he was feeling.

Don't worry, he thought. No one sees you now. He also believed that no one but Tom would know they'd bet this race, and that the only reason he, Tug, had bet was because he loved me. In that sense it seemed good and even admirable that he had done it, and then Tom returned with Tug's ticket and change, all of which Tug folded into a square he shoved well into a front pocket, and then it was post time, and an assistant starter Tug didn't recognize was loading Devilette into the third stall. Tom slouched back in his seat, his eyes, intent and forlorn, on the midnight blue starting gate, and Tug wanted to grab his wrist but told himself they were too old for that, and then the flag was up, and they were off, and Devilette took a bad step and Tug's heart went dead. Jorge let out the reins right then, and Devilette, nine lengths behind, found his stride, and they were all into the turn but the seven horse led by one, and then the pack tightened, Jorge's bumblebee colors gaining, and Jorge took him at least six wide and used the whip. Tug didn't hear it crack until a moment after it struck—and Devilette shot ahead into third, and Tom rose and Tug stood, too, and Devilette, game, closed the gap. Well down the stretch they were even, Devilette and the seven, and Jorge now whipped cruelly, and Devilette nosed ahead, then hung on.

"Sweet," Tug said, though all this victory had done was bring his mood back to even.

Tom glanced off, toward the finish line more or less, then focused on the results board.

"You bet him, too, right?" Tug asked.

"I put him in an exacta with Capizzi's entry."

Tug skimmed race two in his program to see which number Capizzi's entry wore. The exacta, he knew from Tom's past advice, was not a bet Tom generally endorsed.

"Capizzi's was the one horse," Tom said. "She photoed for second with the seven."

The results board showed three in the WIN box, the PLACE and SHOW boxes blank. Tug stared at the darkness inside the PLACE box, trying, for Tom's sake, to will the numeral one to appear in it, and as Tug stared, he knew Tom was watching that darkness, too. Tug tried not to jinx things by wanting more than one thing at the same time, but right then he more than anything wanted to run in the dark with me: He was not, he finally realized then, in that minute of that hour on that day, what Tom would consider an ideal gambling pal. Devilette had gone off at three to one, which meant Tug himself would profit at least thirty dollars, but what did Tom care about thirty bucks flowing from the track to Tug?

And wasn't thirty only a small step toward payment for the diamond earrings Tug now wanted to give me?

Then the PLACE box flashed seven, and Tom said, "Dammit."

"I'm sorry," Tug said.

"For what?" Tom said. "*I'm* the one who screwed up. I shouldn't have gotten greedy and gone for the exacta."

"You didn't bet Devilette straight up at all?"

"No. I lost everything. Which shows you how fucking out of my mind I am."

Lost everything? Tug thought. "How much did you bet?" he asked.

"That's not the issue. The issue is why."

"Well?" Tug said. "Then why?"

Race three's odds appeared on the board, staring back at them.

"I borrowed some money," Tom said.

He assessed Tug unabashedly, as if he'd just explained everything irrational he'd ever done in his life.

"And I wanted you to be an attorney someday," he said. *"And* have your horse farm."

"We gotta be realistic," Tug said, even as he thought: He just lost his ass and then some. He's out of control doubling down.

"Not to mention *someone* had to come up with the cash to pay Jan for those muskies," Tom said now.

"You're saying you won that muskie cash gambling?"

"At first."

"But why? I mean, why pay her to fish?"

"Because Cindy was too proud to take a direct handout. Cindy and Jan were *broke*, Tug. They couldn't pay their rent in Arkansas. Your mother and I—this whole thing started with us trying to do the right thing."

The odds up on the board flashed and changed. One of the outside-post entries in the upcoming race was a one-to-nine favorite, meaning some owner had piled on it so heavily it would barely bring a profit.

"But now you're doubling down with borrowed money?" Tug said.

Tom shrugged.

"And losing," Tug said. "To chumps."

"Don't worry about the chumps. The chumps will never touch you."

"What about Mom? What if they go after her—or Cindy or Jan?"

"They wouldn't. They never touch the women. That's code."

"They got The *Form* Monger's wife."

"No, they didn't, Tug. The *Form* Monger's wife ran off."

"With one of them?"

Again, Tom shrugged. "What's the difference, Tug? It makes no difference. The man's wife left town, and then the only one they went after was him."

Tug couldn't stop shaking his head, unable to say as much as one darned word, shocked as he was that Tom knew so much about crimes of that magnitude.

"So don't worry about that, Tug," Tom said. "You worry too much. Anyway, let's just go. But you do need to realize that you worry too much. I don't know where you *got* that. Your mother— your mother? Your mother probably wants both of us home."

# 31

# DEESH

**SOMEWHERE PAST MILE MARKER 220,** the bus veers onto an exit ramp, then brakes to a halt at a stop sign. It turns right and comes to rest in a minimart parking lot, and I think, Someone's here to cuff me.

The engine clicks off. The driver stands and passengers stir. An old maroon minivan sits in the fluorescent light spilling outside the minimart's front windows.

"Ten minutes," the driver calls, and he heads down the stairs and off. Men behind me glance at each other. I am hungry, so I leave the bus, walk over the gravel parking lot toward the store. Armed as I am, I fear power. A small TV beside the coffeemaker shows cable news, and I see the words BREAKING STORY. I glance off, hear the news reporter explain that, for the fatal cop shooting in the Bronx, police have someone in custody, and this someone, the police are saying, is Cornelius Barker.

*Bark.*

Then a detective being interviewed declares Bark merely a person of interest.

Bark, this detective says, has cooperated fully.

And thanks to Bark, this detective says, a country full of capable law enforcement is now searching for me.

I pretend to read the nutrition information on a small jar of bean dip. I am sweating full-out. The broadcaster talks on, about the shot cop's wife and kids, the hand at my side now a fist. Madalynn and Jasir keep walking up to me in my mind, stopping to face me on that sidewalk in Brooklyn, but mostly I'm trying to keep composed while squaring myself with the truth that, goddammit, Bark sold me out. I fear the suspicion of the redheaded woman at the register and decide not to go back on the bus—Bark knows I was on it. I grab a chocolate bar, then two more, walk to the counter, pull a ten from my cash, trying too late to keep the hundreds hidden. I pay, nod at the cashier as I take the change. She doesn't nod back, and to keep myself calm I tell myself she's just shy.

Then I'm out the door, headed for the bus, the driver, now seated, watching me or someone behind me. I stop on parking lot gravel twenty feet from him, pocket the chocolate bars, touch my toes as if I'm stretching, take a step away from him toward the middle of the bus, where I stretch again. Other passengers leave the minimart, headed toward me. Did they see the news broadcast? Did they listen? I reach overhead as if stretching my arms, step a little more toward the rear of the bus. I am alternately stretching and easing myself toward a spot behind the bus, where I hope the darkness of this night, thicker still here than it was in Jersey, will soon hide me completely.

Then I am back there, five feet behind the warmth and bitter smell of bus exhaust, not stretching, facing neither the minimart nor the bus driver, facing the nearby woods, not doing much except maybe appearing suspicious. It's my fear of wilderness—bears and wolves, yeah, but what's always scared the shit out of me is how even the tiniest mouse can have rabies—that keeps me from sprinting into the woods, the border between this asphalt I stand on and all those trees not even forty feet off.

I am that close. I am that scared. I consider how Madalynn and Jasir would feel if I were arrested, and with them well in mind, I think: Go.

# 32

# JAN

**FOR A COUPLE NIGHTS AFTER** Tom Corcoran took me and Tug to the track's backside, I finally slept well, almost luxuriously, seduced into all but sexy dreams rooted in my confidence in becoming a jock, dreams about crisp morning workouts and braided manes and nationally televised post parades, about turquoise and maroon and lime green silks blurred gloriously as I'd weave a game colt through an unyielding pack, about gearing down graded-stakes champs yards before the wire to save their gas for future wins. In one dream, I sat in this huge chrome grandstand packed with Ecuadorian farmhands chatting and laughing controllably like wealthy folks do, and I woke from that dream certain these people and I had won some revolution, then lay there, on the Corcorans' summer-porch cot, savoring this sense of victory, pushing out my heels to stretch my calves, which felt leaner and not at all sore. And it was then, lolling around like this, that I realized how I could use Arnie DeShields: Ask him to get me a track ID.

That's really all you need, I thought. *Access.* And I faced the lake and rose for the day.

The living room, still untouched by that dawn's sunlight, was soundless as I walked through. In the kitchen, Colleen stood beside the table, staring down at an unopened *Form.*

"Morning," I said, and I headed for the coffeepot, which wasn't on. "And I really do mean it, Colleen. This has got to be one of the best."

I filled the pot at the sink, measured out the coffee.

Colleen didn't move, not even to nod.

"Colleen?" I said.

"Jan," she said quietly.

"What."

"Tom is gone."

And right then the screen door opened, and Tug walked in. He faced Colleen as if he and I had never met. "Nothing odd, really. The pickup's still there, so maybe he went for a jog?"

Tom's glasses lay there, near the *Form.*

"You know the drum's gone, right?" Colleen asked Tug.

"What do you mean?" he said.

"Our forty-gallon drum," she said. "For burning leaves."

"So?" Tug said, sour-faced.

"He didn't say anything to you, Jan?" Colleen asked. "About anything having to do with horses?"

I remembered what Tom had said to Tug and me just before I'd met Arnie DeShields, about the effects of betting horses on the human heart, and I figured Tug would now pipe up about this, but Tug just stepped back to the screen door and stared out.

"Not really," I said, to play things safe.

"You have no idea why he might be gone?" Colleen asked.

I shook my head no, worried she was thinking about the hours Tom had spent without her in the kitchen in the middle of most every night. Was she implying she suspected he'd come on to my mother?

Didn't she know he studied past performances while the world slept at night? Wasn't it common knowledge that, if Tom Corcoran were at all a religious man, the *Daily Racing Form* was his bible?

# 33

# DEESH

**SUMMERTIME IN PENNSYLVANIA'S** woods isn't as hot as it is in the Bronx. But there's brush you can feel trapped forever inside, which can make you sweat fast. And, for real, there is no path anywhere. There are only trees and a darkness more serious than any I've walked through. It's everywhere above and between the branches and down to the rocks and vines and dirt under my feet. I'd fear wildlife more if I wasn't sorting through thoughts about Bark:

The guy stabbed your back.

*And he's a killer.*

Possibly turned on you long ago, when he knew you slept with Madalynn.

Who knows?

Who cares?

And of course I care, but I can't afford to care. Any focus on my past, I think, saps focus from what I'll need to do to survive from now on.

Keeping walking, I think.

Keep training your mind to avoid light.

The less you can see anything near you, the less likely you will be seen.

You can't risk being perceived as the brother on the run.

From now on, there must be no people.

# 34

# JAN

**FOR HOURS AFTER** Colleen and Tug and I realized Tom was indeed gone, we visited every barn on the track's backside, asking about Tom as nonchalantly as possible. We checked the paddock and the crowd near the winner's circle and every nook of the grandstand, and Tug himself checked the jocks' locker room, where he was played off until Jorge Garcia raised his eyes and shook his head no.

Minutes before the first race that day, Colleen said she was thinking of going into town to ask around about Tom there, and her use of that phrase—*into town*—caused Tug's throat to catch, probably because reliance on people like Bill Treacy struck him as a notch above desperation.

And my crush on Tug did not in the least keep me from noticing that catch in his throat, and I right off suggested it might be best if Tug and I stayed on at the track, and Colleen paused to consider this, maybe trying to decide if the track was still a comforting place the Corcorans could use to escape their troubles, then nodded good-bye and headed off. And, standing there, with me and me only, Tug convinced himself that Tom was as likely to appear here as anywhere, and he focused on the action of the first race, then on the uplifting reds and pinks and yellows of the picnics near the snapdragons and phlox.

Then a voice behind Tug said, "Champ."

And Tug and I didn't turn around because it sounded like Arnie DeShields, and Tug didn't want to give Arnie the satisfaction of watching him blink if Arnie asked, "Where's the old man?"—and I didn't want to give Arnie any satisfaction period.

"*Champ*," the voice said.

"Someone's talking to you," I told Tug. Race two's entries were being led from the stables to the paddock, unsaddled, unmounted, just horses.

"I don't think so," Tug said. "I think the sonofabitch is talking to you."

# 35

# DEESH

**I DO NOT SLEEP.** I keep walking through gangs of gnats and mosquitoes and streetlight-forsaken darkness. For hunger, there are the three chocolate bars. For fatigue, there's plenty of fear.

In late morning sunshine on the fourth hill, I hear no birdcalls or traffic noises or swishes from breezes. Bears, I keep promising myself, would hate this much light. My insides are jittery yet my pace stays even. Maybe, I now believe, a guy actually can disappear into woods.

When I see a gravel road, I stop. Everyone knows one road leads to another, and this one is at the very bottom of the hill I'm descending in zigzags to keep hidden behind the thickest trees. Then I see, across the road, a long, barely curved orange-mud driveway leading to a small, moss-stained white house.

And near the dented car in the driveway is a hand-painted sign:

FISHING GUIDE—INQUIRE WITHIN

Inquire within? I think. *That's all I've been doing.*

I remove Bark's gun from my waistband, let a finger rest on the trigger. I still believe I could never kill. I turn off the safety, though, and once I'm in the yard, I stride.

I climb the porch stairs. One hard kick opens the door. I hear television—a CNN report that's probably long past showing some photo Bark took of me—so I dash through a room faster than my eyes can scan all of it, the gun in both hands as far from my face as possible. Just off that room, in a bedroom, on top of the covers with an open book lying on his chest, is a white guy, round, balding, eyes closed.

"Excuse me," I say.

His eyelids open. Neither of us moves. He goes a little cross-eyed, blinks twice.

"You're that killer," he says flatly, and his calmness has me all the more scared.

"Never killed a soul," I say.

My aim zeroes in on him.

"But what's important," I say, "is you're a fisherman."

"Yes, sir, I am."

"And you guide people."

"Been known to do that."

"Well, today you're gonna guide me way the hell into these woods. And on our way, you're gonna tell me what you know about living out there. Then we're gonna say good-bye, and you're never gonna tell anyone about me."

I keep the gun pointed directly at his face. He clears his throat, says, "How do you plan to make that last part happen?"

"I'm hoping to hear some damned convincing talk on your part about how I can forget about pulling this trigger."

He is standing now, beside the bed. He's wearing jeans and a coffee-stained shirt. A breeze from the doorway behind me passes my neck.

"Justice, man," I say. "You could be part of it."

He walks straight toward me, then passes me and leaves the house. On the porch he sits on a gray metal rocking chair flecked with rust, the only chair out there, then looks up to face me as if to say, *Yeah, I'm basically crazy.*

"What kind?" he says.

"What kind of what?" I say.

"Fish. I can teach you trout or bass."

I shrug. "Both?"

"Takes a lifetime to learn either."

In the shade thrown by big trees, his face looks younger than the rest of him. If he ever played anything, it could have been football but not much else.

"Which is easier?" I ask.

He blinks three times. "Bass."

"Then bass it is."

He rocks in the chair, then stands and heads down the porch stairs, and I follow, keeping aim.

"Douglas, right?" he calls over his shoulder.

"Right."

"Sharp."

"Yes. But my friends call me Deesh."

We are headed toward an unpainted wooden shed behind his house, on a clearing of spiky weeds between a propane tank and a stream.

"You do know you're the latest celebrity," he says.

"Kind of had that figured."

"I mean, your name and face are out there."

"A lot of TV watching around here?"

He steps into the shed, and I follow to just inside the doorway.

"They sure aren't reading Chaucer," he says. Here with him, I'm attacked by the darkness in the shed and rushed memories of Bark's gunshot last night. Then, after I take a step back, I'm hit by hot sunlight and fatigue.

He gathers up two wooden oars and a tackle box.

"They watch TV, drink, and hunt," he says.

"So they're armed."

"And they consider themselves the righteous majority."

"But not you."

"If I were armed, Douglas, you wouldn't be here."

I feel myself exhale. It's like he wants me to shoot, thinks I'm down to one bullet and betting his life I'll miss. He takes a fishing rod in one hand, a second in the other, and again we are walking, again with him pulling ahead of me, plodding over flagstones toward the stream. Two varnished oars are tucked under one of his thick arms, each hand aiming a fishing rod at the stream, a fat finger dangling an olive green tackle box. I square myself with the truth that I have never in my life caught a fish, that I tried only once, in Georgia when I was six, with the aunt who took me in during the summer my mother tried rehab and couldn't care for me.

I call, "Think I have a chance to actually live around here?"

"Does it matter?" he shouts over his shoulder. "What anyone thinks?"

"Matters what *you* think," I say. "What I'm trying to ask, Mr. Guide Man, is can I survive out here?"

We are at the shoreline now, roughly beside each other, the gun somewhat lower but still aimed at his chest.

"If you disappear."

And he's looking me straight in the eye. No smirk, no grin, no frown, just suntanned skin over bones over a brain digesting those three words like mine is.

"And therein lies the irony, right?" he says.

"I guess so."

"As for how you'd be received if you run into the typical denizen of this all but virgin wilderness? My guess is not well."

"So I'm lucky I found you," I say.

"Indeed you are."

"You're like an angel."

He nods at the gun, then says, "Ready to fly."

I glance over my shoulder at the gravel road. It's still just us—it seems.

He says, "Name's Gabe, by the way." He's packing a boat chained to the shore of the stream, which is not as long across as the narrowest stretches of the East River near the Bronx. But what really makes this stream unlike any I've seen is how it *glistens* over algae-covered rocks greener than the leaves on the trees. And here's an orange and black bird that swoops twice, then lands in brush on the far shore, which rises into what Bronx folk would call a mountain.

I step closer to Gabe. Sunlight makes me blink. Gabe heads back toward the unpainted shed, and I follow, the gun aimed as he gathers more equipment. Last night's over, I tell myself. He asks,

"Ready?" and again passes me as if Bark's gun is as harmless as dust, this time straining through the arms to carry toward the stream a car battery in one hand, an electric boat motor crammed under an armpit, and another two fishing rods, their tips leading him.

"Yes," I answer, and then the yard goes bone quiet, as if this is the word we needed to say to scare off birds.

He loads the boat, which, tethered at both ends by chains hung from stones cemented to the shoreline, has three aluminum bench seats, its floor an unexpected turquoise blue, its outsides spray painted Desert Storm camouflage. He says something I can't quite hear about knots.

"Say that again?" I ask.

"That's my pet peeve—knotted lines," he says clearly. "One line tangled around itself I can handle. But more than one? Forget it."

I nod, Bark's gun steady. A single bird chirps.

"You get to some fishy spot with the weather just right?" Gabe says. "And then spend an *hour* untangling your lines?"

And as if following someone else's orders, he walks off, up the stone path toward his house. He could phone someone, so I jog to catch up. I realize I could shoot him and take the boat. The gun, aimed well, quivers as he opens his fridge. He moves aside jars and I remember my aunt in Georgia telling me how, when you fish in creeks and rivers, you should proceed *up*stream, since the current takes whatever you dislodge downstream—and this scares fish into not wanting to bite. And I all at once miss my aunt, in this rattrap of a house miss her as badly as ever, though I'm also glad she passed on before Bark lied about me on TV.

With his back to me, Gabe says, "You like liverwurst?"

"Love it," I say, though the truth is I've never tried liverwurst, since liverwurst, this same aunt once told me, was for *them*.

Gabe stuffs something I can't decipher into the bag, so I ask, "What'd you just put in there?"

"Bread."

"What else is in the bag? You got a cell in there?"

"No."

"You got a cell on you?"

"I have never owned a cell phone, Douglas."

"Come on, man. This is really no time to mess with me."

He sets the bag on his counter, holds up his hands. "Go ahead and search me."

I step toward him, and it hits me that this risks him wrestling me for the gun, so I step back and say, "Just pull your pockets inside out."

He obeys.

"You really don't own a cell?"

"Mr. Sharp," he says. "Look at this place. Who am I going to talk to?"

His shabby couch and dusty floor assure me he lives alone. I'd feel sorry for him if the gun didn't remind me of Bark, whose name now means anyone friendly can backstab. I gesture with the gun, and he heads out the door and presses on, waddling toward the boat. The stream all but dazzles me. He kneels beside the boat, arranges the motor, batteries, tackle box, oars, two safety-orange seat cushions, the four fishing rods—each handled individually—and the lunch bag. He points at these things one at a time, as if his mind needs to count to know everything's packed. Is he old enough for Alzheimer's?

"We're set," he says.

"Which way we headed?" I ask.

"Upstream," he says. "And that's always, Deesh. You always, *always* go up."

# 36

# JAN

"TALKING TO YOU, GIRL" was what Tug and I then heard, and I glanced over and saw the usual crew of railbirds along the chain-link, but there, third closest to me, stood that pig Arnie DeShields.

And he had the nerve right then, on that same day Tom went missing, to lift his chin at me the slightest bit, in a way that assured me he rarely needed to try to get women to sleep with him. And after I stayed put right beside Tug, he beelined toward me as if Tug weren't there, and Tug headed off without a word, toward the bet-taking tellers under the grandstand, and I thought: If I were Tug today, I'd probably want to escape the world, too.

"Mr. DeShields," I said.

Arnie held out his hand. "Just call me Arn. Or, if you insist, Arnie."

I nodded and we shook, and as his hand squeezed mine, I was sure he knew something about where Tom Corcoran was.

But all he said was "You know, your daddy jocked entries for me."

"Yessir I knew that."

"And he asked me once if I'd let any of his offspring ride for me someday. And now, young lady? Well, you do look old enough."

All I wanted right then was to be running at night. "You're acquainted with my mother?" I asked flatly.

"Rather well. And I see you're her daughter because you have her same shape." Two of his fat fingers touched his fake upper teeth. "Lemme put this to you directly," he said. "I could use you to help handle my morning workouts. If everything goes fine, we could then discuss you riding for me."

"Arnie?" I said. "Let me put this to *you* directly. I have a few other concerns presently."

"I bet you do, girl," he said, and he winked. "Not a man here would doubt that."

Which removed any doubt in me that I could jock professionally a heckuva lot faster if I slept with him. But all I did at that point was shake his hand curtly, not one more utterance about a future between us, though I'll admit that, with this handshake, the wannabe jock in me squeezed his hand firmly enough to show off my arm strength.

And being "courted" like that really did mess me up on the inside. Because after Arnie walked off, I stood there, roughly where Tug had left me, all jangled in my thoughts and jittery and queasy in my stomach. Plus I felt this sort of woodenness in my face, like my jaw was now suddenly heavier, like I couldn't have smiled if you paid me, and when Tug returned from beneath the grandstand, where I now figured he'd probably made a bet, I was sure he'd say something about how weirdly thrown off I looked, but he just stood next to me, hands clawed to the chain-link.

And after a while of us being together like that, he said, "Let's get out of here."

"To look elsewhere?"

"No. I just wanna leave."

"Because we can keep looking, Tug."

"I know. But I can't imagine where else around here my dad could be."

"He's never anyplace else other than here or at home?"

"Hate to say it, but that's pretty much the truth."

And so there we both were, near the finish yet leaving it quickly, Tug in the lead until, out in the parking lot, we headed toward the woods that bordered the railroad tracks that led to the Corcorans'. As I recall, we passed The *Form* Monger out there that day, and as we did, I glanced at his purple stump, clueless about why his hand had been severed (because, as of then, no one had told me the story about his losing streak and his wife's disappearance), and he ignored me to nod Tug's way and shrug, as if to say *I have no idea where your father is.*

Tug looked over his shoulder to face away from me, maybe because he was set to cry and didn't want me to see, maybe just to take a last look at the grandstand, full as it was of rusting steel beams and concrete and that particular seat up inside it, where his father had usually sat.

So then there we stood, in that parking lot short of the woods, Tug completely still, maybe missing his father, maybe worried about some bet, my insides a little shocked by the uproar of the grandstand crowd, which happened to be cheering now that we'd left.

# 37

# DEESH

**WHAT GETS ME IS** that once I step into the boat, the cool, who-gives-a-shit white dude who so smoothly called me a killer has now turned into a talker. And I don't mean a veteran wisecracker like James. I mean more of the nervous type, a guy who can go off on a blue streak so long you wonder if he's got problems worse than yours.

And in his case I mean mental problems. Or, I guess, emotional. The kind Madalynn would have called "issues."

Like right off the bat he goes on and on about how I should watch my balance and be careful not to fall in and that, of course, I have the gun so I can sit where I want but that, in his opinion, I should take the smallest seat, near the front, as opposed to the wide one in back, and he explains at least twice, the second time at great length, that he'll need to sit in the wide one in back because the motor will hang off the back and he'll need to turn the motor on and off and steer us. "And, see, Deesh, the turning on and off of that motor will prove crucial to your goal," he explains, "because the catching of bass requires that you move along as naturally as you can." And then he takes pains, with a wince that won't leave his face, to explain how a guy can't use a motor of either kind, electric or gas powered, in stretches of the stream that aren't deep enough, because, see, when the stream's going low you don't want to obliterate your prop against river stones, and how we'll need to save battery power to get deep into the woods. It's like he's now all of a sudden into fishing-guide mode, which you'd think would help him relax more about the gun, but instead it's got him all messed up like start-of-a-big-game jitters.

And the longer we sit like that, maybe eight feet apart, face-to-face, with me aiming a gun at the heart of a man I can't deny is a hostage—a gun that's already let loose a bullet to kill a cop—the more I get intensely freaked, too.

Then, on deeper water, he clicks off the motor and begins to row. He's on another blue streak, this one about how his sight isn't perfect because of some "fucked-up open-heart surgery," and an odd twitch from inside me, like a shiver but up my belly instead of down my spine, jolts the gun out of aim. I ease it back down toward his mouth as he mentions as an aside that he's on "several medications," which makes me wonder if, besides being in hyper fish-guide mode, the man is high. Brothers tripping on painkillers have done wilder shit than they'd do after draining a night's worth of forties, so now, here, listening to Gabe, I'm back to using a motto coached into me when I played ball: Defend, defend, defend, but always be set to shoot.

And it's not until Gabe opens the tackle box and grabs a lure and tosses it back in that I realize the twitch attacked me because I suspect this guy is conning me. And I'm not thinking some everyday con like brothers hawking knockoffs on Eighth Avenue. I'm thinking a con that came to his mind twenty minutes ago for the purpose of turning me in, maybe killing me. As in the swindle of my life. As in summer sunshine is now warming my knees and we are gliding up a stream through countryside more beautiful than any I've seen on TV, with the *tat-tweet-tot* of a bird somewhere in branches ahead, but now I will never relax.

Then there's an explosion of birdsong unlike any in the Bronx, Carnegie Hall birdsong, a kind so loud and complex and glorious brothers like me never hear let alone see the source of, and with Gabe going on about some theory of his, something about how to catch big fish, I lean back and hold the gun over the water—so Gabe would need to lunge farther to grab it—then check out the bird itself, which is gray as a mouse, not tiny, not big, just a plain-assed gray bird bursting forth with this odd, bold, loud jazz that, I swear, is all about freedom.

*It's messed up* is the riff this jazz keeps sliding back to. *Freedom looks pretty, but it's all messed up.*

# 38

# JAN

AS TUG AND I WALKED on the railroad tracks through the woods from the track to his parents' house, he faced the woods until I said, "You *are* set to cry. Is it about something he said to you?"

"Jan, I don't want to talk about it."

"Then just . . . listen to me, Tug. Because *I* want to talk."

"Why?"

"Because I care about you and you care about him."

"Then go ahead. Talk. Just remember: I'm predicting right now that you'll end up calling me a baby."

"Why would I do that?"

"A guy cries and a woman at first believes he's sensitive and as such a good catch, but then she decides he's a baby."

And with that word—*baby*—now having been said more than once between us, we walked on as if there were nothing left to say, and I took the lead, letting my steps land between the rail bed's weathered ties, Tug on the soot-colored gravel just outside the rail on my right. We walked like this for a long while, with Tug now and then sneaking peeks toward the woods, maybe to look for his father, risking that I'd think he was again set to cry, concerned, I was sure, that I was already deciding about him: about the way he'd be as a man thanks to his father; about how his father's quirks and habits and, damn, even his father's disappearance might manifest themselves in the person Tug would always be; about how every good and bad trait of both of Tug's parents might affect Tug's potential; about how maybe, right now, Tug and I, as a couple falling in love, were likely to face the same troubles Tug's parents had faced because we were horse people, too. I was already also deciding, Tug probably thought then, about Tug's Attitudes Toward Women and Tug as a Possible Lover and Tug as a Simple Partner, maybe even Tug as a Future Husband, and, what the heck, Maybe as a Father Too.

And I asked him, "Why would I think you're a baby?"

And we walked. And we walked. And we walked.

"Because babies cry," he finally said. "But that wasn't my point, Jan. My point was that you might believe you want a guy who cries, but you don't."

I studied the splintered ties, considering this.

I asked, "Are you figuring he won't come back?"

"I told you. I don't want to talk about it."

"He's coming back, Tug. Mine never did after he got stuck in those weeds, but that was different. I mean, be real with me, Tug. What are the odds that, with us being this young, *both* of our fathers would leave us for good?"

He shrugged, as if here, this far from the grandstand, things like odds didn't count.

"He's coming back, Tug. He has to. How could he not? After seeing what my father's absence did to me and my mother?"

And for a while there, my silence had Tug appearing calm and well-adjusted, as if I'd consoled him, and, for a few moments, I felt that I'd just made the only relevant point. Then, maybe because I'd asked, maybe because he just wanted to be honest with *someone*, he came out and said, "I don't know."

"You don't know what?"

And his voice went all quiet:

"I just—I just have a sick feeling."

And he shrugged without glancing at me, even though he was now directly beside me, making no bones about hiding his face.

Then, all male and female pride be damned, I said, "When you're set to cry, Tug? You should. Because if you don't, bad things can happen."

And then there I went, too, trying to spot a bird or squirrel or something alive other than trees in those woods, wishing I could run off to someplace far from everything that was happening to us.

And Tug let me do that. He let me look off for as long as I wanted.

Then he said, "What sort of bad things?"

And we faced each other, both of us frowning. We had this new mutual dead seriousness.

"Like your heart could go sour," I said, and I remembered Tom's recent speech about heart and luck and losing. Had Tom really wanted both Tug and me to hear that speech—or just Tug?

"Or *you'll* run away," I said now. "And never come back."

"Who would I run from?"

"Your father. After he comes back. Or your mother. Or anyone else you might love."

"Who said I ever loved anyone?"

"You love your father and you know it. And that's the problem here, Tug. You got yourself all wrapped up in pretending you don't care about a guy who, given how he behaves, cares only about placing bets on horses. That's a big mess, Tug."

And there, after I said that, I pretended I was captivated by something deep inside the woods. To Tug I probably looked like I despised the world, and in a way I did, because right then it hit me that there were plenty of folks now gossiping about the Corcorans and me and my mother as viciously as people had gossiped back in Arkansas.

Then Tug said, "Just don't ever call me a baby, okay?"

I smiled a little at that, with one of those smiles Tug knew all about, the kind that force themselves on you when things feel at their worst.

And with that smile refusing to leave my face, I glanced over.

And I said, "Tug? If I'm with you and I happen to call you *baby*? Trust me—you won't mind it at all."

But what's probably most important about this whole business of Tug not wanting to be called a baby was something I learned the next day: that despite all the adulthood and manliness Tug aspired to, he could not dismiss a rule Tom had declared for him back when he'd been a kid, which was that if ever Tug and Tom were together in the grandstand, Tug was to consider himself the Stay Putter and his father the Always Come Backer. This rule, of course, was meant for whenever Tug felt lost; Tug was, according to this rule, supposed to continue sitting or standing wherever he and Tom had last spoken, then wait there confident of his father's return.

And no doubt Tom had laid down this rule to keep them from chasing each other in circles, but back then Tom never explained it to Tug as such, instead telling him that he should take pride in any departure of his father—since Tug was the luckiest kid, since he had a father whose eventual return was as certain as the fastest, most honest-running sure-thing horse.

And sometimes back then, Tom would be gone long enough that a grandstander would ask Tug if Tug was lost, and Tug would say no, then say, *My dad is no loser,* and the grandstander would laugh hard, as if Tug had made the perfect joke, and then Tom would return and the grandstander would recognize him from back when he'd jocked, and they'd shake hands and ignore Tug and talk the highs and lows of the game.

As a result, when Tom's disappearance had continued on into its second day and beyond, Tug would spend his mornings in town or in the woods near the track looking for Tom, but he then spent his afternoon hours in the grandstand, in that same upper-tier section his father had claimed, the one overlooking The Crux. On the first day Tug did this—that is, essentially, *wait* up there—I went with him, and as we sat there, right where his father had, he explained to me, after I suggested we again check the backside, that he believed it was wisest to follow his father's advice to stay put. Whether he actually believed his father would return and we'd all end up happy was something I quickly learned not to discuss, because the one time I asked him about this he acted as if he hadn't heard, just stood and excused himself and headed off, to bet two of his father's dollars on a long shot.

And while we watched that race, it occurred to me that Tug had made that bet sentimentally, doing what his father would have done, almost, you could say, as a surrogate, carrying on the Corcoran family tradition, and I did not in the least want to mess with that, but it bothered me, and it bothered me all the more when I admitted to myself that, as we sat up there watching horses run, the hard-core grandstanders Tom had long known were obviously giving us the silent treatment.

Among these hard-cores I should probably mention now was The Nickster, a portly, clean-shaven Sicilian who had once scowled at Tug and called him a pussy for caring about retired horses—though now, with Tom gone, The Nickster would neither scowl nor react at all when he'd see Tug. At most he'd lick his thumb and turn a page of his racing program while letting his steely eyes drift.

There was also The Show Stopper, a gregarious loser who'd once famously bet ten grand on "a lock to show" (his words), only to see it leave the gate and stop, and whose gregariousness, now that Tom was gone, had suddenly pulled up lame, too.

And as always (in his usual place at the bottom of the pecking order), there was The *Form* Monger.

In fact, it was then, after Tom disappeared and Tug and I sat up there, that Tug finally told me the whole story of the absence of The *Form* Monger's wife, including the part about how The *Form* Monger's compulsive betting had led her as well as his hand to disappear pathetically forever. And what was odd was that, as Tug told me this story, all three of us—Tug and I and The *Form* Monger—were all right there, all three of us up there in the flesh in the grandstand, still making bets on horses despite the likelihood that, right then, as we gambled, Tom Corcoran was very well facing his own gambling-related horrors.

I mean, here, smack in front of us, was a guy whose right arm was a hideous purple stump because his attraction to betting had caused *his hand to be sawed off,* and he just kept cruising around in that grandstand in search of *Form*s, kept following losers out to the parking lot in case they'd drop anything—kept on aspiring to stand out there and scalp used past performances and return to the grandstand to bet.

And even though The *Form* Monger kept his distance from us, never once stepping foot in the section that overlooked The Crux, Tug kept wanting to be near men like him.

# 39

# DEESH

**GABE'S LATEST BLUE STREAK** changes direction as sharply as my first right turn after Bark shot the cop. Gabe has a little something to propose, just a little idea he's saying just now popped up in his head, an idea for a possible plan for me. The plan, the *plan*, his plan for me, is that he and I both keep on together, keep on heading upstream in his boat, for a good couple of hours. And that while we stick together like brothers and continue on, he'll teach me all the finer points of baiting a hook and casting a line and catching bass, because a guy can't live more than a week or two without protein, and I myself can't risk shooting squirrels, or shooting anything, for that matter, since regardless of how much ammo a guy has to spare, the sound of a gunshot in these woods risks a warden rushing toward him faster than wildfire.

And, yes—of course—I would need to put down the gun in

order to cast, so he won't push any of these fishing lessons on me, certainly not now, not right at this moment, because he understands me, he *gets* how I need to keep the gun on him—he'd do the same thing if he were me—but of course, being himself, he also would like me to put the gun down, not only for his own personal safety but also for mine, because, if I, Deesh, think about it, I don't need another count of murder or even just kidnapping added to the list of the counts already piling up against me. He's sure I've already thought this through. But he really does want me to know he's been thinking it through also, because, see, he really does want to help me, really does want what's best for me.

"You saying you believe I didn't shoot that cop?" I ask, to slow down—or, shit, end—this particular blue streak or, if not, to remind him that if he, (a), really does have heart problems, and, (b), truly wants this boat ride to be good for both of us, he should probably take a breath now and then to let a brother say something.

And his answer to my question wastes no time:

"Oh, no," he says. "I think you shot him."

So now my eyes stay as riveted on his damned white-guy face as his are on the gun.

"I just think he deserved it," he explains.

"Why did he deserve it?"

"Because he was racist."

"But man, you weren't there."

"I didn't need to be. I've seen this scenario play out enough on the news. How many times do we need to see it reported after the black guy is killed? How many racist cops do we need to hire and suspend and put on trial and finally stick in jail? And you *know* we probably hear about less than a tenth of the shit."

"But—"

"Deesh, this is a fucked-up country. It is totally fucked. It's just one big old melting pot of hatred. And it just keeps boiling."

"But how do you know *I* wasn't the hater?"

"Because I've been around haters. Been around the best of them, and you can tell. Just listen to how they talk, and you can tell."

And this, he then says, reminds him to give me the matches in his tackle box. And to show me what kind of tree branches to use to make the fires I'll need to fry the bass I'll catch. And I'll need to remember never to make a fire during the day, or even at night unless it's cloudy, since neither he nor I will want anyone to notice smoke rising past his land's treetops, which of course would provoke suspicion.

Because, well, we both now need to remember these *are* his woods, but they're not. He alone is paying the mortgage that says he owns them, but when it comes to land in this part of Pennsylvania, long-held land prime for fishing and hunting and hiking and fracking and whatnot, there are always rights-of-way and shared borders and so forth, and of course there are also state laws that apply to every hunter and hiker and gem collector who might want to encroach, at least theoretically speaking, but that's not his point.

His point is the plan. That wasn't the *whole* plan, what he's told me so far. The whole plan, he explains after his eyes cross briefly and he blinks them back into alignment while he takes a ragged breath—the whole plan ends with him taking me to the empty hunting cabin that sits in these woods, these woods that are mostly his except for a right-of-way owned by a contractor from Philly who comes up very rarely, *maybe* once a year, sometimes not at all—but certainly, definitely only in fall—when deer hunting is legal.

Deer hunting, if he, Gabe, now can remember correctly, begins in October. October 15th or 20th or 25th. Or something like that, but it's definitely in October. Which means the cabin's always empty now. The cabin's all mine. The cabin's all mine for the summer at least and, with any luck, pretty much forever.

# 40

# JAN

THERE WAS ALWAYS another place to look, certainly always Bill Treacy's feed store and the tavern in town, and every morning Tug checked the shed in the woods behind Jasper's cabin, and Tug and I again and again asked around at the track, and after eight days of such checking and looking and asking, we returned to the Corcoran house almost as a couple would, and Jasper, anchored across the kitchen table from Colleen, glanced over at Tug, and Tug said, "Nope."

"Well, let's face it," Colleen said. "This isn't good."

And I thought, It's *horrible*. But I didn't dare say that.

And that was the thing about being in that house. The Corcorans acted as if you solved problems by simply not talking about them, which I *knew* made them worse. But at the same time it kind of lent you hope, so soon you almost liked keeping your mouth shut—or keeping on while waiting for someone else to speak.

So I did that for a good while, as my mother reheated Tug and I a lunch of fried bluegills someone had caught from the lake. And I did it a while longer as Tug picked at his food and I ate nothing at all. Colleen then suggested that Tug join her and Jasper that afternoon, because today, finally, after eight days of Colleen's consternation about whether they should or whether they shouldn't, she'd decided that they'd skip the Podunk sheriff and go straight to the state police district headquarters forty-some miles away. And Tug nodded a yes, as if nothing being said were at all a big deal, much as he still seemed to be trying to keep me from knowing how undoubtedly fucked-up everything was.

And when he and Colleen and Jasper got there, to the non-Podunk state police district headquarters, a trooper eyed Tug on and off while he asked Jasper about Tug's father's gambling pals, and Jasper answered some of those questions reluctantly, some maybe dishonestly, but always, Tug thought, for his family's own good. Then an older trooper had Colleen sign a missing persons report, which he said he'd file immediately.

And it wasn't until after Tug and Colleen had finished their business there, on their way down those headquarters' concrete stairs, that Tug eased up on worrying enough to imagine running in the dark with me, and again he wanted to buy me something I'd like that would show he'd always care, so right there, within earshot of Jasper, he gathered the spine to ask Colleen the kind of question Tom would have considered too intrusive.

"Mom, I need some of my tuition money—could you get it?"

"What do you mean *get* it?" Colleen said.

"I mean withdraw it."

"Tug, that cash went into an account only your father can touch. You'll have to ask him when he comes back."

And on those stairs Tug tried to accept what she'd meant.

She'd meant: *Honey, that cash is long gone.*

# 41

# DEESH

**EACH BEND IN THIS STREAM** presents the threat that we'll sail directly into the range of a loaded firearm held by a redneck or a warden or a trooper or a strapping buck from the FBI, though so far we've seen no such life-forms here, just the hind legs of an orange fawn leaping between Christmas trees to escape us, then a pair of small yellow butterflies tumbling over each other, and then, way up there, a hawk or an eagle, who knows which, circling so high it seemed closer to the rolling gray clouds than to us.

But now there seems to be more to Gabe's plan than he first told me. Or so he's now informing me. The plan also includes his suggestion that he and I never be in contact once he drops me at the cabin. Of course he'll give me all this fishing gear, the tackle box no problem, matches included, the lunch bag of bread and liverwurst and so on if it turns out we get to the cabin before we feel hungry enough to stop, and, now that Gabe thinks about it, he'll need to replenish my stock of matches every few months or so. But he can do that, he's *willing* to do that—just "happen" to drop a box of kitchen matches on the shore near the cabin when he's up that way guiding a client—even though there is some risk involved—for both of us—in our being in contact after he drops me off, since, from his point of view, of course, he'd be thrown in jail for having given me refuge like this. For me, of course, the risk would be less significant. But there would be *some*. For me the risk would be that, if I felt that he and I had struck up a little friendship, I might be tempted to head downstream to hang out with him now and then, which would mean that if, say, by an almost inconceivable coincidence, he had a visitor, maybe some woman—maybe this one particular woman in a plaid jacket who, twice now, has hiked past the road just beyond his driveway whistling that one show tune, that one show tune he should be able to remember right now but can't—he just can't—what the fuck—it must be the synergistic effect of all the damned medications he needs to take thanks to his botched heart surgery.

But the point, the point he's trying to tell me, is there would be risk for me, too. There would be risk for both of us if we stayed in contact. So the plan that stands in his mind right now, albeit sketchy, is that, after he navigates me far enough upstream and we take the short walk through virtually virgin woods to this basically unused hunting cabin, we'll never see each other again, much as we would both, at that point, if I was happy with where he'd taken me, be on the very best terms, wishing each other the best of luck and all that.

And I think, He thinks I shot the cop.

He thinks I'm guilty.

*Everyone* thinks I'm guilty.

And everyone includes Madalynn and Jasir.

And I, right now, in this boat, wonder if I can abide this. My aunt wouldn't abide this, none of my people would abide this—if my father somehow showed up right now, he'd resent it as much as I do.

And I keep on resenting it while Gabe rows around a bend with the tight-lipped look of a man who has just spoken his peace and a damned righteous one at that. And I resent it well into Gabe's next blue streak, which, since I'm barely listening, might be about his heart surgery or the woman in the plaid jacket or—yeah, I'm sure he's right that he *could* probably go on for days about his ex-wife if I let him.

But I'm not going to let him. Because I can't stop thinking that he thinks I shot the cop. And of course I need to think. Everyone does. And sometimes everyone needs to think on their own, and it's now, as I realize this, that I can see myself pulling this trigger. Because the more a guy who thinks you're a killer yaps on about his owned fucked-up life, the more he can get on your nerves, to the point that you start thinking things like how shooting him right now, smack in the middle of him talking about shit you hardly care about, would be doing him a favor, too.

And of course he has no clue I'm thinking any of this. How could he, with him not giving me a chance to talk? So now here I am, waving the gun wildly in front of him, wildly for sure and still pointed in his direction, kind of aggressively, hell-yes risking that it might go off and put a bullet into *some* nearby life if not his, and finally, right about when he notices enough to shut up, I say, *"Gabe."*

"What?"

And here another twitch comes up through me, startled as I am that his talking's stopped, but I absorb this one to keep the gun aimed. "How do you know so much about hatred?"

"What are you talking about?"

"You said you thought I shot the cop because you know so much about hatred. And I'd just like to know why you think you're such an expert."

"I didn't say *you* hated the cop," he says. "I said the cop hated you."

"I know. But what made you such an expert on hatred that you knew the cop hated me?"

"Oh," he says. "You don't want to hear that whole story."

"But I do, man. I really do. Otherwise I wouldn't be asking."

"Fine," he says, and off he goes, on blue streak number eight or nine or, fuck, ten, and the thing about listening to a guy talk on and on for several hours is that it does help him get into your head—you start hearing his rhythms when you think—maybe you're even starting to want what he wants, which can be a problem if you're holding a gun on him and he wants you to put it down.

But that's just me. Just me telling you how it feels listening to his eighth or ninth or tenth blue streak, this one about a woman, another woman, a woman he's certainly lost contact with, a woman he doesn't love at all. A woman he calls The Man Hater. And a Man Hater, he's now explaining, in a shy but lecturelike mode, is exactly that: anyone who hates anyone born male. Yes, most Man Haters are female, but not all of them, he says. In a sense, he says, a Man Hater is not different at all from people who've despised me because I'm black—both a Man Hater and a racist like the cop he's sure I shot won't empathize with you, or hear you out, or even as much as give you the benefit of the doubt. Once they see you're born with that certain physical characteristic they despise, they plug themselves into their hatred and let it rule you and them. No doubt, he says, there are also Woman Haters and White Haters. He's sure there are haters of all the various ways that people are born to be. American citizenship, he thinks, encourages hatred. But it's beyond America, he says. It's international. It's why there's war, certainly why there's terrorism. 9-11, he's sure, happened because of Haters of Christians and Jews. He guesses most everyone in the world has been hated at least once. In fact, he says, he would bet on this.

"You're talking about discrimination," I say.

"I'm talking about hatred," he says. "Hatred, Deesh, when you really stop to think about everything? Hatred is the world's most wanted public enemy."

I nod. He's freaking playing you, I think. This is all just to get you to lose the gun.

But he hasn't once glanced at the gun since blue streak number six. Though maybe that's all an act. Either way he talks on, rowing, yeah, and sometimes studying a shoreline but mostly talking, about how this Man Hater he knew was the chair of the English Department at the university where he last tried to be what he's always wanted to be, a literature professor—poetry. About how this Man Hater's hatred of him contaminated his love of teaching and even his marriage. How, when he proposed to his wife and she said yes, they'd thought he'd bring in at least his modest salary as a professor, so when he was later denied tenure, their finances were screwed.

All bullshit, I think. All a freaking con. But I know how to deal with cons—give them time and ask questions. Any con man anywhere, on Eighth Avenue or on a hoops court in the Bronx or, probably, on any stream where guys like Gabe fish, will eventually lie to you so long and often that something will stop making sense.

So I say, "You hadn't factored in The Man Hater."

"Exactly," he says, and now he's swallowing hard, touching his face, scratching the side of his scalp—the guy is nervous.

"No one warned you about her?" I say. "When you first started teaching at this university?"

"Nope. Then again, most of my colleagues were female."

"Like most dudes on Wall Street are white."

"Exactly," he says, and our eyes meet, then part ways.

"What did your wife think about all this?" I ask.

"Didn't believe it either. At least not at first. She thought I was just a shitty professor. And then she simply didn't want to talk about it. I mean, it was just too tense and confusing for both of us, with all my students giving me positive evaluations but my boss telling me I wasn't going to get tenure. There was kind of this vibe that if I was a good husband who really loved his wife, I'd figure out how to keep paying the mortgage. You know, from my wife's perspective, at some point it became more about the bills and the credit cards than it was about how I and this Man Hater felt."

Talk on, Professor, I think. Talk.

And right then, as if Bark's gun betrays my mistrust, he shuts up on me. He casts. Reels. Casts again. He sighs. I doubt that, right now, he cares at all about catching fish.

I say, "You stay married?"

He sets down the fishing gear, rows intently. It's like he wants to disappear more than I do.

"Not for long," he says.

"And?"

"And what."

"She didn't love you?"

Rowing harder, he grins for the sake of making a show of it. "Man, you go right after what counts."

"Can you blame me?" I say. "I just want to know if you're bull-shitting me."

"About what?"

"This." I wave the gun. "Who shot this gun, why we're on this boat trip, why you have these stupid theories about Man Haters—*everything.*"

He glances at the gun, blinks hard. He faces the shoreline and rows on.

Cliffs flank the stream, purple wildflowers crowded up against both shorelines. It's tight here, the only way through.

"At some point after my boss began messing with me," he says, "my wife became mean."

And that's all he says, with no blue streak attached.

And I feel sorry for the pudgy sonofabitch. Really feel sorry, like you would for a real friend.

So I say, "Mean's hard to love, man."

"But, see, Deesh, my wife was cool before we got married. We understood each other. We were on the same team. But that all changed when The Man Hater began making sure I wouldn't get tenure."

"How'd she do that?"

"Assigned me goals that no human being could possibly reach. And made up lies about me. You make up one good lie about a male professor in a department of women hired and chaired by a Man Hater, that male professor can kiss his *career* good-bye."

He rows on, and I keep the gun aimed, maybe a little lower, but still set. Gnats try to distract me, and I swat at them.

"So what, then—your wife divorced you?"

And I feel both of us, on our insides, sinking down.

He lets go of the oars, grabs a fishing rod, wings a cast that lands his bait smack between two gray rocks. There are plenty of ways not to tell the truth, I think. One of those ways is to run from it.

Then, after nothing but a sneeze from me, off Gabe goes, on another blue streak, this one about the heart murmur his doctor found just after his divorce, how the sound of that murmur led to his botched surgery, how he now needs to take all sorts of medications, blood thinners and beta-blockers and statins and "whatever," how side effects from the statins have him trying to replace the statins with plant sterols and red-rice yeast tablets of various dosages. How, yeah, there's been Percocet as well as on-and-off reliance on anti-depressants, how, yes, it causes him shame but he probably needs to admit to depression, how he has these "little episodes."

"What do you mean, 'little episodes'?"

"It's just a little hard to see sometimes," he says. "Things get blurry. Sometimes I black out. But usually not for very long."

And there I sit, across from this ill man in his boat, my own body perfectly healthy as far as I know, holding a gun on him.

"Because you *need* me, right, Deesh?" Gabe says. He rows very hard, but he's playing it up, grinning like a maniac. "Without me," he all but shouts, "you can't get to that cabin!"

He's jacked up for sure. Reminds me of drunken Friday nights with Bark and James back when we were all cool, and yeah, yeah, I'm smiling, but fuck him.

"Which I'm happy to do," he says seriously. "But you do realize a guy can't expect to be a hundred percent, particularly after they saw him open and slice up his ticker—right?"

Bullshit, I think. *Bull*shit.

Get him talking again. About heart surgery. He'll mess up fast if he's not being completely straight.

So I say, "From what I've heard, man, not too long after heart surgery, a lot of people feel great. Hell, they run marathons."

"That's if you had a little bypass," he says. "I had two new valves put in."

"Valves are a bigger deal than a bypass?"

"Mine were." He inhales slowly through his nose, lets a breath out through his intentionally open mouth, and I think, He is *unreal*, with this bullshit. But there's no bringing him back now, gone as he is into a new blue streak, this one about how, in his case, the surgeon "bungled" the suturing on of the new valves. How anyway that was if you asked Gabe's lawyer. How of course if you asked his surgeon, his surgeon did a perfectly fine job, and how the surgeon has a team of fourteen doctors and nurses and technicians to back him up. How what he, Gabe, was now trying to say—to me, Deesh, today—was that these fourteen people were all trained professionals who were there, completely awake, doing what they did for a living. And he was of course *out*, completely anesthetized, so who was he to say that the surgeon botched it?

And I notice his face has gone bone pale, with sweat dripping through his sideburns.

I gesture toward his heart and say, "But he botched it."

And he nods. After inhaling and holding his breath to maybe decide something, he goes off, this time half softly, to let me know, just between me and him, that he *did* have a stroke four months after the surgery, right about when he was supposed to be feeling—as I aptly put it—like running a marathon. That when any heart surgeon saws a guy open and cuts out two of his valves and sews on new ones, a primary goal after they staple the guy shut is that there be no clotting, and clotting is what caused his stroke. That a clot did in fact go to his brain, and this clot "almost certainly" formed near one of the new valves.

And everyone, Gabe needs to tell me, knows there shouldn't have been clotting. And based on all this, the lawyer he hired more than a year ago has been badgering the offending heart surgeon for a monetary settlement that would make things at least somewhat close to fair, if not a do-over surgery. But, see, this lawyer of Gabe's has been getting the runaround for months. He's just a rinky-dink personal injury guy from Scranton, so he and Gabe are, in the eyes of the world, just poor suckers in Pennsylvania up against a renowned heart surgeon and a hospital owned by a billion-dollar conglomerate. Realistically speaking, Gabe has a piss-poor chance. Between his failed marriage and a few other "mishaps" he doesn't want to get into for my sake, his general prospects have taken kind of a hit lately.

And you're blitzing on Perc, I think.

And, no, he's not done talking. And sweating more. And still pale if not another shade near pure white. But I'm with him again, listening, if for no other reason than to keep the gun aimed. And he sure is now off again, about how he's no longer represented by this rinky-dink Scranton lawyer—not really, since this lawyer just last week demanded another retainer to keep on fighting. How there's no money, certainly no cash anywhere Gabe is aware of, for another retainer. He's already taken out a home equity loan on that shack of a house his fishing guide business barely keeps afloat, and his ex-wife, who has been remarried to a jackass for years now, would never give or lend him cash.

How his failure at trying to be a literature professor left him bad-mouthed and isolated and "fairly friendless."

How, so, yeah, he has no one else to go to.

And we let this sink in some, too, on top of everything else, and I think, Damn.

And then I need to admit: I'm close to believing his whole story.

It's almost to the point that, if someone's out there offering a reward for my capture, I want this guy to have it.

# 42

# JAN

**TWO DAYS LATER,** Tug and I and Colleen and my mother and Jasper and a couple volunteers who were strangers to the Corcorans joined sheriffs to begin searching the woods and meadows within a five-mile radius of the track for any sign at all of Tom Corcoran. We checked abandoned fox dens and kicked aside fallen leaves, turning up pop bottles and twelve-pack cartons and cigarette filters but little more, and often, while we searched, Tug lagged behind to check areas the others might have glossed over too quickly.

This part of the search lasted nearly three days, Tug insisting on there being a third after the volunteers had quit to tend to personal matters.

And then, on the day after that third day, Tug returned to the grandstand convinced Tom would be there, only to get another choral refrain of the silent treatment, and I have to admit it was that afternoon that I, too, found myself generally unable to say much around Tug, because, really, the more you saw business at the track and elsewhere carry on as usual without Tom, the less it seemed possible that he would return—and, well, who wanted to dish truths like that in some conversation you could never take back?

What I'm saying is, I didn't want to lie to Tug about my lack of hope, or, for that matter, encourage him to feel like his family's future was rosy when pretty much everything suggested it wasn't. So the best default reaction for me to have to Tom's absence, it seemed, was to say nothing around Tug, to even let Tug sprint off on his own after we'd left the house to run together at night.

At dawn on the following morning, Tug convinced Jasper to join him in a search of the lake's entire shoreline, including a far stretch that was part of a nature preserve. After they did this using both a canoe and fishing waders, Tug decided that his staying put in the grandstand had been sentimental foolishness at best. Late that afternoon, he persuaded Colleen to have internet service connected despite the long-held Corcoran family belief that they, being down-to-earth horse folk, would always avoid the lure of social media, and Tug spent his first day online googling *Corcoran* and *Tom Corcoran* and *Tommy Corcoran + Jockey* and so on, finding that there was very little information about Tom posted, mostly just county records of Tom's previously secret DUI arrest back when Tug was roughly two years old.

There also wasn't much about my father, but then again my father's jockeying glory days had happened going on decades ago now, and soon Tug was back to searching in the real world, jogging up and down dirt roads near the track and the Corcoran house, sometimes on lanes cleared through woods for the sake of electrical transformers and wiring, sometimes down exercise paths leading to streams feeding the area's numerous lakes, some public, some private, some on easements subject to dispute. Tug's hope felt strongest on the various grown-over paths leading to three generally unfished ponds; he took his time on these, trying his best to see through the thick brush, grateful for any sunlight that helped him decipher mammals as small as woodchucks beyond the layers of leaves and branches, even though this fondness for the sun made him wish we were running in the dark.

And he was on his way home from the last of those unfished ponds when the Galaxie stopped beside him and Jasper rolled down its window and said he'd just learned that Tom Corcoran's file was now middle priority.

And it wasn't long at all after Jasper said those words—*middle priority*—that the deepest breaths Tug could take couldn't reach the bottoms of his lungs.

But Tug didn't tell me about this then.

He acted cool, often keeping as still and quiet around me as a veteran thoroughbred cooped up in a dingy stall, waiting knowingly.

# 43

# DEESH

**THE STREAM GROWS WIDER**, all flat and curvy and snaking its way toward thicker woods, the current slower. Gabe is breathing easier, and he's not sweating, as far as I can tell. "Obviously you have problems of your own," he says. "Probably one or two no one out there has a clue about."

"Not really," I say, and it hits me that I might try to match his hell-on-earth story with one of my own, if for no other reason than to let him know that I, too, can mess with a stranger's head by going off forever on a blue streak. And, yeah, maybe I'm falling for a con now by giving him what he wants—a story about me he's earned by telling me all about himself. But I'm doing it. I'm telling him one, a good one. I'm telling him the one about me that very few men know, the one about how I was walking to school one morning on 212th Street, back when I was maybe in fourth grade, maybe in third—either way, just a kid. How I was barely awake that morning and walking alone and doing exactly what I always did when I walked alone back then, scanning the pavement for money. How, more often than you'd expect, I'd find a penny or two. How once I'd found a twenty tucked behind the cellophane of a crumpled cigarette pack. How on this particular morning I saw no money, saw nothing until it was too late, because four of my classmates had surrounded me. How they held me. How three of them yanked me off the sidewalk, then lowered me headfirst down a manhole. How the fourth kid replaced the steel cover to trap me in. How I was freaked as much by claustrophobia as by how quickly a bright morning could turn dark. How I felt too scrawny to remove the cover. How I clutched the slippery footholds. How, after I would finally raise the cover maybe an inch, the wheel of a car or truck or bus would slam it down.

Gabe, listening to this, has quit rowing.

"That is *some* shit," he says. "Not exactly like heart surgery, but similar. I mean, that feeling you get right when you start to go under—"

"That's not the point, Gabe," I say, and I realize that, damn, I actually want him to hear me out. "My point is they did this to me because they knew I had a crush on a girl. And you know how it goes when you're a boy that age. Liking girls so much that it shows is for sissies."

Gabe nods, possibly cool with this, cool with the truth that, between him and me, I have personal shit to say, too.

"You're right," he says. "That *was* how it went. I forgot all about that."

And it's then that his eyes remind me I'm still holding the gun, which has gotten good at keeping aim.

Then there's nothing but the sound of the tiny splashes made by his oars.

The blue streaks, it seems, are over.

Gabe says, "So what was her name?"

"Whose name?"

"The girl you had the crush on when they put you in that manhole."

A crow launches itself across the stream. I think, Why can't the gray-assed bird be singing near us now?

"Madalynn," I say.

"And was your crush on her . . . requited?"

"Not at first. She was like the other girls; she hated boys, too. And a few years later, when liking boys was cool, she was into older guys—I mean high school guys. But she'd give me these little looks when I'd catch her on the street acting lovey-dovey with one of them."

"Her being with them didn't tick you off?"

Keep the gun close, I think. He's just trying to win you over.

I raise the barrel higher, loosen my wrist.

"No," I say. "Or if it did, I got over it. I mean, back then I never believed I had a chance with her. Plus, you know: I *loved* her. Anyway I finally won her over when I was in high school myself."

"When you were the basketball star."

I nod.

"And *that* didn't tick you off?"

"Why would it?"

"Gold digging."

I shrug. "There wasn't a one of us who wasn't trying to get out of the Bronx, man."

"So let me guess," Gabe says. "You finally dated her for a while, but when you proposed, she said no."

"No. Loved her like crazy, finally slept with her, then slept with her every night for a while. But, no, I did not ask her to marry me."

I check the woods on both sides. I wish Gabe hadn't started us talking. I wish I'd never been through a lot of what my memory feels loaded with.

Plus, now I can feel Gabe studying my face.

He says, "But eventually she *did* care about you."

"Eventually."

"Loved you?"

"I suppose."

"You don't think she felt it from the start?"

"I don't know. Can a girl love a kid who's scared?"

And it's just after I ask this, just after we've passed pink, silver-flecked boulders, that Gabe stops rowing. He holds his oars at most an inch out of the water, his focus on what I'm guessing is some hick near the shoreline not far from us, and I think: If I'm going down today, shoot me dead right now, while I watch this glistening water.

But I hear no shot. Gabe keeps the oars still. Then there's a rustling from the brush that he, pale again, keeps watching. Lime green branches near the rustling move, and I aim Bark's gun at this movement, and out struts a cat smaller than a tiger but far bigger than a tom. Black tufts raise its ears into points, its legs long and anchored by monstrous paws, its tail looking like most of it got left in some trap.

"Gabe," I whisper, and the cat stiffens to check me out. Its expression says *Try me* as its eyes seem to deepen. Quick breaths appear in its underbelly only. Mostly, though, it comes off as cool, as if it's not showing off how cut it is, as if, because of its looks, it owns every nearby person and tree and squirrel and fish, and fear in you swirls when you admit that its paws, three times wider than you'd expect, hide claws you'd need to be crazy to mess with.

"Assume it's rabid," Gabe whispers, and I remember something my aunt once said: *There are fools, there are damned fools, and there are goddamned fools.*

And now, all these years later, in this stare-down with this wildcat, I realize her point: *Don't be a goddamned fool.*

"Stay still," Gabe whispers, though he himself lowers the anchor slowly.

"Even if it attacks?" I whisper.

"Just . . . maintain your presence."

"I'm trying."

The cat dips its head, takes three steps toward us while keeping us in view, stops in mid-stride to growl at Gabe.

Sprint to a tree you can climb, I think.

But no such tree is within fifty feet.

And the cat closes the gap. If I weigh 180, it goes 130, though again, it has those claws.

I aim Bark's gun.

"Should I shoot?" I whisper.

"No."

"Why not?"

"Just stay still."

But Gabe isn't still. He's standing, gradually, even as his movement seems to draw the cat closer. The boat drifts toward the shoreline, and now we're at max five feet from the cat, then maybe three: one pounce and it would be on us. Its snout is surprisingly wide. Its chartreuse and gray blue eyes, full of hatred so understandable you could almost love it, shift from mine to Gabe's, and it growls, this time at me.

"Should I?" I whisper.

"One gunshot means a warden on your ass."

"You're just saying that."

"And if you miss, we're *both* screwed."

The cat steps into the stream, and now here's Gabe, lifting an oar.

And he holds the oar up there, over his own head, not the cat's, and the cat hisses, raises a front paw, swipes in my direction—then turns and sprints off, into the woods.

Somewhere out there, a stick snaps.

Then there's nothing but the sound of the current.

Gabe is still standing, the oar well over his head. He could bring it down on me, seeing the gun is aimed at the cat. Yet I don't move. It's like we might trust each other.

"What the hell was that?" I ask. And I'm sweating full-out.

"That was your bobcat."

"Sonofabitch."

Gabe lowers the oar. After he finally sits, I aim the gun his way. If you trust him, I think, put the gun down, and I keep the gun aimed.

"Thing probably associates humans with food," he says. "That's what makes them aggressive."

"So why did it leave?"

"I don't know. Because we didn't?"

"Oh, come on, man."

"If we'd run from it, Deesh, we would have defined ourselves as prey. But we didn't run."

"But it could've kicked our asses."

"Yes, it could've—even with one of your bullets in it. It was the oar that saved us, Deesh. It was you deciding not to shoot or bolt, and the oar."

"What did the oar do?"

"Made us bigger. The bigger you are, the more their instinct says not to attack."

Gabe pulls up the anchor, sets it in the boat. Rows enough to make progress, and his eyes cross briefly but he blinks them into place, and then his forehead's creased like he's trying to solve some problem. He sticks two fingers in a front pants pocket, pulls out an orange prescription bottle, cranks it open, shakes out a pill he tosses into his mouth. The current begins taking us back.

"For your heart?" I ask.

"Blood thinner."

He rows, aimed straight upstream.

"Something I should probably tell you about blood thinners," he says. "Let's just say I bump my head hard? We wouldn't even know that an excess of unnaturally thin blood is pooling up in my skull." He snaps his fingers and says, "Could kill me in minutes."

"Seriously?"

"Take one of these oars and smack me over the head," he says. "And you'll see a man die fast."

# 44

# JAN

TUG STILL WOULDN'T SAY BOO, which would have been fine if we'd been running, but we were walking, just walking, so I came right out and asked him, "What do they mean, 'middle priority'?"

"I don't know, exactly," he said. "Maybe no more active search?"

To keep things hopeful I said, "You mean active search by *them*."

And we walked on, a solid five feet apart.

"Yes," he said. "That's what I meant."

"You ever consider that they might stop looking for certain people because they figure them still alive?"

He nodded. "Not exactly a comforting thought for *you*, though, huh?"

"That he'd be alive?"

"That he'd have run off. I mean, of course, I'd rather the guy be alive, but if he did run off, he's probably not what you'd consider an ideal role model for me."

"You think he's with some woman?"

"Possibly. But he could have run off for any number of reasons."

"Such as what?"

"I don't *know*, Jan. You tell *me*. I'm tired of always trying to figure that guy out."

Tug was now walking faster, as if he, like me, had learned the beauty of speed.

I caught up and said, "Anyway, where else?"

"You really still find my family worth your time?"

"Of *course*, Tug. Because you need to know what happened. I mean, do you want to go through years of questions like I did? Years of people gawking?"

We fell more into stride, some from me speeding up, some from him slowing down.

"Yeah, but the thing is," he said. "Where else is there?"

"There's not one place left that makes a tiny bit of sense?"

He snuck a glance at the clouds between treetops ahead. He sighed loudly, in a huff almost.

"Saratoga Springs," he said. "Just after he retired, we'd always vacation there this time of year. It's got a track that's like a hundred years old, and there's a ton of money up there."

"He'd be there to—what, start all over again?"

"I don't know, Jan. You're kind of the expert on the answer to that question."

"I am?"

Tug nodded.

"I mean, seriously," he said. "Why did you leave Arkansas?"

And of course this made me wonder if he was trying to tell me he'd heard some of those rumors about me, maybe the same ones Arnie DeShields had obviously heard.

So I said nothing, just walked on beside Tug, as if we had a complete understanding.

And the next day, after Jasper drove our mothers and us to Saratoga Springs, I told myself to gear down the last of my hope as the Galaxie rolled onto the grass parking lot near the Saratoga training track. Though given the look on Tug's face after we all got out and began for the track proper, I was sure they actually believed he was minutes from again gambling with his father, as he had so many times when he'd been a kid.

Then, from behind the rest of us, my mother called, "I'll be in the car," and we turned and saw her already walking back to the Galaxie.

And right away, Jasper called, "You'll need that unlocked," and off Jasper went, toward her.

And then there went Colleen, toward a dusty riding path that led west, away from the grandstand.

And I, feeling hurt because Tug hadn't said a word to me since we'd left the house, found myself veering off, too, in my case toward the white shedrows east of the track.

And, sure, I figured Tug now wondered if, here in Saratoga, with the promise of a racing day ringing out from the chatter of the patrons, we, the final stalwarts in the effort to find Tom Corcoran, were quietly giving up.

But if we were, how could anyone blame us?

# 45

# DEESH

**SOMETHING'S GETTING TO ME** in that festering, gnawing way you notice but don't quite feel and then can't ignore. Yeah, I'm hungry, and no doubt I need sleep, but this is something else, some mess made of nerves and impatience and nausea and awe about the steep pitch of a gorgeous green hill too close to me.

"So what happened with Madalynn?" Gabe asks. He places the oars inside the boat, lowers the motor, clicks it on.

"Like I said, we ended up kind of serious."

"You lived together?"

"For a while."

"But you never quite took the bait."

"The way I saw it," I say, "marriage meant a life of two people committed to having kids and then telling each other what to do."

I brace myself to hear Gabe ask, *Plus you found a hotter woman?*

But for now at least, he just gives me one of those looks, the kind people give when they're thinking better of speaking up, the kind that lets you figure things out on your own. It's a better look than the one he was giving me when he was telling me about his plan for me and his cabin, all intent and hopeful and insistent—the look Madalynn gave me back when she was pregnant and she and I talked about marriage.

"And what gets me now," I say, "is that this little part of me never stopped loving her. I'd loved her since the first time I saw her in grammar school, and I would go *on* to love her. As the years just, you know, kind of went by."

And it's with these words now out there, said by me to another human being, that I want Gabe to go off on a blue streak, about fish or bobcats or his own fucked-up heart. I need to hear someone talk about something other than me.

But he just navigates on.

He clicks off the electric motor. We're in slow-moving shallows. He works his torso forward to grab up the oars and, again, rows quietly.

"Real but unsustainable," he says.

"Huh?"

"Real but unsustainable love. Saddest story ever, and it happens all the time."

And he goes off talking about how, for any wannabe stand-up husband, there's the need to afford the financial costs of a marriage, not to mention, he says, that the prospect of having kids destines most any guy to a life burdened by debt—but how not having kids threatens to make him resented by the woman he loves if she comes to want motherhood.

I'm nodding as he says all this, realizing that, right now at least, he does sound like some kind of professor. Maybe he really was one, I think, and we cruise onward upstream, splitting a patch of evergreens.

"You used to hear the expression *'living on love,'*" he says. "But you don't anymore. And you know why? Because it's bullshit. Because, man, people in love have basic needs. People in love need to eat, shower, and sleep. Not to mention that, if people in love want to *make* love, they pretty much need to do it indoors, so a roof over their heads is probably a decent idea, too."

He reaches into his tackle box, finds a second prescription bottle, cranks it open. He shakes out its last pill, which he slaps into his mouth and swallows dry.

"Blood thinner?" I ask, stuck less on worry about his heart than on what Jasir might be doing right now—and what he'll always think of me.

"Yeah," Gabe says. "Without these, I'd be in more trouble than you."

"Hang on a second, man. Let me get this straight: If you take those pills and bump your head, you'll die very quickly. But if you *don't* take those pills, you'll have a stroke."

And right then he stares directly at me like a son might, all eager to portray himself as earnest.

"Not necessarily a stroke," he says. "The other possibility there is a heart attack."

"Well, that definitely sucks."

"It does. Either way, six feet under, or might as well be. But as I see it now, Deesh, it really only puts me right back in the same mortal lot as everyone else. I just have less leeway to fuck up in."

And for a second there, I want to toss the gun. This guy's a *lamb*, I tell myself. He really is trying to help you.

And he's letting me in on some theory now, his Theory of The Big One, which he admits boils down to one thing and one thing only—*In order to catch your biggest fish ever, you must believe it swims where you are*—but there's no chance this blue streak will stop even though he's already summed it up, because he's already getting into some of its ins and outs, its examples of how, if you believe your biggest fish is nearby, you'll behave like it's actually there, always making sure that the "presentation" of your bait is perfect, its implication that accuracy of casts is more important than losers who catch small fish think, and he slows down a little, maybe for emphasis suited to me personally, to add that I'll need to adjust my reeling speeds to find the one ideal for my biggest fish, who hasn't lived long enough to grow big for no reason. Fishermen pass up their Big One probably every time they fish, he makes clear more than once, the last time very loudly, almost angrily, but there's more of a love than anger here, I think after he holds up a hand to catch his breath. And ninety-nine times out of a hundred, he is saying to me quietly, man-to-man yet still intimately—ninety-nine times out of a hundred fishermen have no clue what they're passing up, so my best bet will always be to act, *at all times*, as if my Big One is near and aware of me.

And the longer this blue streak goes on, the more I think: Jasir.

Still, I keep the gun riveted. And again it becomes Madalynn's face my insides focus on. Madalynn's stateliness, Madalynn's way, in bed, of closing her eyes to pretend to ignore me until, an hour later, she'd finally touch me. Gangly Madalynn in grammar school. Curvaceous Madalynn just out of the shower. That better-than-ever Madalynn I ran into with Bark in Brooklyn last week.

And I remember for the thousandth time how, two years after

Jasir was born, Bark proposed to Madalynn. About how Bark and I, cool as ever, never talked about that proposal, never got into whether it meant Bark had slept with Madalynn or had just tried to use Jasir's need of a father as a way into her heart. How I learned of that proposal through James. How from then on Bark and I and James at most joked about my troubles with women, and how, whenever we laughed, I'd always, everywhere inside me, think *Madalynn*.

Gabe reaches down just behind the tackle box, grabs up the lunch bag, opens it, holds it toward me.

"Sandwich?" he says.

"No, thanks."

He flips the bag down between us, starts rowing all downcast and serious, maybe moping because I didn't take him up on his offer to share a meal.

So I say, "Got a question for you, though." And I'll ask it to be nice, but I've been wondering about this all afternoon.

"What," he says.

"How long after your divorce till you stopped loving your wife?"

He considers this, maybe trying to figure out why I asked it. He considers it long enough to be hung up on some huge argument he had with her.

"You mean when did I start telling other women I no longer loved her?"

"Yeah."

"Something like two years after we divorced."

I wish it would rain now, hard, a kick-ass downpour with lightning and all so we'd need to dock and leave the boat. But there's just ruffled gray clouds over us. I ask, "That long, huh?"

He nods. "But that was hogwash on my part," he says. "Because *now*, Deesh? All these years out? There isn't a damned day I don't miss her."

And this lovesick guy, I realize, still thinks I shot the cop.

Maybe everyone except Bark still thinks I shot the cop.

And everyone keeps on including Madalynn and Jasir.

# 46

# JAN

**AS TUG WOULD TELL ME DAYS LATER**, the antiquated Saratoga grandstand turned out to be far smaller and less grand than Tug remembered, and by the time he was walking up and down its wooden aisles among the well-heeled bettors, littered losing tickets and crumpled napkins and nearly finished cups of beer already lay here and there. Three loudmouths were making a hullabaloo about their profits while toting smelly cigars, no clue of Tom Corcoran anyplace, and as Tug accelerated toward the bluegrass band near the paddock, it was not lost on him that, at one time, his father's race-riding on this same hallowed track had been cheered by loudmouths, loudmouths who had since aged considerably, and then, as he watched the bluegrass band play, fatigue and disappointment and hunger ate at him.

Worst for Tug was not knowing how he'd greet Tom if he did

run into him. Would they hug? Would Tug ask what in hell, precisely, had happened? Would he lose his temper about how the Corcoran passion for gambling had screwed up the chances of healthy love between him and me?

And while all this uncertainty kept Tug's mind away from whatever he felt for me then, I was off, away from him, too, asking after Tom in the stables and barns on the Saratoga track's backside. And I'll be frank right now about how, back then, in Saratoga, I didn't exactly like how Tom's disappearance seemed to be testing whatever Tug and I had sparked the night we'd first run together through the dark. But I will now also always understand that any woman entwined with male desperation as much as I was then with Tom's and Tug's—that, well, there are times when she, like the most desperate of men, will do whatever she needs to.

# 47

# DEESH

ON MY HEAD THERE'S SUNSHINE shot toward me from around the edge of a rain cloud, and inside all of me, not just in my mind, there's that invincible sense of a decision already made.

So I say to Gabe, "I want to go back."

"What?"

"I want to go back to the Bronx."

"What are you talking about, man? You'll get your ass kicked in the Bronx. Plain and simple."

"Then let the ass-kicking begin."

And there Gabe goes, diving into a loss of words that threatens to last longer than his worst and bluest blue streak, maybe thinking through insights, maybe not. But I try to imagine. I imagine his gray eyes looking in. And what I imagine is that, here, in this boat with me—and inside him—there is still love for his wife, has been all this time, throughout his marriage and long before it. I imagine he loved her back when he was being hated by The Man Hater. I imagine that, for years since The Man Hater messed up his chances to teach, he's mostly felt like hell and wanted to do something significant, something good, and I see how I, Douglas Sharp, America's most recent notorious black man on the run, have been giving him the chance to do that good thing by asking him to help me hide. But now here I am saying, *No, you can't help me. I don't want your friendship. I don't want to live near you. I don't care if you've been hated because I have real love waiting at home, and—hell—maybe it's sustainable.*

"You're being very foolish, Deesh," he says now.

"Matter of opinion, bro."

He sighs. He goes cross-eyed but seems not to mind. Then his eyes seem fine, though he's again gone pale.

"Then at least," he's saying now, "at least let me—you know—at least let me show you how to fish."

And I fuck that up, too, by saying, "That would mean putting down the gun."

"*So?* You're about to put it down anyway."

"Not around you."

"Then who you gonna put it down around?"

"A sheriff or whatever."

"You plan to have me drive you to the nearest sheriff's station so you can walk up to the building with a loaded *gun* in your hand? The gun that'll end up making your conviction a sure thing?"

"It's not a sure thing. I didn't shoot the guy."

"Just put the fucking thing down, Deesh." He flails an arm into pointing at a flat clearing past a sunlit shoreline behind us, and then he's waving both arms more wildly the louder he talks. "Or throw it in that marsh. Nothing's going to happen here—can't you see I'm a dying old coot? I'm just a washed-up wannabe; I've failed miserably in my career and marriage and health. I have no kids, no siblings that care, no money besides the two tens and six ones in my wallet, just a mortgage on a piece-of-shit house I'll never pay off. Hardly anyone ever hires me as a fishing guide. I'm depressed! I'm on a million meds! And you think I'm gonna kick your ass? Can't you see I'm dead tired of hatred, Deesh? Like anyone hated eventually gets to be? That I'm done with the endless *argument?* Can't you just—if you're not going to stay in the cabin—fish with me for two minutes?"

And then he goes still, other than to row to keep us in place in the stream.

And the guy is glaring at me.

So I say, "Fine."

And he nods but does nothing. That one word from me seems to need to sink in.

Then, as he hands me a fishing rod, I set the gun beneath my thigh, the perfect compromise, if you ask me, then say, "Let's do this, man."

"Remember how I've rigged it," he says. He is blushing, maybe embarrassed now that he's won, or maybe it's just a dogged collection of side effects. "Split shot fourteen inches from the hook," he says. "Worm hiding the whole hook except for the barb."

And it's right then, committed as I am about returning to the Bronx, that I realize that, push comes to shove, I like this guy. Like how, dammit, he's still trying to teach. Like how his blue streaks made for conversation between two dudes in a boat with little in common. Like how even though he's old, white, out of shape, and generally uncool, he isn't the racist prick I thought he was. Like how there's still a kid left in him. How he *did* want to do something to protest hatred. Maybe mostly like knowing he cares about me.

"Purple rubber worm hooked an inch and a quarter from its thickest end," he's saying now. "Know how to cast?"

I doubt I do. But I remember that aunt showing me how in Georgia, so I nod. Then this gear, belonging to this Gabe I will never forget, is solidly in my hand, mine to keep if I wanted it, I'm sure, and, with all of this in mind, I try. The purple rubber worm falls short of the opposite shore. As I reel in, Gabe says nothing. No praise, no criticism—nothing.

Then: "Deesh."

"Huh."

"You ever envision a place after you've left it?"

I shrug. I think, This is an extremely odd man. "I don't know, Gabe," I say. But the truth is I have envisioned such a place: the Bronx. I've envisioned it often in this boat, most every time I've thought of Madalynn and Jasir.

"I mean, *specifically*," he says. "I mean, you ever picture exactly how it would look to someone else?"

"Can we just fish, good brother?" I ask, since I'm not sure what he's driving at, and since right now what I'm picturing, if anything, is Jasir and Madalynn and me *here*, on this very same stream, maybe in a matter of weeks, maybe in a few years, maybe with Gabe teaching us all to bait hooks using this same kind of purple worm I've just cast again.

"I mean, a guy's supposed to get over love, right?" he says.

I say, "You telling me you believe I should be over this Madalynn?"

"No," he says. "Not at all."

Good, I think. Though already what this man believes matters far less than it did an hour ago, since, dammit, I am going home. And I'm not entirely hopeless; I'm less like Gabe than he thinks. Still, now that I've reeled in a second time, I check my "presentation" for his sake, maybe a little for mine, too, and then I cast again, for the heck of it, a last-try-before-we-go effort if ever a guy made one, this time showing improved aim, and then I reel quickly, slowly, quickly-slowly-quickly, as Gabe's Theory of The Big One seemed to suggest, wondering if that theory or any theory of his— or of anyone's—is ever completely right. How could he be an expert? How could I be an expert? *Who* could be the expert on what a lover is or isn't supposed to get over? The most I know, if I know anything about love, is that, right now, I want to talk with the stateliest woman any man in the city has ever laid eyes on, then get to know her son.

And that's why now, as I reel, I feel a lot less freaked. There is only this world full of beautiful and ugly things, and I, a runaway brother casting into water smoothing down this world, am still one of them.

And it's not long after I think all this that one of my fingertips, the one against the line just after I cast it, feels a very light tap, then another, then something more like a tug. I stand and yank the gear over my head, and then I'm still standing but trying to regain my balance, jerking both arms higher to keep what's on the line hooked.

And Gabe has stopped rowing. We are in a calm pool. "It's big," he says, and he uses an oar to turn the boat to help me face what I'm doing. The fish cuts through deep water, possibly pulling us slightly. I am reeling fast—until I can't. I kneel on aluminum, yanking, reeling, yanking, reeling, Gabe's arms out at his sides to steady the boat, and as much as I'm charged by having a monster on the end of this line, I am now wholly committed to leaving this stream. I will, as soon as I land this fish, insist that Gabe and I return downstream so I can find a county sheriff, tell him every detail about how Bark shot the cop, then return to the Bronx to face Madalynn and Jasir, and embrace whatever love they might still share with me. I might be arrested; I might be questioned harshly for days; but as sure as I'm standing to reel and now yank this darting fish within three feet of me, I believe my truth will win out over Bark's lies—this monster bass has put fight in me.

And it's right then, as I pull the bass straight up toward me, that I hear the gun's report, which is quieter than I would have expected, probably because Gabe's mouth smothered the volume. Pale pink insides from his skull—pieces of a brain he'd trained to read and remember poems and teach, I realize—are sinking into the pool, the rest of him already floating on his back and begun downstream, limp and more rotund than I once figured, the gun nowhere visible, nowhere near the tackle box or on the fishhooks scattered across the boat's blue floor. An orange prescription bottle rolls toward me as the boat spins, taking me, as it spins, downstream, too. I am sitting now. Only one oar is intact. The gun is no doubt in that pool now well behind me—I can't see it at all and believe I never will.

But I can still see Gabe. Barely, but I can see him. He's still on his back, bobbing, and we're both spinning downstream, he still in the lead, me clutching the aluminum sides to keep the boat upright, the lunch bag already trapped inside an eddy, the gear gone from my hand, the rod and the reel just now underwater in sunlit riffles back there, my big bass taking it, escaping with it, headed upstream in a wisdom of its own.

# 48

# JAN

A FILLY WARMED UP ALONGSIDE ME, her tongue hanging out despite the bit, her eyes strained to see the pinks and yellows and magentas on the dresses and wide-brimmed hats, and I thought, Get into your stride, girl, wanting to watch her run rather than worry about trying to find Tom Corcoran, but then, near the finish line, I saw Jasper, patting his forehead with a folded handkerchief as he waved at me, and he was walking toward me, his own stride so fast I was sure he had news.

Then, closer to me, he shook his head no, and Colleen appeared from beneath the grandstand and waved, but took her time walking toward us. After she reached us, she stood directly in front of me, her face too close to mine and her eyes sort of mechanical, I thought, and she said, "Let's go see your mom," and it hit me that, on this trip to Saratoga, she'd been treating me like I was Tug's girlfriend—and I mean *really* hit me, to the point of confusion greater than my confusion about where Tom could be, since to me it was obvious that, today, Tug had as much interest in dating me as a muskie did in chomping down on an exposed hook. Of course neither Colleen nor I then mentioned any confusion, keeping to the entrenched Corcoran manner of not saying shit when anything important hung in doubt, and as she and I and Jasper walked back to the Galaxie, I wondered if there'd ever be a time when I'd know that, in actual fact, she cared about me.

And then there we were, she and I and Jasper, bearing down on the Galaxie, and my own mother, from the backseat, asked Jasper if he could take her to a church, and Jasper, as if relieved to have an option, said, "I don't see why not."

And now here came Tug, from the direction of the grandstand, loping steadily if not passionlessly, arms crossed, making it clear to the entire world, it seemed, that he no longer cared enough about me to as much as glance my way.

And the rational, unselfish part of me sensed this was because Tom's disappearance had Tug despondent, but let's be real—there was also the other part of me that wished I could be at the top of the list of the people Tug worried about.

I mean, doesn't everyone want that?

To be considered, by at least one other living person in the world, as the body who's most important?

# 49

# DEESH

**AS SMOTHERED BY GABE'S MOUTH** as his gunshot sounded, I keep hearing it in the back of my mind. And I know he was right that any gunshot this time of year will have a warden hauling ass toward it quicker than wildfire.

So I'm back on land, walking. Again in woods, this time hoping to see a road. The gun is still in the stream, where I should have tossed it before I fished.

But the gun doesn't matter now, I keep telling myself. I need to approach someone peacefully before anyone stalks me and shoots. I need to explain I just want to go back, so it would be stupid to run—I need to stay within myself, like I had on those sweet shiny courts in my hoop-playing days.

And it's here and now, in these woods in Pennsylvania all these years after I ran fast breaks over those courts, that I finally realize why I loved that game. Ball's a team sport if there ever was one.

The more you play it and win and pursue championships, the more you cherish teammates whose flow and moves click with yours.

Y'all pushed that ball, I think.

Fast and together, and that's why you won.

And that's why you clicked with Gabe.

Old white man was on your team.

He got what you're about. Understood your shit. Even had a term for it.

Fucking real but unsustainable.

And I walk on, crunching last fall's leaves, trying to understand exactly why he offed himself.

Maybe what he had with his wife was never real.

Maybe that's why he was all messed up about hatred.

And hatred of hatred ain't enough to get by on.

Maybe you also need love.

I try to focus on tree roots, fallen branches, any birdsong anywhere, anything but my memory's insistence on those bloodied pieces of the man's brain sinking into that pool.

You're in shock, bro, I think.

This is how a brother in shock feels.

But you need to keep hanging in.

You don't need an out like he did.

Sustainable or not, that Madalynn love was real.

Get your ass back and sustain whatever's left.

And it's right about then that I hear something, or someone, kicking up leaves.

And from behind trees emerge four figures, two ahead and two to my left, each stone-faced and white as hell, all of their guns black and aimed square at me.

"Okay, Sharp!" one of them yells. "Picnic's over!"

# 50

# JAN

JASPER WAITED IN THE GALAXIE while my mother knelt between pews and prayed and Tug and Colleen and I stood in the
aisle. I was beside Tug then, both of us more or less facing the altar,
and I thought about my own father's early departure, about whether
my mother felt about him back then the way Colleen now felt
about Tom. It occurred to me that, no, back then my mother had
probably felt quite a bit differently, since here she'd been, pregnant
with me, on top of still maybe feeling that swirled feeling you get
when you're with the love of your life, and the longer I thought
about all this, the worse I felt, because now, with Tom gone—a
supposedly responsible adult I'd actually known enough to have
fondness for—a sudden disappearance like that felt to me like a
very real thing.

It also occurred to me that, back then, in those days of my

father's passing, my mother had had to endure plenty of talk about her pregnancy with me, gossip so widespread it would reach Jasper and someday me, too, as well as invade my father's heart and mind and maybe even his soul. All that speculation about whether I'd end up proving to be Ronny's daughter—Jasper's granddaughter—it all seemed so old-fashioned now, this whole business of how the color of my skin would supposedly tell the world which man my mother had loved most. Still, I now also sensed, by my mother's persistence in remaining on her knees, that nothing back then had been easy for her, and I wondered, as she kept right on kneeling between those pews, if those days struck her now as being buried deeply by time, as they always had seemed to me. Today I know that, most probably, my father's passing has always hit her as having just happened, because I now understand how, after you've gone through certain things, there's this acceleration in the passage of time that can scare you almost as much as the disappearance of anyone, but on that day, as I stood in the aisle of that church in Saratoga, I was still unaware of how quickly time passed for her. I was, you could say, far younger in my thinking at the start of this summer than I am now, prone then to focus on only myself, at most on Tug's prospects and mine to end up together.

And then, after I thought through all these things, about mothers and fathers and the progression of time, Tug's arm bumped mine, maybe accidentally, and it occurred to me that if Tom hadn't won and lost the races he'd ridden and gambled on, Tug and I might be all out in love—I mean, crazy enough to marry. I knew impulses to marry at my age were unwise, especially for a woman who wanted a career, but still, right there, in that gray stone church in Saratoga Springs, I let a few dance through me.

And I think it was right about then, just after Tug's sticky skin touched mine, that it began to really sink in that the chances of Tom returning were slim, that I'd been looking the other way when it came to why Tom was gone. Obviously he was gone because he'd gambled too much, and it was also very clear he'd lost far too much—so much he couldn't borrow from even the cruelest of loan sharks—and I, like the rest of us, needed to deal with this.

And it was also sinking in that he'd lost to the kind of people no one should bet with in the first place, heartless, greedy men who see in racing not the beauty of speed but the chance to book bets made by people shocked by loss and therefore sure to lose more.

And it was then, in that church, that I first sensed why gamblers like Tom bet on horses in the first place: Every person on earth ends up trying to love someone else, and let's face it—it shreds your heart to try at love and lose, whether it's because love was never destined to come your way, or it was but your lover's moved on. I mean, the thing about trying to love is that no victory in love lasts. No matter how joyful you feel, no matter how young and healthy your beloved and you might seem, you can never, in truth, rely on love, because as love plays out, if you get right down to it, there's never any permanence of victory.

But in horseracing there is. There are races of certain lengths, with certain numbers of entries. And there's always a definite finish line, with the first horse to cross that line the winner and everyone else a loser. And, yes, sometimes there are jockeys' objections, but soon enough it's true that a winner is declared official. And once things are official there's an official reward for the second-place finisher, too, and there's even recognition of the mediocrity of taking third, and it goes on like that, all orderly and numerical and charted out for posterity to read in the *Form*.

And it was in that stone church in Saratoga Springs that it grew undeniable to me that there's this whole community of people who live for such certainty, such unchallengeable declarations about the results of races that are as heated and full of surprises as love.

My mother wasn't one of those people, maybe because the results of the love she shared with my father had ended as officially as you could imagine.

But Tom *was* one of those people, as are most grandstanders.

And I will always understand such people, always hope that, despite the infinite number of ways they choose to risk their time and money, they could all—somehow—win big.

# 51

# DEESH

"LET'S GO," A TROOPER SAYS, as I sit on a guardrail alongside I-80 with my hands cuffed behind me. "Up."

I stand as four or five hands keep me balanced.

"You read him his rights?" one trooper asks another. All but one of them—and there are dozens—are white.

"Yes, sir," I hear.

"Straight off the yellow card?"

"Absolutely."

"Did you *hear* your rights, sir?" the first one asks me.

And to spite him, I don't answer. Maybe there's wisdom to this: If I didn't hear my rights, I wasn't truly told them?

"Sir?" I hear.

Again I don't answer. At least twenty marked and unmarked cars and SUVs have gathered here, on this stretch of I-80, traffic funneled into one lane by orange cones.

"Do you hear *me*, sir."

Traffic beside me has stopped, more staid white folks staring.

"Then I'm going to read your rights again," I hear. "With these three—Tierney, get over here. I'm going to read your rights again, Mr. Sharp, with these four officers present to witness."

And again come my rights, this time shouted distinctly. A bus in traffic rolls ahead, followed by a parade of semis and pickups and cars. Three older guys huddle near an unmarked SUV, one of them, in a suit, on a skinny cell he snaps shut as he heads toward me. There is shouting, between him and Tierney, between Tierney and the trooper who arrested me, between the guy in the suit and the latest caller on his cell.

Then the guy in the suit approaches me. He says, "You took him down, you take him in," and I'm confused—until it hits me that he's talking to the white guy who first cuffed me.

"Yes, sir," that guy says.

"Do you have an attorney, Mr. Sharp?" the guy in the suit asks calmly.

I shrug.

"Do you want one?" he asks, and here I understand why people confess even after they've heard their rights: There are things you want to say, *need* to say—and here someone is, a person the world has deemed important, paying you attention, waiting somewhat kindly for any word from you.

And maybe it's because of this kindness that I say, "Possibly."

"Then I'll get the folks in the Bronx started on that," he says. "Okay?"

Again, I shrug. I don't want an appointed attorney, since the street taught me Legal Aid does little but hold your hand as it walks you into prison—because no Legal Aid lawyer wants to lose at trial. But I can't afford my own lawyer, certainly not for this mess. And now two troopers, one a woman, guide my shoulders toward a squad car's backseat, and now I'm put there and the woman closes the door. I'm inside the stink of hot vinyl.

There is silence, then radioed static. For a long time, I watch armed men chat while my guts and lungs rise toward my throat.

And now here's the guy who tackled me headed my way, and now he's here, with me. He closes the door, adjusts his rearview to check me out; I'm dizzy and blinking and, yeah, taking slow breaths like Gabe did to calm my own heart, because we are rolling ahead into traffic, back toward the Bronx, merging with people free to flee their troubles, squad cars behind and in front.

"You have any idea how much this all costs?" the trooper asks, and his rearview image makes eye contact.

And I won't answer, of course. But I wish I would. I wish I would speak up right now to say, *Yes*, I know. I know this costs a lot. And I know that some of its cost is to pay your salary, probably also to pay you for as much sweet overtime as you want. And I know that, because this money ends up in your pocket, you can afford to sustain any lover who loves you.

Then I tell myself to chill.

I will not speak to this jerk.

I will let him avoid the question Gabe and I never discussed: How long can my lover's love stay real?

And to face this question myself, I look pointedly away, at the green blur made by the thousands of trees we rush past.

Because, *man*, are we moving.

We will not be stopped.

We are flying down a long, steep straightaway.

# 52

# JAN

**PROBABLY, I TOLD MYSELF,** you're thinking about marriage to him to avoid thoughts about his father and yours, and then my mother nodded at the cross behind the altar and stood and side-stepped toward Tug and me, appearing so childishly in need of the nod Tug gave her, I about bawled. I mean, it hit me right then that her struggle to handle what horseracing had done to her had led her to pray on her knees, and I hadn't as much as sat beside her, and my standing out there, in the aisle with Tug and Colleen, was kill-ing her. So right then and there, I actually tried. No, I didn't use my actual voice, not even a whisper, but I allowed myself to think thoughts that might have been prayers, asking only one thing— that we would again see Tom Corcoran—but almost as soon I doubted this prayer since, first of all, it was kind of selfish, and, two, the sight of Tom Corcoran could never by itself guarantee happiness. And then, whether praying or not, I thought hard about happiness, about what it really was and how it truly felt, and I couldn't stop remembering how it felt to ride Equis Mini, that electric sense of joy and freedom he and I shared, and I also remembered how, even after he'd crossed the finish line and we both had won, he would have kept running if I'd let him.

And gratitude for that experience welled up in me in that church, and I wondered if welling up meant I was indeed praying, but I also felt very alone right then, with no sense inside of anything God-sent. All I felt was an accumulation of logical thoughts, earthly, selfish thoughts that urged me to never let anyone know what I wanted—because it was clear to me now that, in horseracing at least, there would always be people who'd use their knowledge of what you wanted to take advantage of you. Why people like Arnie DeShields enjoyed treating jockeys like meat was something I still didn't understand entirely, but what mattered right then and there, in that church aisle near my mother, was that I finally accepted the truth about what had happened twenty-some years ago in the Corcorans' shallows: My father had committed suicide.

And the reason I could accept this was that, thanks to my stay in the Corcorans' house, I now knew how it felt to ride racehorses for money, and generally it was a feeling of being used, a feeling you wanted but then also despised. In my case I'd wanted Tom Corcoran to bet on me when I'd jocked Equis Mini in that secret sprint—but then came Tom's using me to get that tip from Arnie DeShields, and then came Arnie trying to use me for sex, a sleazy intent on Arnie's part that still appeared to have no end to it. And, yes, it was probably true that women who jock feel used more than men, but even if you *were* a man—even if you'd been my father, the

Great Jock Jamie Price—it was all still *use*—of your body but also your mind and the best of your spirit.

And, sure, winning felt good, very, very good, but a victory in a horse race takes very little time, a very small fraction of your life. And then there ends up being the whole rest of your life, where you feel caught in this tangle of beauty and ugliness.

# 53

# DEESH

**FROM THE GEORGE WASHINGTON BRIDGE** on in, my mind jumps as quickly as it did when I first saw Gabe's house, this time from thought to thought about Bark's selfishness and the Belmont trifecta and James's wisdom in bailing on us in Queens, then about Gabe and Madalynn and Jasir. I try to focus on Jasir, but now there's Bark's chat with Madalynn on that sidewalk in Brooklyn where I faced Jasir, and then there's me in those days when I made careless love with Madalynn, then James telling me that Bark proposed to Madalynn but Madalynn said no, and then there's Gabe rowing that blue-floored boat and, now, there's Gabe's body lying on that water, after his last attempt to connect and do good.

And then there's Gabe's ex-wife and her gutless love, and Gabe's ex-boss The Man Hater, and the mother and father who gave me a life but never quite got into it.

And under all these thoughts is the realization that, now that I'm back in the Bronx, I'm also in the world of law, and law, I should have learned long ago, never lets go of you.

And where law takes me now, in a motorcade led by NYPD, is to the precinct building on 230th Street. I've walked past this building countless times, been inside it one Halloween long ago, when word was cops gave candy bars to any kid who stepped inside, and now, just outside it, well-dressed folks, not all white, wait with cameras and mikes. As I'm taken inside I neither shy from these people nor face them, just pass them with the pride I have left. Inside, all eyes welcome me in their casual but intense way, and I keep silent. They want fingerprints, which they uncuff me to get. They want name, address, and digits, and for these they make do with what's in my wallet. They say they'll take me to be arraigned, ask if I know what an arraignment is, and, for that, they get a nod. And then, after they cuff me again, this time with my hands in front of me, one of them says, "Good luck, Deesh," and they take me back outside, where a livelier crowd gets as much of me as their cameras can. And then I'm in another squad car, again NYPD, again alone in the back, cuffed hands on my lap, no escorting vehicles in front or behind, though the two cops in the front seat obviously wish they could kill me, and, shit, this squad car ain't stopping. I have never fainted in my life, but now, on and off without warning, comes this sense of sinking into myself, as if, you know, my mind is sort of a black hole quickly devouring the rest of me, maybe because I know, from my time in school and on the streets, that I'm up against official City of New York rancor.

Will it *really* help Jasir to see you back here like this? I think.

Won't it just make his matters worse?

And what about Madalynn?

Can any love, real or not, withstand arrest and incarceration and the lust of millions for conviction?

Then we're near 161st, approaching the beige, soot-tinged building etched with the words CRIMINAL COURT and flanked by more media, and we turn twice and roll into an underground parking garage full of cop cars and trucks. I remember Gabe and I watching the stream swirl and glisten, but here, trapped as I am by concrete, Pennsylvania seems like it never existed: no birdsong, no bass, certainly no friendship with a washed-up wannabe lit professor.

And now we've stopped. I'm taken out and passed to four armed courthouse guards, who take me up an elevator to a floor where people wearing dark blue uniforms take more fingerprints, these digital and probably instantly online. And after a young white woman brings me a worn chair, here, across this large but stuffy office, stand two guards, brothers I'd bet were once Marines, taking turns glancing at me as one reads a computer printout. And as they stroll back toward me, the other lifts his chin at me and says, "Just so you know? You're a forty-one."

I play this off, and the other brother says, "He don't know what that means."

"Know what it means, being a forty-one?" the first asks.

And here my eyes answer: *Just tell me.*

"Means you're a badass."

"Means you'll need more than Legal Aid," a sister behind me calls.

But I can't afford more, we all know, and now three other guards, these white, take me via elevator to a higher floor, which is simply an open area, no hallways or rows of doors, just a worn-shiny concrete floor under four holding pens constructed of gray bars, the largest pen with twice the floor space of the others, maybe a third of a basketball court. In this large pen stand five cuffed-silent suspects of maybe forever-untold crimes, one tall and Asian and the four others black, and I'm being escorted toward them when a guard shouts to an old Hispanic guy at a desk against a wall: "Should we put this forty-one alone?"—and the old guy nods.

So I'm walked and locked into the small pen farthest from the five suspects. The first words I think inside are *This is it*, because avoiding the inside of a cell has motivated me for practically my whole life, and I wonder if maybe avoidance of anything for so long somehow finally becomes attraction.

The four brothers in the big cell are staring me down. Instinct says stare at the wall opposite them, which I do, but that makes me remember Gabe gazing off into Pennsylvania's woods. Then I get why people behind bars off themselves: If I didn't have Madalynn and Jasir to pin my shoulders back for, what would be the point?

"You the *cop* shooter," shouts someone.

I don't answer, don't even breathe. Then I inhale motionlessly.

And then all of us waste more of our lives in silence.

Then I hear, "Hello?"

A short white dude with cut-to-the-nubs gray hair stands just outside the bars, one finger readied inside a closed manila file.

"Douglas Sharp?" he says. He wears a green suit, three piece but discount, the skin on his face, just above and beneath his eyes, chapped to bright pink. "I'm Larry Gerelli, your attorney."

"How do I know that?" I say.

He looks me up and down and says, "You don't."

And he walks off, then out a side door.

And I feel like I did in that manhole years ago. Yes, smarter than some, but alone.

# 54

# JAN

**AS TUG AND I AND OUR MOTHERS** left the church, my mother asked me if I preferred to leave for Pine Bluff that week or the next, as if our return to Arkansas were something we'd discussed of late, and even though we hadn't talked about going back there, I got all petty on Tug and answered casually, as if I'd never cared about him in the first place, and what I said was "As soon as you want."

Then I glanced toward Tug, to see if I'd gotten his goat.

But all he did was glance away, with this put-off look on his face, and accelerate on ahead. Like he was thinking, *This is what happens when you hang out with three women,* like he was determined to never again step foot inside that church.

And I knew he knew what the popular songs said, that if you cared about someone, *really* cared, you'd fight against all odds to keep that person close. But I was also sure he knew, from having watched his parents try to coexist after their arguments, that if you pursued love from your lover when pride was at stake, you could lose respect and maybe love itself.

So there I was, on that sidewalk between the church and the Galaxie, walking well behind Tug even though I cared about his thoughts as much as I did mine, feeling abandoned despite being squeezed in between our mothers, trusting the sudden headwind we faced was full of my father's spirit, then asking it:

*Daddy, why did you let us live here?*

# 55

# DEESH

**WHEN I'M FINALLY LET OUT,** I'm taken by three guards down an elevator and through narrow white hallways, then out through a blue metal door to a courtroom, where the blond-wood onlookers' benches, set in rows like church pews, are about full, most everyone seated on them dark haired and dark skinned and dressed in dark clothes, the few whites there restless—reporters, I figure. Front and center, up behind the judge's bench, waits a robed white guy not much older than I, the guard beside him a freckled brother in a white long-sleeved shirt who calls, "Douglas Sharp, docket number ending 6374—charge number 125.00."

Guards' hands urge me toward a chipped Formica defendant's table, where, to make matters worse, I'm forced to stand beside the short guy with the cut-to-the-nubs gray hair.

Damn, I think. Then a sister in nice clothes, standing at the worn table to our left—for the prosecution—all but shouts facts from a manila file folder of her own. Facts like the name of the shot cop, the time he was pronounced dead, and the address on 216th where the shooting of him happened. Facts like the willingness of Bark to come forward as an eyewitness, like the cop's and Gabe's names as well as their mailing addresses, so now there's no question that, yes, there are two homicide charges against me, one for Gabe's death, the other for the most recent shooting of a member of the NYPD.

And now the judge says, "Mr. Sharp, I understand you had concerns about whether Mr. Gerelli is the attorney appointed to you. And I want to commend your caution in that regard. But foremost I want to assure you that he, the man just to your left, is indeed Mr. Gerelli and your appointed and astute legal counsel, one and the same."

Great, I think.

"Do you understand me, Mr. Sharp?" the judge asks. Behind him, dusty windows reveal branches of a tree reaching between buildings across the street.

"Yes, Your Honor," I say, and a twitch attacks one of Gerelli's thumbs.

"Would you like to speak privately with counsel before you plead?" the judge asks.

"No, sir," I say to the judge.

"Then how do you plead?"

"Innocent," I say.

"In my court, it's either guilty or not guilty, Mr. Sharp."

"Then with apologies for that mistake, sir," I say, "it's not guilty."

And I expect a buzz of whispers from the onlookers behind me, but then I get it that no one who stands accused where I do is guilty—unless guilt can be traded for freedom.

"Well," the judge says. "Mr. Sharp is indeed a flight risk. There can be no arguing that. So he gets a remand to Correction in lieu of bail. In a few minutes we'll tell Mr. Gerelli the date of your pretrial conference, okay, Mr. Sharp?"

I nod, and the judge nods back, but more as a signal, it seems, to the guards behind me, who guide me by my elbows back to the navy blue door, which, on this side, says, CORRECTION FACILITY—DISPLAY SHIELD AT ALL TIMES. Another guard throws a dead bolt and opens the door, and I'm headed back through the bright hallways, then up the elevator to the holding-cell floor, where, now, at least ten guys stand in the large pen.

And when I'm entering my smaller pen, someone behind me shouts, "I need privacy with Sharp," and a guard yanks me to a halt, then into a small, mostly yellow room, where I stand alone until Gerelli walks in and closes the door.

"Why the *hell* did you say that," he says.

"What," I say.

"*'Mistake'!* It's on the *record*, man! You admitted to making a *mistake*! You—"

"I was just referring—"

"No, you did *not* refer! You merely said, without an explicit referent, the phrase 'that *mistake*'! Which could therefore be argued, down the line by *prosecutors*, to refer to one of the murder charges! And you might also care to know, Mr. Sharp, that you are up against *life*, and as such my *client*, so therefore, all of my boundless respect for your natural intelligence and homespun ambition notwithstanding, I am, for your own legal and personal darned good, asking that you and I, right now, stipulate that I, your attorney, know what the *fuck* I'm doing!"

Wow, I think.

"Fine," I say.

And we stand in what's now relative peace.

"You need me, man," Gerelli finally says, as if using this peace to persuade me.

"Fine," I say.

"So I have two questions for you," he says, and he gestures to have us sit, which we do. "One is what happened? Two is what do you want besides freedom?"

He opens his briefcase, takes out a pen and a legal pad, aims the pen down to write.

He says, "I trust you understand that your friend Bark has signed an affidavit saying you shot the cop."

"And his bullshit is still on the news?"

Gerelli leans across the table. "At the top of every hour."

I swallow hard, imagining Jasir watching Bark's televised lies.

"To answer your second question first?" I say. "I want to see three people. My son, his mother, and a buddy of mine named James."

"Full names and addresses?" Gerelli asks.

I answer this as best I can—James, I figure, is still at his grandma's in Queens, and I don't know Madalynn and Jasir's address in Bed-Stuy—and I watch Gerelli write, and he asks, "Why this James guy?"

"Been tight with me and Bark since high school."

"So we need his testimony." He underlines James's name twice. "And, of course, I'll try to contact your wife—"

"She's not my wife."

"What, divorced?"

"No. Just . . . you know, never married."

"But this Jasir is your son."

"Yes."

"And you've supported him over the years."

"Not exactly."

"Not always?"

"No."

"Ever?"

"Not ever."

And here my face radiates. And Gerelli leans back and slaps his thighs with both hands, then inhales and holds his breath.

"Well, this is all a *problem*," he finally says. "Because—Mr. Sharp—not being your spouse, this Madalynn could be asked to testify *against* you. So I would need to watch what you say to her, and—"

"I don't care," I say.

"But Mr. Sharp—"

"She loves me, man."

Gerelli frowns cynically. "And let me guess. You also love her."

I nod, and he snares me with a pout that commands:

*Don't be a goddamned fool.*

"I know what you're thinking," I tell Gerelli. "But I don't care. You asked what I wanted, and I told you. And you gave me your best advice, which I took. And now I'm asking you again: I want to see Madalynn and Jasir."

"Mr. Sharp, the existence of Jasir, a son unsupported by you, will *not* win over a jury."

"You don't get it," I say. "Jasir is why I'm back here."

Gerelli's adoration of law, I sense, tries to grasp this love I've finally found for Jasir. In the margin beside Jasir's name, he jots a question mark.

"Okay then," he says. "Tell me what happened."

*I just did,* I want to say. *Madalynn and Jasir happened.* But instead I talk about the phone call Bark got from the woman up near Poughkeepsie, and I make it clear that Bark got this call only two days ago, and that I'd never met this woman before that call and haven't seen her or contacted her since. Gerelli writes in a scrawl I doubt he'll be able to read, and I tell about how, two mornings ago, Bark drove James and me upstate, how we three teamed up to take the drum. How I helped carry it but barely. How we left it on that straightaway upstate, then how we went to Belmont Park and won the trifecta. How then Bark wanted his gun and James said no and I stuck with Bark out of friendship. How the gun always scared me and Bark double-parked to get beer and I got in the driver's seat. How the cop baited Bark and Bark fired.

"And that's the truth?" Gerelli says.

I nod and say, "I wish it weren't."

"And then what?" Gerelli asks, and I tell about how I drove to Passaic and agreed to ditch Bark's gun someplace remote. How Bark and I agreed to park his truck and take separate buses, how I saw the breaking news in the minimart and abandoned the westbound bus for the woods. How I then hoped to find someplace where no human being lived—but then met Gabe and couldn't stop thinking about Madalynn and Jasir.

"So you headed back for love," Gerelli says with a straight face.

"Yes," I say, and I inhale until my throat catches. Am I nervous about Madalynn and Jasir, or is Gabe's death finally really hitting me? I vow not to break down—not around Gerelli.

Gerelli stands and grabs his pen and legal pad and says, "So I'll get right to contacting these people." He packs his briefcase and his cell phone rings. He cusses but answers, says "Right" distinctly, folds the phone closed, pockets it, holds his briefcase at his side, turns to face me.

"Is that it?" he asks.

"You tell me."

"We'll talk tomorrow," he says, and all I can do is picture Gabe last I saw him, watching me, with Bark's gun just beside me, as I fought the bass in that sparkling stream.

And not long after Gerelli leaves, I'm walked back by guards to my holding cell. The big pen now holds close to twenty. And it holds more still as evening gives way to night, brothers always the majority. At some point, a guard brings me a bologna and cheese sandwich, which I eat while wishing I'd tried that liverwurst. I'm given a pint carton of milk I sip slowly. My answer to catcalls at me from the large pen is to remain seated on the concrete floor faced away from them. I sit like this for hours, shoulder blades numb against the gray bars, trying to think good thoughts, like about the years I taught myself basketball, but any good thought ends quickly.

Then I hear, "Douglas." A guard has opened the pen, and he and three others, without another word, take me out and past the big pen, which is now packed, then down flights of stairs and outdoors.

We cross a sidewalk crammed with media. I wonder if Gerelli knew I'd be relocated this soon, and if so, why he didn't mention it. I still keep emotion from my face, or think I do until I'm headed toward a white van whose windows are caged over with painted-white steel grids, ten huge Carolina blue letters on the side facing me that together spell one word:

## CORRECTION

# 56

## JAN

**I SAT IN THE BACKSEAT**, on the far left, watching the orchards outside the window, my mother beside me, Colleen in the passenger seat directly in front of Tug while Jasper drove in a quiet of his own.

Then Jasper clicked on the radio, changed music to news, and dealt with an incline by giving the Galaxie more gas, and Colleen stared out her window but down, at the yellow and blue wildflowers sprouted through emergency lane gravel. Tug would later tell me that right then he was trying to decide which was the better time and place to ask me to delay my return to Arkansas—right away, within earshot of everyone, or as soon as we got home and found time alone—and those wildflowers kept rushing past, yellow, blue, sometimes a purplish blur, and, in this stubborn reticence of everyone's, Tug remembered overlooking The Crux with his father during the last silence the two of them shared. Maybe, Tug realized only now, his father had been silent then because he'd been planning to run off from the Corcoran household to someplace remote, someplace where no loan shark or wife or anyone could further bedevil him, and then, on the Galaxie's dash radio, a forecast called for clear skies to the south, and the broadcaster went on to announce that a corpse had been found in a forty-gallon drum discovered by someone on the Saratoga County Highway Department's cleanup crew, the identity of the body being withheld until the next of kin knew, and Jasper braked hard, and my mother actually cussed, and Tug said, "Turn around."

And the Galaxie changed lanes violently to make the next exit, then hairpinned using the overpass and sped east, and everything Tug saw was radiant. He saw radiance through the clouds, radiance on the grilles of oncoming cars and bouncing off the slow lane— Tug's thoughts themselves *felt* radiant. He told himself this radiance was a result of the angle of the sun at this time of year, but whatever it was, it had begun too suddenly to be explained away so easily, and it grew stronger as the speed-trap trooper who'd clocked the Galaxie gave chase and pulled us over, stronger still as the trooper and Jasper talked, maintaining this great strength as the trooper sped to escort us, and when the Galaxie finally stopped near the cluster of black brick buildings, the parking lot asphalt gleamed. And then there stood Jasper, on that lot, Colleen staying put in the Galaxie as if there were no way out, and I opened my door just after Tug opened his, and Tug said, "Jan, please just stay here," but I followed him and Jasper and the trooper to the building, and nearly caught up with them just after they stepped in. The trooper told a sergeant why all of us were there, and this sergeant gathered up forms and a clipboard and a pen but kept calm, very calm, as if he, too, knew Tug's father as the same Tom Corcoran who'd once jocked, and then this sergeant told Jasper to take a seat in the lobby but said nothing to Tug—this sergeant was just leading him. Tug was then walking in a hallway he perceived as being the color of radiant milk, and the sergeant kept on leading, and Tug wanted every gesture between him and his father's body long past over and done with: the nod Tug would give, the squeezing of the wrist by Tug one more time because they'd squeezed wrists in the grandstand while his father's winners had won, the touching of the hair, the thank-you. But Tug also kept thinking his own feet were taking him toward his father too fast, and the radiance, whose existence made even less sense in that hallway, seemed to have grown worse.

Then, from maybe four feet behind, I whispered, *"Tug."*

And he turned and saw me.

"I'll do it if you can't, Tug."

"But I need to do it myself."

"But I'm not sure you should."

"He's my *dad*, Jan. The guy's my father."

And we kept on, toward a door the sergeant held open, and now, inside the room Tug entered, any radiance or brightness seemed cast by the room's overhead lights, and the sergeant neither spoke nor nodded but Tug kept right on past him and kept going, and soon Tug kept his gaze fixed on one of the table's silver legs, because he had known at first glance. He had known from the shape and from his father's height, and from having seen all that radiance, and all he could think was: There's no need.

And I stood behind Tug, in the doorway, and Tug quickly said, "It's him."

"Yes, but we need a direct visual ID," the sergeant said.

"But it's him."

"Mr. Corcoran, I need to be able to swear you saw his face."

"No, you don't," Tug said. "Because his face is beside the point. Just let me sign that it's him."

"Mr.—"

"I'm not scared, sir. It's just that I *know*."

"Tug, get it over with," I said.

"I can't."

And I set a hand on a hip and walked straight over and lifted the sheet. The head was enlarged, swollen or waterlogged, the neck ugly as hell, and the hair looked oddly dry, like a clipped-off horse-hair braid I'd found as a child in the hot-walker's dilapidated stable. But the hair here had thinned precisely as Tom's had, and it had receded that same distance past his darkest age spot, and what helped me endure this viewing of this ugliness was Tug's motion-lessness, and our silence.

# 57

# DEESH

**THE THING ABOUT BEING RELOCATED** this time is that I now appreciate it more for what it is, a chance to see as much of the world as someone in custody still can, the world of bright storefronts, of striding employed people late to meet someone they care about, of the grins on kids being made fun of by their pals.

And then I am there, in Queens again, this time blocks from LaGuardia Airport, rolling onto a tree-lined road divided by a guardhouse, the bridge to Rikers Island, the only way on or off the island other than a swim that would kill any escapee, and it hits me that the city bus just ahead must be a Q100. In my youth I made jokes about the Q100—about how desperate women used it to visit their bad-boy lovers—but now, as this rattling van I'm in keeps close behind such a bus, I imagine how Madalynn and Jasir would feel riding a Q100 to see me, or waiting for one in Queens while innocent residents walk by.

Then we roll off the bridge and onto the island itself. And it turns out Rikers isn't just a building or two. Goddamned Rikers is more like its own town, and my mouth goes dry, one breath almost a gasp, though I'm also trying to see as much as I can, guessing which brick structure will house me, which loops of razor wire might be my view. Then I know which structure, since the van has stopped beside it. And then I'm being escorted out of the van and into that structure, joined by more uniformed guys, two, then three more, each with holstered black guns and varnished billy clubs, and they take me up flights of stairs to the third floor. They leave me untouched as we head down the only route possible, a narrow concrete walkway flanked by opposite and adjacent cells, one cream-colored steel door to my right, one to my left and so on, until the walkway dead-ends at an unpainted cinder-block wall, which I stop to face directly, maybe four feet from it.

To my right, a steel door has been slid open, into the wall. A guard uncuffs me and says, "Okay."

And you don't feel the claustrophobia until you step inside, but for me the sense of panic sure does then come on fast, my face well beyond flushed by shameful heat when one of the guards slides the door closed and it clicks. I am shivering. I am chilled yet perspiring. I am up against the door to try to see out my only window, fingernail-etched Plexiglas maybe a foot square over steel bars painted the same cream color. And looking straight out, I can see only the cinder-block wall of the cell across the narrow walkway, though if I try hard, I can decipher part of the Plexiglas window on the cream-colored steel door across the walkway roughly six feet to my left, behind which someone, a brother maybe, tries to see me until our eyes meet.

And, no, there will be no hearing him. There will be no hearing anyone but myself. There is stillness here about as pure as the stillness that welcomed me into those woods in Pennsylvania, though this stillness conveys terror more than that one did freedom: Neither moonlight nor sunshine will reach me here. There's a mattress on a bed bolted to the wall, and there are two thin blankets. There is no pillow. And the toilet is kid size. The floor is gray, unfinished concrete. As is the low ceiling. If I look at the ceiling, I feel so trapped I get dizzy.

So you won't sleep on your back, I decide. I also know there will be no sleep tonight. Feeding the stillness around me is hunger inside me that wants people more than food. I would beg out loud for Madalynn right now if anyone could hear me. I caution myself to focus on innocent, grammar-school memories of her, since any desire for her tonight, as the woman she grew into and still is, will no doubt prove to be foolish.

I sit on the edge of the mattress and stare at the blank wall. I have no reliable sense of time, but it must be hours before I accept that I will have a view out of the barred window only—that is, no window through which to see the outdoors. And often, throughout these hours that I sit here alone because of what I've done and haven't done, I think of Jasir's future.

What will he tell his friends about me?

Will my time here be a secret he never shares?

Of course, I'm trying not to consider who I'll meet in this building. There will be mostly brothers, so if I'm known as the cop killer, will I be a hero? And if so, will I be spared from the jailhouse horrors no ex-con ever talks about?

Questions beyond these run through my mind. I sit down. I stand. I remember Gabe's kindness. At some point I'm sure Gerelli is bound to visit momentarily, but he doesn't. I promise myself he is now working for me, and after this promise wears thin, I start to doubt Gerelli the man—his resolve, his smarts, his goodness.

So when the door slides open and I hear, "You have a visitor," I have roughly as much respect for Gerelli as I do for Bark. Again there are guards, this time two, and again I am handcuffed, the three of us led down the stairs by a black administrator too large to take shit from anyone. He nods me into a room walled by Mets navy blue cinder block, where he alone uncuffs me, has me undress completely and raise my arms and widen my stance; he sees all of me but touches none of me. He stuffs my clothes into a metal bucket marked with the same number as the one on the gray jumpsuit he hands me. He never once looks me in the eye, and he cuffs my wrists tighter than anyone has yet.

Then he has me leave the room, and we are walking again, his palm on my left shoulder blade, pushing in a way that hints he's behind schedule. And then we are cutting through a small office to enter a room centered by a white wooden table with three stainless steel rings bolted into it, a visiting room. And here, I notice as I'm cuffed to one of the rings, stands Gerelli, behind the table, wearing that same green suit, setting himself up on a folding chair while I sit. He places his briefcase on his lap and says, "Not so great news, Mr. Sharp."

"What is it?" I say.

"I contacted the three people you wanted to see."

He opens the briefcase, pulls out a legal pad, flips his way to a new sheet, pats his inside jacket pocket to find a pen he clicks twice.

"And?" I say.

"Well, they're not here," he says with a glance behind him.

"Did you expect them now?"

"To be honest, Mr. Sharp? People who will visit an accused generally do so right away."

"Generally," I say.

"Correct. The pattern is more visitors sooner and very few later."

He jots phrases on consecutive lines.

"Let me be candid with you, Mr. Sharp. You've been charged with murder. Nine out of ten times, that means the people you know would rather not think about you. Let alone visit."

"So who's my one out of ten?" I ask. "You?"

"I'll tell you who it *isn't*," he says. "This friend of yours, James."

"You saw him?"

Gerelli nods. "First thing this morning."

"What did he say?"

"It's what he *didn't* say, Mr. Sharp. Didn't and thus very likely won't. What he did say was, essentially, that I should contact his attorney. Who, as it turns out, is the same guy who represents your friend Mr. Barker. Which, of course, means we need to prepare a case that assumes that both of these lifelong friends of yours will, as character witnesses, prove hostile."

"You're saying James will lie, too."

"No need to lie to harm character, Mr. Sharp. I mean, we've all lived lives." He jots something, again with a question mark. "And of course nothing's for certain," he says, but then I wonder exactly how much extra cash Bark gave James last we all saw each other—plus, Bark, I realize, has been James's only employer for years.

Then Gerelli says, "Your buddy James did request that I ask you one thing."

My gut guesses James's question—Who would *you* side with?—but all I say is "What's that?"

"His precise words were 'Why run?' And I hate to say this, Mr. Sharp, but those two words kind of sum up what we're up against. Let me be clear here: By no means do I, personally speaking, want to second-guess anything you did or failed to do in the past sixty-some hours. After all, you are, right now, still alive, and survival itself, no doubt, has been a great challenge for you. But all of my compassion for you aside, Mr. Sharp? People *will* ask why you ran."

"I know," I say.

"And unless we can give them an adequate answer—which, trust me, I am already working on—we're going to be up against it."

What I'm hearing right now in this room, I tell myself, is lawyer talk, and its essence is that Gerelli has already lost hope. And now here this Gerelli is, glancing at his watch, which means he has other work to do, for other clients if not for me, not to mention he might have his own love and children and all of that.

Then he leans back in his chair so far it tilts, and now, rounding the doorway behind him, is Madalynn—Madalynn as stately as ever—and I see no speck of her that's not knock-dead beautiful, her hair pinned back off her strong cheekbones and delicate neck.

"Hey, Deesh," she says.

I want to say *Maddie!*—but all I do is nod.

"Now what you done?" she says with a hint of playfulness, and I glance at Gerelli, who stands to let her use the folding chair on his side of the table, gets a folded one from against the wall, sets it up a bit behind her right shoulder, which she glances over before her eyes kill mine.

"He needs to be here?" she asks.

"Mr. Gerelli?" I say.

"Yes, I do," Gerelli says, and, already, I'm sure, I'm losing her.

"Well," Madalynn says, "I figured you could use seeing me."

And I say, "Always."

Then she and I sit, her eyes searching my face, looking, I sense, for anything at all having to do with me that's to-the-core true, and here goes another rush, up my neck, of that now familiar heat I give off with shame, and as it leaves my face I know that, yes, since grammar school, it's been her, Madalynn, one way or another, here and there and wherever I've been, who has drawn such heat from me.

And I want to tell her this, but my thoughts jump to where she and I might now be if Bark hadn't pulled that trigger, or if I hadn't joined him to haul junk as a way to make cash, or if I hadn't kidded myself by thinking Jasir didn't need a father just because I'd done without one.

"But the thing is," Madalynn says, "is that you never *did* see me." She huffs out a sigh. "For pretty much every day of our seventeen-year-old son's entire life."

It hits me that she said nothing at all like this on that sidewalk in Brooklyn. Then again, she was talking with Bark. This is what she was saving for me, I think, and I feel both lucky and empty.

"I'm sorry, Maddie," I say.

"Of course you're sorry," she says.

"I'm sorry because I love you," I say, and with these words I'm not trying to play her, just plain sharing what I've felt for years.

She jabs a thumb over her shoulder at Gerelli. "He tell you to say that?"

"No, Maddie. He—"

"See, but, Deesh? I will *always* wonder if he did."

"Why?" I say. "I swear, Mad: You don't need to wonder. Why do you need to wonder?"

"Why do I need to *wonder?*"

"Yeah."

"Deesh, *you*, the man who is now *here in prison*, are *the reason I have* wondered for almost twenty years. You think love can just, that far down the line, up and turn wondering off?"

And all I can think is: She said love.

"Anyway what does all of that really matter today?" she asks. "I mean, Jasir's been talking about signing a piece of paper to agree to get blown up in some war."

"You're saying he wants to enlist?"

"No. But he might *need* to. The point is, Deesh, we're all a lot older than you think we are. I realize you want to be all lovey-dovey with me now, but it's not like you can suddenly just start . . . *being there* after you've been gone for so long. I mean, face it, Deesh: People, you know, *adjust.*"

"But Maddie, you also have to remember something. That, you know, my being gone caused *me* to adjust."

"So?"

"So, for what it's worth . . ." And here, rather than go off on some blue streak like Gabe might have, I think, Forget it. You screwed this up long ago. You should've stayed in those woods, away from everyone, Gabe included.

Then Madalynn says, "What?"

"Nothing."

"Just tell me, Deesh. You don't now, you might never."

I picture myself fishing in Gabe's boat as I did—with Bark's gun no longer in my mind—and think: *Stupid.* I take a deep breath and notice Gerelli watching me closely, ready, it seems, to do what lawyers do.

"It's just," I say to Madalynn. "That I—"

"Mr. Sharp?" Gerelli says, and I wave him off with a frown that says chill.

"It's just that—you know," I say to Madalynn. "I want you to believe me."

All three of us, Madalynn, Gerelli, and I, wait.

"I mean, believe that I didn't shoot anyone," I say.

And here I can actually see, on Madalynn's face, the brunt of an onslaught of thoughts running through her mind, Bark's story on the news among them.

"Maddie?" I say. "I'm telling you. I didn't kill anyone."

# 58

# JAN

"WE DON'T RUN FROM FUNERALS" was what my mother whispered to me and me only before we'd left the state police parking lot over in Saratoga County, so now here I was again, snug beside moonlight reflected off the lake that had swallowed my father. But now, as I lay on the Corcorans' summer-porch cot, it occurred to me that my mother must have gone through a hell of her own waiting for my father's cremation—before she could pour his ashes into the lake and leave New York State to start her life with me. I reminded myself that I was lucky to have had at least one parent who'd stuck close to me, but now, on this night, even though I was in the same house as this parent, I felt more alone than ever.

Then I heard footfalls, and I sat up and saw Tug emerge from the strip of lawn along the south side of the house, jogging toward the shoreline, where he stopped to face the lake. That he'd run through the dark heartened me a little, though now I couldn't deny he'd chosen to run without me, and with this well in mind, I actually missed Arkansas.

Then he walked out onto the pier, in that slightly thicker darkness you see when a cloud obscures the moon, and he kept on walking until he stood at the very end, his arms at his sides, the whole of him reverently still, as if, right now, he might be trying to give the benefit of the doubt to his father's best intentions, but my gut told me that, most probably, Tom's love affair with gambling would always lead Tug to disgust, and that this night, for Tug, would probably be unbearable.

If nothing else I knew well that a dead father never stops being dead, and no wish or forgiveness or run through the dark can change that. And I knew, too, all about the hardest part: Learning that, between you and your dead father, only one of you is now capable of change—you—and then after you *do* change, the new you comes to feel all the more distant from him, and the longer Tug stood out there on the pier, the more these lessons hit me all over again, and I hated them.

And I wanted to walk out there and explain all this to Tug and tell him it was only natural, but I sensed that, as bad as I'd had it growing up, Tug now had it worse, because I, being born after my father's death, couldn't possibly have done a thing to cause it, whereas Tug, if he felt so inclined, could second-guess dozens of things he'd done and conclude that, hell, if he'd avoided doing just *one* of them, maybe Tom would be out there right now, standing on that pier with him. Any insolence of Tug's, any rolling of his eyes, any decision as recent as the one he'd made to run with me in the dark the night Tom had driven off in a huff—anything could be turned over and over in Tug's mind as a possible fault, and as I watched his stillness I wondered if, instead of being in love with him right now, I might just be feeling sorry for him.

Then I realized that my hatred of what our fathers had put us through assured me I didn't want for there to be pity, from Tug to me or from me to him. What I wanted was plain and simple—to be with Tug—and it hit me that what I liked most about running in the dark was picturing myself with Tug some night long from now after some run, doing whatever we wanted without concern about our parents' troubles or anyone's gossip, doing it until we'd see that little smudge of light the sun can push between branches at dawn. And it was then that there was simply no more kidding myself that, sure, I was capable of feeling sorry for anyone going through hell, but that my desire to put an end to Tug's hell right now—so we'd be free of it—meant I loved him genuinely, maybe invincibly. And it was then that I felt how quickly the summer was flying past, how, even if he and I lucked into having long, healthy lives, we would each someday go quickly, too.

And that's why I stood and then left the summer porch.

And why I walked across the moonlit lawn, privy to that same tightness in my chest I felt when Tug and I first met.

And why I stepped onto the pier, setting it into its seemingly microscopic quiver over the black lapping water.

And why I kept right on walking.

And I don't know why Tug turned around, but when he did, he saw me and sized me up carefully and said, "Yes?"

And I said, "Yes."

And he stepped toward me, then stood directly in front of me, and we kissed, just once, but there was this sort of gravitational pull between us, and there was no shyness.

"Out here?" Tug said.

I shook my head no. "On the porch."

"But they'll hear."

"No, they won't, Tug. I'll be on top, and you won't move. Just one rule: No squeaks from the cot. They'll think we're just sitting there talking."

"And that could actually . . . work for you?"

I nodded. "I like our chances."

# 59

# DEESH

"I *DO* WANT TO BELIEVE YOU, DEESH" is what Madalynn says. "It's just that . . . well, for you to be innocent makes no sense. Since you—you know. Ran away and all."

"But I was *scared*, Maddie. It's as simple as that."

She shrugs. She doesn't cry. "Scared will never make sense, Deesh," she says, her voice higher. "If you love someone, there's no *scared*. There's no running! Unless it's from something like . . . responsibility for a *life*."

You blew it, man, I think.

"Or several lives," she says.

Just shouldn't have run, I think. Ever.

"You know?" she says. "When I first saw Bark talking about you on the news, I pointed straight at his face on my TV and said, 'That Bark is a *liar*.' And I said that because I believed in you. But when the news showed you being escorted in that *Pennsylvania* trooper car? I started *shaking*, Deesh. Because, all of a sudden my *body* couldn't take it anymore. Because, dammit, Deesh? It wasn't just Bark talking anymore. It was *you*, all the way out in those big hills covered with all those trees. It was a man obviously caught on the run, and I needed to finally stop denying that that same man *was* you."

Gerelli's gaze at the ceiling has me certain he's thinking the worst.

"You can say caught," I say, to Madalynn but him, too. "But not on the run. Because I wanted to come back, to own up to you. To you and Jasir. That's what my heart felt, Maddie, and I promise you that. I wanted to *come home*, Maddie. You just need to believe I saw home as someplace with you and Jasir. And that's pretty much all I have to say."

"And all I have to say, Deesh?" she nearly shouts. "Is that I can't believe you!"

"Not ever?"

"Not that I can foresee."

The sting of these words leaves me unable to move.

Finally I manage to say, "I still need to talk to Jasir. I need to know that at least *he* might believe me."

"*Jasir* needs to believe the *truth*," she says. "Like he always has."

"Then please tell him the truth, Maddie: that I want to talk with him. So I can see all this through. So he can know the whole truth on his own."

"No way, Deesh."

"Huh?"

"Jasir is *not* going to step foot near any Rikers prison."

"No, Maddie: Jasir is not going to *end up* on Rikers. Which is exactly why he needs to talk with me."

"*Needed.*"

"What's that supposed to mean?" I ask, knowing full well the answer to this question.

"Means it's too late to be his father now, Deesh. Too late by years."

And she nods at me, once but with aim as lethal as Bark's and Gabe's aim of that gun, then gets up and walks out of the room, no slowing down or stopping, no turning back.

# 60

# JAN

**TUG TOLD ME THAT THE FIRST THING** he heard when he woke in his bed the morning after we first made love was nothing for a long time, just a quietness similar to the silence he'd grown up fearing in the house, save the fact that this silence said less about frustrations between spouses and more about shock that another retired jock had passed on. There was also, if you asked me, a certain relief to this silence, a calm because now, among this jock's survivors, fewer bets would be made, and then, as Tug lay in his bed, he heard *"Tug"* whispered from behind his opening door, but rather than me it was his mother who stood there, in the doorway, dressed for a trip into town.

He grabbed jeans from the floor, pulled them on.

"Maybe you'd rather not talk about this," she said. She closed the door behind her. "But I think we need to."

Tug yanked on a shirt. "Okay."

Sunglasses and purse and keys in hand, she sat on the edge of the bed.

"We're getting money," she said. "From the insurance. And, Tug, your father and I had *two* mortgages. And our worst fights always happened when those stupid payments came due. So I want to pay both mortgages off—so we can be done with them. Just pay both in full so we can own this place. With no resentments."

Tug smelled her dabbed-on lemon juice for the first time in weeks. "You'll get enough from the insurance to do that?" he asked.

"Yes, but not by much."

"Then—I don't know. Do what you want, I guess."

"I'm thinking I will, Tug. But I wanted to tell you first. Because from now on, you and I need to be much more open about things like finances."

Tug nodded. Then, despite himself, he sighed. As open as she was being, this was her unspoken way, it seemed, of proposing a deal: She'd keep this roof over their heads if he'd find work and pay for everything else.

"Can I say something then?" he asked.

"Sure."

"I mean, if we're going to be open?"

She nodded.

"First thing I'm doing today is buy another forty-gallon drum."

"*What?* Tug, why would you—Tug, we really need to consider—"

"We need to send a message, Mom. We need to say we consider all of his accounts closed and paid in full."

"You'll do that by going to the *track*, Tug."

"You're right. You're right. But if I show up there today with a new drum in the truck bed, those chumps'll have no doubts about *why* I'm there. I'm there to say: Got another drum, gentlemen. You want me to keep talking to sheriffs, go ahead and steal this one, too."

Colleen sat there for a while, lips pressed. She stood, stepped to the window, and gazed out over the lake.

She cleared her throat and said, "And you actually think that will work."

"I do," Tug said. "Plus consider how you'll feel the longer a new drum stays put in our yard."

She didn't move, not even to breathe.

"I mean, seriously, Mom: Wouldn't you sleep a lot better?"

"I really do want to say yes, Tug. Except there's this one little thing."

"What."

"Your dad always asked that exact same question."

Tug let this truth sink in, among the others, new and old.

Then he asked, "Well? How did you usually answer it?"

She shrugged.

"Apparently not well enough," she said, and the way she both turned and stepped away from him, as he sometimes had from me, assured him that he was his mother's son.

So he tried for a hug, but she stiffened.

Nor would she let him see her face.

"Go," she said. "Get the stupid thing. I'll give you the cash—that is, if you really think it's for the best."

"I do," Tug said. "Believe me: I wish I didn't, but I do."

"Then just buy one and let them see it at the track as quickly as you can. Just get this whole damned thing over with."

She glanced over at Tug, and Tug kept his eyes on her.

"But then, Tug?"

"What."

"I don't want to see it. I don't want to see anything *resembling* a drum sitting in our yard. I don't want to stand in my kitchen and ever have to as much as notice it."

"Okay," Tug said. "I'll put it on the horse farm. We should probably quit burning the damned leaves anyway."

# 61

# DEESH

**THIS TIME IN A SPORT COAT,** his head shaved clean, Gerelli takes his place on the other side of the table in the visiting room and says, "Someone's been found," and all I can think is *Jasir.*

But then Gerelli says, "Upstate," and before he adds another word, my mind takes me back to the stench I smelled in that crawl space, and now there's no chance that my gut feeling then—about death being in that rusty drum—was misguided, because here, now, is my attorney talking about the discovery of an adult white male corpse identified as Tom Corcoran, a retired jockey who was strangled.

And this attorney of mine and I are not teenage hoopsters shouting laughter. We are not two men who've loved the same woman conning ourselves about the tightness between us. We are not two experienced souls at wit's end on some stream spilling our guts about love. We are, as Gerelli puts it, *the accused and his counsel*, and now, as he also explains, we are the *apparent perpetrator of a third homicide* and the public defender who, at this moment, feels tempted to *quit this insane profession altogether*.

And, now, we are quiet.

Until Gerelli says, "You look upset."

I shrug. "Why would I be?"

"I don't know."

"Are you accusing me, Mr. Gerelli?"

"I'm asking you."

"But are you *accusing* me."

"I'm your attorney, Douglas. I'm trying to help."

"How can you help when you don't believe—"

And here my mind jumps to Madalynn to Gabe and back to Madalynn, and heat rushes quickly into my face, and I turn away from Gerelli: I am welled up, yeah, a jailed-stupid brother welled up.

But not crying.

"We're going to have to work on our credibility, Mr. Sharp."

"Fuck you," I say. "I didn't kill anyone."

"Mr. Sharp, a footprint that matches your sneaker precisely was found near the drum. And traces of similar dirt were found on your shoestring."

"I didn't kill the jockey, Mr. Ger—"

"And the gun that killed the cop was, without question, the same gun that killed the guy in Pennsylvania. Do you hear that, Mr. Sharp? Do you know what all of this means?"

"I didn't kill anyone," I say.

"And the problem is," Gerelli says. "You want to know what the problem is, Mr. Sharp? The problem is you didn't tell me about this retired jockey when I asked you my first question, which was the simple inquiry of what happened. So now it appears you had something to hide."

Gerelli grabs his chin with one hand, blinking nonstop.

He drops the hand but keeps right on sitting there, staring at me incredulously.

# 62

# JAN

TUG KNEW WHERE YOU COULD BUY a new drum, the lumber-yard on an unnamed east-west road just past the second town north, but it would more than help his cause, he figured, to first off buy a *Form* and visit Bill Treacy's feed store, to ask where a guy could get a new forty-gallon, the kind used to burn leaves.

And Jasper's presence there, on the decrepit wooden chair beside Bill, meant that Jasper was finally getting out again, holed up as he'd been since Tom's wake the previous week, but, still, the only greetings between Jasper and Tug were nods, Bill Treacy then taking the conversation's reins to ask Tug how Colleen was managing, whether my mother and I planned to stay much longer, whether Tug still had aspirations about law, all of which Tug answered as straightforwardly as he could.

Bill then recommended that same lumberyard north, which

strengthened Tug's resolve to do what he told his mother he'd do, and Tug pressed on during the drive north and bought a drum painted the same orange as the first, not at all rusted but otherwise quite the replica. And with this new drum on the bed, kept there by a discarded chunk of cinder block, he returned south to make his showing at the track, which hadn't yet opened for the day.

But the regulars were there, on the edge of the parking lot near the grandstand, strung out in a line that stretched to the turnstiles, smoking, clustered in groups of two and three, all reading *Form*s except The *Form* Monger, who apparently felt no need to hide his bewilderment—or was it respect?—thanks to Tug's presence in Tom's pickup with a new orange drum. In fact, The *Form* Monger stood pathetically for well into a minute, unconscientiously agape, eyes shifting from the drum to The Nickster and back to the drum, the scarred wrist beneath The *Form* Monger's phantom hand all the more purple in the late morning sunlight.

And after The *Form* Monger stared like this for so long Tug was sure every chump at the track today would get the message, he went ahead and waved in their direction, at all of them, he thought. And The *Form* Monger waved back, then turned to interrupt a conversation between a very young gambler and The Nickster, and The Nickster looked up and over at Tug, then gave Tug a nod more resolute than any Tug had hoped for. And Tug felt the sense of worth he'd sometimes felt months earlier, back when he'd done chores to benefit the horses on his farm. Then, to make sure The Nickster knew Tug's days of feeling intimidated were certainly over, Tug made a show of gathering up something from the pickup's passenger seat: the first issue of a *Daily Racing Form* he'd ever purchased for himself.

And to convey even more nonchalance, Tug, on his own accord, spent a few minutes pretending to read results in that *Form*'s past performances.

And soon there Tug was, actually reading some of those results, probably seeing, in some racehorse's officially documented win, an indisputable quality that he, like Tom—like everyone, really— could never possibly find in love.

# 63

# DEESH

"WELL?" GERELLI SAYS. "Why didn't you tell me?"

"I hadn't gotten around to it," I say. "Anyway here's the question you should be asking prosecutors: Why would I leave the gun there?"

"With this Gabe Cutler's body?"

"Yes."

"You didn't. It was found well upstream from where his body was found. Not to mention, Mr. Sharp, you'd just used your last bullet on him. There was, of course, another bullet from that gun in the cop's head. So as a result, the prosecution is now saying, you didn't know what to do after you shot Gabe Cutler point-blank. I mean, the sight of a third person killed by you is presumably a tad more disturbing when you yourself are now no longer ably armed.

So you panicked and tossed the gun in the stream, maybe hoping Gabe's death would look like a suicide."

"But it *was* a suicide," I say.

"Mr. Sharp, I do need the truth. We both do."

"I'm telling you! Gabe Cutler killed himself. I've been telling you this since day one."

"Yes, but how do we *know* this?"

"Because he was depressed."

"Yes, but *how do we know* he was depressed?"

"Because everyone is. Because the world is extremely fucked-up."

"Oh, for God's sake," Gerelli says, and he leans back and tosses up his hands.

And it's right here that I lose all doubt about whether, if I ever do find myself on the streets of the Bronx again, I won't be best buds with Lawrence Gerelli.

# 64

# JAN

"THEY CAUGHT HIM," my mother said.

And she sat down beside me on the cot, the same cot where Tug and I had made love, and she did her best to ignore the lake as I squeezed one of my knees and said, "Who?"

"The guy who strangled Tom."

"Well, good," I said—I actually said that.

"Thirty-seven years old. Unemployed and, bless his heart, about as black as you are white. Named Douglas Sharp or some such."

"Rest in peace, Douglas Sharp."

"You're saying you prefer him dead?"

I shook my head no. "Just that now that they caught him, he's as good as it."

She studied a sunlit oak and it struck me that there were too many men to think about. My father and Tug's, Tug himself, and now whoever it was that had killed Tom—men were always running roughshod over the brighter future I'd long ago hoped for.

My mother leaned a little toward me—or maybe I had toward her.

"If I were you," she said, "I'd tell Tug to forgive him."

"Of course you would," I said. "It's just that there's one not-so-small problem with that."

"Huh."

"You will never be me."

And here my mother was, definitely leaning in, pressed against me so intently it was clear she wanted to keep touching me. "I'm aware of that, Janny," she said. "All I'm saying is that here I am, feeling sour because *you're* feeling sour because Tug's off every day watching horses run. So it seems to me that—maybe?—if he'd forgive this Douglas Sharp . . ."

"Maybe what."

"Maybe some of that sourness would leave us all."

"Yeah, well, Tug Corcoran isn't just watching those horses. He's betting on them. And if you ask me, that's your basic problem here."

"That he'll turn out just like Tom? All in love with betting and in debt up to his eyeballs and gone for good from his fine-looking woman?"

I felt a smile threaten then, and I thought: If only men loved as easily as mamas could. "Something like that," I said.

"Then all the more reason to forgive Douglas Sharp. Not that this should be repeated, Jan? But Colleen and I have been talking, and if you ask her, neither she nor Tom were all that prone to forgiving—or apologizing, or accepting apologies, or making good out of bad—or anything along those lines. It was all stone-cold business around here, and now she believes it stayed like that because she and Tom never forgave."

"And you didn't prompt her, even the tiniest bit, to adopt that belief?"

"Maybe a little. But if so, barely. Anyway forgiveness is only a matter of saying three words. I mean, from Tug's point of view, there'd be very little to lose."

"I kind of doubt just saying *I forgive you* is all it takes," I said, and right then, out a window to the south of us, a healthy-looking leaf fell straight from an oak. It appeared to be a big, fine leaf that was still shiny and dark green, but it fell.

"And how would you know," my mother said.

"You're right, Mama. I wouldn't. Just making my best guess, really."

"Jan, no one's asking anyone to join some church or tithe instead of gamble. I'm just saying come out with those three words. I mean let's be serious, girl—how could that hurt?"

And of course I'll never like when anyone tries to force beliefs on me. But then again, it really did feel like Tug was starting to get stuck on gambling.

If nothing else, he kissed differently now, all eager to pull away.

# 65

# DEESH

"SO LET ME GET THIS STRAIGHT, Mr. Sharp," Gerelli says. "You actually want me to argue . . . *now* . . . after this damning discovery of Tom Corcoran's murdered body . . . that you killed neither Tom Corcoran nor the cop in the Bronx. *And* that what happened in those woods in Pennsylvania was that a despondent, underemployed, aging white male willingly navigated you away from his house and well into the woods, then peaceably came into the possession of the same gun used to kill the cop in the Bronx, then freely decided, with you sitting in his boat and looking on, to end his own life."

"Well, I wasn't looking on, but—"

"What were you doing, Mr. Sharp?"

"Looking overboard."

"At what?"

"The water."

"Because it was so freaking beautiful?"

"Because I was fishing. And deciding I would come back here to talk to my kid."

Gerelli rolls his eyes, then closes them and covers his face with his hands.

And I let this silence play itself out, my hope right now being that maybe he's prepping me for how it'll feel to be cross-examined.

Then he says, "Well, we can argue that, Mr. Sharp. But before we decide what to argue, I need to know every single one of the facts. Because we just can't walk into another surprise."

I nod, dumbstruck all over again about how it didn't matter who pulled the trigger in Gabe's boat, since I should have known better than to put down the gun around Gabe in the first place. Then it occurs to me that, in fact, I am guilty of kidnapping Gabe, and that Gerelli and I have yet to discuss this.

"So what the fuck do you want me to tell you?" I ask. "A list of every wrong thing I've ever done?"

"That probably wouldn't hurt, Mr. Sharp. I realize you have no priors, but there are also certain exigencies a public defender like me and a client like you need to address. Such as how much fucking time do you actually expect me to dole out to you when I have other clients—who are far more upfront and grateful—waiting encouragingly for me?"

"What are you saying? You want me to pay you something after all?"

And it's here that he just stares across the table at me, lips pursed.

*"That,"* he finally says, "was really not the kind of question you should feel the need to ask me."

And now's when I realize that if he isn't suggesting that I arrange for him to receive some kind of payola, he's just playing judge and punishing me by messing with my head.

# 66

# JAN

**EVERY GRANDSTANDER TUG HAD KNOWN** had harbored a tragic tale that explained why he, that poor, poor grandstander, wagered on horses every day, as well as a story about the *giant* trifecta he *almost* bet on, as well as a nonstop stream of anecdotes about his *unbelievably* persistent losing streak.

And whether Tug had wanted to hear about gambling or not, every grandstander had blabbed on about some horse race wherein the long shot he'd bet was numerous lengths ahead of the pack down the homestretch; about how, when this long shot was mere feet from the finish line, another horse came *flying* from out of nowhere to win by a nostril; about how, had this nostril not been flared, this particular grandstander's life would be far easier than it now seemed cursed to be.

So Tug didn't bother me with all the facts about his wins and losses during the twelve days he spent at the track after he showed up there with the Corcorans' second orange forty-gallon drum.

Other than to suggest, by way of his various moods when he'd come home every night, that he, too, had welled with the joy of winning.

And that he, too, had experienced how victory can urge a wounded soul to want to win more.

And that he now no longer questioned his father's belief that if a man with a modicum of intelligence hunkers down alone and handicaps obsessively, he *can* know who will win.

And who *will* win—as Tug had long known—is the track.

And when a guy is down to his last six dollars, and then four, and then two, and he bets those quivering two on an even-money favorite to show, and it lopes along ahead by eight only to pull up lame and finish last, that guy can face the horror of his father's death all over again—with his own eyes dulled and his lips joined as if one and his heart certainly overworked.

And if it's not until minutes *after* this guy's last possible bet that he realizes he's just lost the cash he'd once promised himself he'd use to buy a gift for the woman he loves, his heart feels pretty much gone.

And when he therefore flips down his *Form* to announce to everyone in the grandstand that he, too, is a profound loser, and the bare legs of this same woman appear as she takes the seat directly to his right, wearing shorts and a sweatshirt and a frown across her face, this guy will indeed struggle, like the true bastard he now feels he is, regarding what, precisely, he might say.

And what Tug said, after such a struggle, was nothing. Instead he just faced me directly, tried and failed to make eye contact with me.

But then, in consolation, he had these thoughts to think:

You no longer owe him that fifty.

You gambled it—and more—*for* him.

You are done.

And then I tried to make eye contact with him, and when I finally succeeded, I pointed at the disheveled *Form* at our feet and said, "I take it this means you lost."

"Yes, it does," Tug said.

"A lot?"

"A good amount."

"Good as in harmless? Or good as in large?"

You understand now, Tug might have thought then. You understand how your father felt.

And he said, "I don't know how to answer that, Jan."

"Then why don't you just show me your wallet?"

"What?"

"If you're such the Mister Money Bags that you're able to sit here betting every day, let's see your fucking thick supply of cash."

This is how your mother felt, Tug probably thought then. This is why she and he argued.

And I slumped back in my seat, but still I was glaring, though now my eyes were aimed at the concrete aisle just beyond the *Form*, as if I were having this lovers' spat with the charts rather than with Tug.

Then, finally, I asked a question I'd wanted to ask for a while. I asked, "Ever think you'll have kids, Tug?"

And he, too, glared at the aisle.

And I could almost hear him thinking: *Okay. This is it. Don't waste any more of her time.*

And, to me then, he simply said, "Nope."

"Good," I said.

He shrugged again, this time making a big show of it, then slumped back, barely behind the line of fire of my eyes.

"Because as much as you'd suck as a husband," I said, "you'd suck even more as a father."

Give her that, he probably thought. And let her enjoy having it.

Then he must have felt he owed me an explanation, because he said, "So now you know why."

"Why what?"

"I grew up wanting a horse farm."

"Actually, Mr. Tug? I have no idea why being a jerk means a guy would want a horse farm."

And there, right then in that grandstand, Tug might have finally understood why his parents' arguments had never ended. The gambler sees more of the picture than his lover does, and the gambler knows that what he sees spans plenty of time—more time than his lover is considering—and the gambler sees that, for all this time, he has never stopped wanting the best for her.

He *sees* this.

And it's not so much that she lacks confidence in him.

It's that she refuses to see.

And no one can make anyone, especially a woman who's strong enough to love a gambler in the first place, do a single thing, Tug probably thought right then.

Because he said to me, "The upshot, Ms. Price, is that I'm good with horses."

And I took a deep breath, then held it.

Finally I said, "Uh-huh."

"As opposed to people," he said.

"Okeydokey."

"And I feel comfortable with horses as opposed to people."

"Gotchya."

"So why wouldn't I just take care of horses—instead of fathering some actual human being who I'd definitely raise to be a completely fucked-up member of society?"

Now I was shaking my head no, looking at every grandstander there except Tug. But as I did this, I asked, "Why would you fuck anyone up?"

And Tug's answer was "Why wouldn't I?"

"You're saying you're fucked-up because you were raised by your father?" I asked.

"Yes."

I nodded once, quickly. I said, "I'd go along with that."

"And my mom," he said, and he shrugged again, a shrug he might have thought I didn't notice, but now I seemed destined to notice things like that, and I felt smaller as I folded my arms.

I said, "Well, that's just sad, Mr. Tug."

"Not if I end up with a horse farm."

And for quite a while there, we sat like that, side by side as if stuck in those old grandstand seats with each other, watching a green sunlit tractor comb the homestretch dirt free of hoof marks.

"Or so I used to think," Tug said.

And then—maybe—he noticed that I was holding my head slightly off center, as I had when we'd first met.

I said, "For what it's worth, my mother thinks you should forgive Douglas Sharp."

"Who's Douglas Sharp?"

"Guy who killed your father."

"They caught him?"

I nodded.

"He confessed?"

"No. I mean, I don't think so."

"Jan, I'm no expert like your mom," he said. "But I think the forgiving's supposed to happen after the guy fesses up and says he's sorry."

I sat up straighter. I ran both hands over my clipped-back hair.

I was as calm as ever as I said, "So you're saying you're not ready."

"For what?"

"Lots of things."

"I'm telling you, Jan. I'll forgive the man as soon as he confesses."

"And what if he never does, Tug?"

"Then I'll do it when he's convicted. I mean, if you still want me to then. But I really don't get how this whole forgiveness thing's supposed to work. I mean, let's just say I visit this Douglas Sharp and forgive him. How does doing that make my average day better?"

I shrugged and said, "Hell if I know."

And here, dammit, I had Tug smiling so hard I was sure I had him hooked.

And I said, "My mother would probably say that, somehow, good would eventually come from it. Like somehow you and this Douglas Sharp might, you know, think about each other more or whatever, and as a result one of your problems gets solved."

"My problem or his?" he asked.

"Whoever's," I said. "I have no idea, Tug. But if you plan to ignore the guy anyway . . ."

"All I said," Tug told me then, "was I'd wait till we know for sure that he did something wrong. I mean, let's just say he turns out to be innocent. Forgiveness from me would be kind of rude, right? I mean, think about it, Jan. If this Douglas Sharp is innocent, we both probably owe him an apology."

"For letting him sit there?"

Tug nodded.

And I said, "I still say having more forgiveness than you need isn't the worst thing in the world. Because, damn, Tug, people screw up."

And here was where my voice had gotten shaky, when Tug was probably sure I would cry, but I didn't. I hadn't cried at his father's wake or funeral or burial or at any time since, and I hadn't cried all summer, not that he'd seen, not with tears falling, and it struck me then that maybe he thought I was one of those people who cry only when they're happy, and he sat looking at the odds board, apparently ticked off at himself and maybe the world because he, Tug Corcoran, had followed his father's footsteps and as a result gambled away cash he could have used to buy me a gift.

Why had his family bet? I wondered silently then. Why had each Corcoran continued when everything felt jinxed? There'd been very little good in all that time they'd spent in the grandstand, and now, as always, there was even less time, good time and bad time both. There was never, ever good in not being able to buy something small and nice for a lover you actually loved. Today offered every grandstander there a gloriously clear sky and newly blooming flowers on the infield, but now that Tug had lost, what good was all of that doing us?

Then, to our right, we heard, "Do you need this?"

And there, weak chinned and crouched on the concrete stairs and pointing at one of the strewn *Form* sections at our feet, was The *Form* Monger.

"No, pal," Tug said. "It's all yours."

And The *Form* Monger didn't thank Tug or me, just reached for the section closest to his grimy self, unmarked past performances worth pennies at most since the eighth race was just now leaving the gate. Using both his purple stump and his good arm, he struggled somewhat, and I, no doubt red-faced, maybe from fading anger with Tug or new embarrassment over how close the purple stump was to touching my legs, bent to help The *Form* Monger, and he thanked me, once as one potentially kind human being to another, a second time, it seemed, as a man enamored of me if not of gambling only.

Then he and I had roughly all of it gathered, various sections now secured between his torso and the stump, his hand taking the last of it from me when I said, "Wait."

And I was reading a past performance while his hand pulled at it.

"You can't have this," I told him.

"But Tug said I could," he said.

"But I need it," I said.

"But—"

"Sir, this *Form* is ours and I need this particular section," I said. "Take the rest of it if you want, but please just go away."

"But you have the ninth race," he said. "What I have is worthless."

"I know, sir," I said. "And we thank you for recycling it. Seriously, mister, I need to study this race."

And he walked off without even a glance in our direction, no doubt pissed at me for my lack of respect and at Tug for being a cocky liberal who took pride in respecting women to the point of embarrassing every old-school grandstander present, and then

I pointed at the newsprint and asked Tug, "Did you—did you *see* this?"

"See what," Tug said.

"Equis Mini. He's running in the next race."

"Here?"

I nodded. And I will always, always have to admit that, right then, I was excited.

"Today?" Tug asked.

"With morning line odds of fifty to one," I said.

"Don't play with me, Jan."

"I'm not. Look."

And I held that *Form* section closer to his face, so he could see that there, beside the numeral nine, were the words EQUIS MINI.

And Tug no doubt again felt stupid for having blown all his cash.

Though of course there was also the thought any gambler could think: Nothing's for sure anyway.

And Tug said, "He'll probably get his ass kicked."

"I kind of doubt that," I said.

So Tug then went ahead and did it despite his better judgment, skimmed over Equis Mini's past performances.

"Look at the results of his last real race," he told me. "He got killed. Twenty-plus lengths behind the pack the whole way."

"That was a year ago," I said.

"Which means today he's rusty."

"You just saw him fly in that secret sprint, Tug. Which is not listed here as a workout. Which means it's still more or less secret. Which means his odds will probably stay high."

"You think so, huh," he said.

And I hunched myself up to pull cash from a back pocket, a

wad rolled tightly and secured by one of those black elastic bands he'd seen me use when I washed my face.

"Where'd you get all that," he said.

"Fishin'."

"I thought that muskie money went to your mom."

"It did. She gave it to me when your dad went AWOL. She was scared she'd disappear, too."

I pulled off the hair band, uncoiled the bills, the top one a ratty hundred.

"Why would *she* have disappeared?" Tug asked.

I held the cash against my chest. "Why does anyone?"

And I knew this could be taken as referring to my possibly moving back to Arkansas, though I still suspected Tug figured I'd left Pine Bluff because of all the rumors there about me. Then I realized Tug might have taken it as referring instead to his father's death, which obviously needed to take precedence over anything else, and for a while right then, both Tug and I just sat. If we could just keep being this honest with each other, I thought during this silence, we could probably make this work.

*Lovewise,* I then thought.

And then the unsaddled entries for the ninth began trudging from the backside toward us, single file along the rail so each could get tacked up in the paddock, and there, maybe fifth or sixth in line, was Equis Mini, too sharp to wear a blanket, shiny but not at all from sweat, nimble, proud, on his toes about as much as a thoroughbred could be. And now there was no doubt I was holding my head that tiny bit off center, because I was taken more by Equis Mini now than I'd been when I'd ridden him, like he was some son of mine I'd stay proud of regardless of wherever his running days would take him.

And I glanced at the odds board, then said, "Forty-five to one."

"Those odds'll drop," Tug said.

"Not if that sprint stays secret," I said.

"But like you said, Jan: Gambling is stupid."

"For you."

"What does that mean?"

And I said, "You and you only are your father's son, Tug."

"Yours didn't die and leave things messed up also?"

"Of course he did. But he didn't mess up my head."

Tug tried not to smile right then. And he said, "You sure about that?"

"Uh-huh," I said. "The man killed himself, Tug. I accept that. I flat-out forgave him for that in that church in Saratoga, so I'm good with him."

"Fine. Whatever. I mean, I'm glad to hear that, if it's true. But you do realize that this talk of yours about him now is just you rationalizing, right?"

"Rationalizing what?"

"That you want to bet, Jan. But, hey, I understand."

"I don't care about the betting, Tug. I hate the betting. I will always hate the betting. I just love that horse, Tug. I just love that Equis Mini, and I know he's going to win. But you know what the main thing is? The main thing is that this cash right here is my money."

"Actually," Tug said, "it's your mom's."

"Actually, it's your father's. Right?"

"We'll never know that for sure, sister."

"Nor will we ever disprove it."

"Okay, fine," Tug said. "That cash, right there in your hand, probably did come from my father. But does that mean you need to risk even a penny of it on a forty-five-to-one shot—just because he would?"

"I'm not talking about risking a penny of it."

"Then what are you talking about?"

"If I bet a hundred on Equis Mini to win," I said, "and he goes off at forty-five to one, I can buy him. He's a three-thousand-dollar claimer, Tug. He could be ours—living on your farm—for three grand. With cash for feed and vet bills to spare."

"Yes, but you yourself said my farm needs a barn. Who's gonna pay for that?"

"Then I'll bet three hundred. And we'll have enough for lumber for a barn *and* a new fence—and for labor to make sure it's all perfect."

"You have three hundred bucks there?"

I nodded. And it was fun, being able to nod like that.

"Anyhow, I need to get a job," Tug said. "This whole horse farm idea: It really was just a stupid kid's dream. An actual, legitimate horse farm owner needs backup cash for when times go lean—"

"But I know Equis Mini, Tug. I know him like probably no human being in this grandstand knows him. And Tug? That horse simply loves the act of running."

"Jan—"

"And I know he could get bumped coming out of that gate and have zero chance. But I also know he can break in full stride easily. And if he gets out in front alone, Tug?"

And it was now, all these days and years after the deaths of Tug's father and mine, that tears finally came from me in Tug's presence, two of them falling fast, plenty more gathered in wait.

"If he gets out there alone, Tug?" I managed to say. "They simply won't be able to catch him."

And it was maybe my tears right then that had Tug lost for words. Why did everyone we loved end up making us sad? The early evening sun had us both marigold orange, as it did the infield and the homestretch and every grandstander, and it was in this orange light that it must have struck Tug that, yes, if his father's efforts as a gambler had ever brought the Corcoran family inside information worth betting a pile on, Equis Mini today, at forty-five to one, was it.

# 67

# DEESH

"SO I GUESS," GERELLI SAYS, "I do feel obligated to make it clear to you that, in my professional opinion, we should probably consider other options."

"What are you saying?"

"I'm saying you should consider making a deal with the prosecutors, Mr. Sharp. I think I can get you a life sentence in New York to keep you off death row in Pennsylvania."

"But I'm not guilty, man!"

"I'm saying even so."

"But a *suicide*," I say, and the need to swallow quiets me, barraged as I am by thoughts about what I'd say to Bark if somehow given the chance. "I mean, an expert . . . a forensics expert could tell that Gabe shot himself, right?"

"And another could say Gabe didn't. We don't want to rely

on bullshit games like that, Mr. Sharp. As you can probably imagine."

Fuck, I think. Fuck everyone.

"Mr. Sharp, three of your actual peers—your two pals and a woman who loves you—think you're a killer. A jury would be comprised of *theoretical* peers."

"Yes, but one of my pals knows for a fact that I'm innocent."

"Yet that's not how it appears. Remember, Mr. Sharp, we're not talking about truth here; we're talking about *legal* truth—which, for you, when you get down to it, is defined as whatever your jury will believe. And in Pennsylvania, as you might well imagine, a person or two on any jury—regardless of how carefully we screen—might happen to hate you on sight."

Then we both do nothing but sit facing each other, not even blinking.

"Well, that's true," I say.

"Unfortunately," he says, and for a while there, rather than thinking about Pennsylvania, I think about the pigeon-toed sister whose phone call to Bark started this whole business with that drum in the first place.

About how she probably made that call as a favor she owed to the mob because she'd messed herself up by tricking or using.

About how I, sitting here, assume she tricked or used because, after all, she was black.

And I'm pissed at this.

I'm pissed at how my own blackness made me so confident in judging her.

Finally I say, "So at least we agree I have a color problem."

And Gerelli shrugs at this, sour-faced.

"Mostly, Mr. Sharp?" he says. "You have a belief problem."

And it's now clear to me that he's long ago convinced himself that, unless someone out of nowhere takes up my cause, I can't possibly win.

And that if a guy like me fears he was born to lose, he should stick himself behind four walls that will never let him run anywhere.

# 68

## JAN

**THEN THE BUGLE SOUNDED**, and out came the post parade, Equis Mini now officially wearing the nine, diminutive, yes, but on his toes, sort of bouncing on them. I pulled myself together as the apprentice on him murmured into his ear, and then there I went, up and off and away, certainly gone from Tug, probably, as Tug saw things then, to bet three hundred though he could still hope not, with there now also being that speck of chance that I, like anyone, could soon prove to have left him as permanently as his father had. He avoided thinking like this by admiring Equis Mini, then finally stopped admiring Equis Mini to check Equis Mini's odds, which, right then, bumped up to fifty to one, which would mean I'd clear $15,000 if I bet three hundred—and if Equis Mini won.

And then there were eight minutes to post, a rather long time for any gambler, inveterate or not. And for the first few minutes of those eight, Tug no doubt considered me impetuous and foolish in my desire to bet. Maybe he figured that for me today—after everything I'd been through this summer and in my life—impetuosity and foolishness were virtues of sorts, and maybe he knew, for certain now, that he would always love me. Maybe he imagined me on a line behind numerous eager gamblers, probably all male, some twitching here and there, most of them compulsive, probably one or two he knew shallowly, and he probably wondered how I would decide how much to risk—and if I was considering hedges like place or show or going across the board, and whether I'd grow tempted to try something greedy, like an exacta.

If she isn't greedy, he probably thought, she'll bet simply to win, then never bet again.

And if she wins, he might have promised himself, we'll never again sit in this grandstand.

Then it was only two minutes to post, and I was still gone, and, if I knew Tug, he seized up like his father had when people kept the Corcoran family from a wager on yet another sure thing, and then he alone, Tug, sweated a hot swath down his back and well up into his scalp. He'd told me nights earlier that he considered this quick sweating a symptom of mourning, but now, in the grandstand, this was no way to mourn, not when a guy might also grow faint, and maybe he would've left the track for good right then if it hadn't been for my absence.

And absence, I realized then, means nearly nothing if you've never loved whoever is absent, whether they're someone from your past or from a future you've conceived. And for Tug right then, I knew, Tom Corcoran would always be absent, powerfully absent, but for me right then, as I waited in line to place that bet, the most powerfully absent person was Tug.

And then a TV monitor overhead told me it was post time, and behind the starting gate beyond the pond stood Equis Mini, well back of every horse except the ten and the eleven, dwarfed even by the teal saddlecloth worn by every nine, and an assistant starter was loading the four, a roan muscle freak who glowed in that blood-orange sunlight. And I was still waiting to bet, and Tug hadn't told me to seek out the shortest line, and I'm sure Tug remembered the countless times his father had cursed crudely while some chump at the front of a line delayed progress by rereading a *Form*, and for Tug and I both right then—for our future—time was now passing too quickly, because things just kept happening as if they were out of control, as if there had never been a way we could stop them, and then a hand grabbed Equis Mini's bridle, leading him, and the teal number-nine saddlecloth slipped from sight as he entered the gate, and the ten walked in without delay, as did the eleven, dammit, and the flag was up, and they were off.

And no one near Tug cheered or stood, but this was race nine, the last of the day, most grandstanders silenced by losses of their own, losses of cash and sanity and respect, losses of the aspiration any day's first few races bring, losses of children and siblings and parents and spouses and youth and the brightness of this sun be-fore its orange hue had collected them, and now here I was, my legs maybe more splendid to Tug on those patched concrete stairs, standing still, out in the aisle, poker-faced, maybe uncommonly pretty in that way he sometimes found me, green blue eyes aimed well beyond him to decipher if Equis Mini had indeed broken well. And on the backstretch there did appear to be only one entry out in front, its saddlecloth the teal of the nine reddened by that sunshine—or were we seeing the purple of the eleven?—and I drew close and said, "That's him, Tug. That's him. He's out there."

"Did you get it in?" Tug asked.

I handed him a tote ticket, and there, on that square of thin white paper, was this:

**$1,100 Win #9**

"Jan, this says you bet eleven hundred dollars to win."

"Correct," I said.

"Why did you—"

"We want him and the farm forever, Tug. And he's three lengths ahead. And the next horse is a length ahead of the rest."

"He's flying. He's going too fast."

"No, he's not, Tug. This is what we wanted."

"Jan, don't get excited."

"Tug, he's out in front."

"I know. I see it."

I had him by the wrist now. "Tug, he's out there," I said. "He looks comfortable. He looks like he's not even trying."

"Did the jock even ask him?"

"Don't ask him, jock. Don't ask him!"

"Just let him run. Just let him enjoy taking that turn."

"Don't even show him the whip—Tug, he's ahead by five."

And no one in the grandstand was cheering. There was one scream down near the finish line, an incredulous, touristy shriek, but that was it, because, as the odds board attested, Equis Mini had gone off at sixty to one, and now here he was, halfway down the homestretch, still unwhipped, his elongated shadow a good seven lengths behind him, the closest contender a length behind the shadow itself.

"We're gonna do it, Tug," I said. "We're gonna do it."

And that little colt of ours ran on boyishly, without a single glance over at us, as game out there, above that familiar dirt, as any soul we'd known.

And as he crossed under the wire, neither Tug nor I shouted or screamed or made a sound.

Tug, though, stood beside me with his arms raised over his head, a well-pronounced fist still on each, as if, I thought, trying to cajole fist bumps from both of our fathers. He stood like that watching Equis Mini continue to run well past the finish, as if he, like I, feared for Equis Mini's physical safety, and then he kept right on standing like that. Maybe, I thought, he was thanking his father's spirit for having arranged this miraculous coincidence, and then, as if finally realizing he'd been drawing attention to himself, he lowered his arms and sat back down and nodded and winked at me.

"This is huge," he said, and he grinned. "Do you realize how much you won?"

I wouldn't look over, trying as I was to read the odds board.

But I did say: "We."

"Pardon?" Tug asked.

"We won, Tug."

"No," he said. "You. You were the one with the guts to put down the eleven hundred."

And for a white-hot while then, I couldn't think. Or maybe it was just that my mind couldn't choose now that it swam inside its own suddenly privileged new wealth of good thoughts.

When I could finally speak, I said, "Still. I want it to be *us*, Tug. Us. I want Equis Mini to be *ours*. But the money—I can't imagine. I really, really just can't. This isn't like anything else, Tug—you know what I mean?"

"Sixty grand plus," he said. "You could walk it right down to that winner's circle," he said, "and buy him with just a fraction. If they won't sell for three thousand, you can offer four. Or five. Or, hell, whatever the fuck they want."

I handed him the ticket. "Can you go?" I asked. "I mean, do you mind? I want to see how he looks in the winner's circle. I want to see if he likes it."

"You might see me down there buying him," Tug said, and he was grinning more impishly than he had all summer, and now I wanted to go with him but he was already off with the ticket in hand, bounding up the grandstand's concrete stairs, and I told myself it was better this way. I had no idea how I'd react with cash like that in my hands—who knew *what* I might do—it was out of this world, really, everything that was happening—I couldn't believe it.

And then I could believe it, but hardly. Maybe belief was difficult because I'd never had luck like this, the kind people in love had and shared with each other, the most excellent kind, I thought. Anyway I liked how it felt to have so much. Luck scared me and made me feel like a stranger to myself, but, really, I really did like it.

And I liked watching Equis Mini run on, how he kept going even though the race was getting to be long past over, how he resisted the reins and the jock's command to take it easy, how he must not have wanted this run (ahead of so many bigger, professionally trained horses) to end, must now have been trying to savor that feeling of having burst from the get-go into the lead, of knowing so soon that everyone who cared had to admit that he was the very best. And I liked how he obviously wanted to go around again, in order to feel more of that caring. To him, I believed, crossing under that wire would now always mean this pleasurable business of being patted and petted and lovingly kissed and talked to. And Tug, being his father's son, would know how to handle getting the cash, would then know how best to first approach the trainer and owner, so all I needed to do was keep watching Equis Mini cool down; if I just kept doing that, I believed, Tug and I—and Equis Mini!—would all see one another soon.

So that's what I did: kept watching. And then, with no apparent prompt from his jock, Equis Mini downshifted into a canter, his tendons intact, I hoped, and then, after he again made the bend around the far turn, I watched him ease into a loping walk toward the finish. He was a beautiful horse, truly. There was beauty in his smallness. And I could see this beauty all the way from the rusted blue steel grandstand, could see it better here than when I had ridden him in my sprint, and any grandstander who hadn't left his seat for the day could now certainly see it, too. And I remembered the feeling Equis Mini had given me as we'd won that sprint, that sense of actual physical flight he lent, the notion of escape but mostly of running *with*. And now here he was, again evoking that voice in my head, the one I'd considered my father's back then, the same voice now saying to me, *You did keep on; I'm proud, and I'm still with you*—and now he, Equis Mini, would be mine to share with Tug, and maybe, if he ate well tomorrow and struck us as eager a month later, we'd consider letting him race here again.

And in case my father's spirit was now actually—in real truth—with me, I let myself whisper, *"Thank you."*

And the jock patted Equis Mini's withers as they entered the winner's circle, where, finally, without command, Equis Mini stopped completely, wanting to nod, it seemed, but keeping within rein, letting his tongue hang out the left side of his mouth—playfully, I hoped—and all around him were handshakes and smiles and pats on backs and hugs and pumped fists and the raising of fingers done by proud men when victory finds them. Maybe they won't sell, I thought, but I was too happy to worry, and I was all the happier now because Equis Mini was in his element, nodding as freely as he was then and there, engaging as he did in a tossing around of his head I'd never quite seen a horse of any breed try, a sort of dance done by everything above his shoulders while the rest of him remained beneath the jock and within the jock's command to keep still. And I wished Tug could see Equis Mini dance like this, wished I had gone with Tug so Tug and I and Equis Mini could all the sooner dance like this together.

But this way I'd gotten to watch Equis Mini run beyond the finish eagerly as any, and now that I'd seen this, I thought, I could talk about it with Tug. That was the way it was and was always supposed to be, all three of us winning and sharing victory's good results, sometimes all together, sometimes not but with one watching another and soon telling the one who'd been gone, and we were good at that, Tug and I: We were good at talking and listening.

And I was still happy now but already missing Tug. And I wondered: Was I becoming a sap this way—was I becoming a *sap*? No, this was no sap. This was natural. This was just the process of love, just two peoples' love becoming one and the same. It happened all the time. Love like this was no privilege. I was privileged to have been fathered by a jock, and Tug had been privileged to have had a father who'd jocked, too, much as Tug and I both had sometimes privately cussed our fates for having been intertwined with gambling, and Tug and I and our mothers and Jasper and everyone at that secret sprint past Geneseo had been privileged to witness Equis Mini's speed, and now fewer people than that, far fewer, had been privileged to bet their life's savings on that same speed at sixty to one, so there was *some* privilege. There was, and there would always be, some unfair privilege, if only a little. And now I had to admit that, yes, I, like those upper-crust folks I had long envied and resented, had benefited from privilege, but still: When it came to love itself? Love itself had nothing to do with privilege.

Love, the more I thought about it, was the opposite of privilege. And then I thought: Come on, Tug. Let's go buy us a horse!

But Tug didn't appear then or anytime soon, probably, I thought then, because collecting winnings this sizeable took a decent amount of time. I had heard men on the backside whine about IRS windows, and I had seen an IRS window when I'd made this very bet, three lines over with no one but a teller at it, which must have meant IRS windows existed for cashing in huge tickets only. And if the IRS needed some of these winnings, there were probably papers to sign, and I was fine with that; I was fine with the IRS; I was fine with sharing a few dollars, even if politicians would then kick some of those dollars back to their wealthy friends; I wanted only Tug and Equis Mini and the horse farm as well as just a few remnants of this happiness I felt now. I didn't want to worry about the IRS.

And now the handshakes and hugs and dances in the winner's circle were over, a stable hand now removing Equis Mini's saddle, the proud men inside forming a line so each could follow the next out, Equis Mini then led out, too, the stable hand guiding him back onto the track, then walking him slowly enough to allow him the slight nods caused by the steps he took. And I thought: Okay, Little One. Talk to you in your stall. And I watched him complete the clubhouse turn and leave the track for the backside, and when he was gone from sight I missed Tug all the more, to the point of impatience. I told myself that this meant maybe something was wrong, wondered if impatience could live in me if there really was true love between me and Tug. Shouldn't I, ideally, trust that he was doing his best to return?

And the longer this question bothered me, the harder it was to wait, because, dammit, I just wanted to be with Tug. I considered going to look for him but then remembered his father's old rule for Tug when Tug was a kid, the one about there needing to be a stay putter, and, with this rule in mind, I sat still longer and waited.

And it was this rule of Tom Corcoran's that caused me to stay put for what seemed to be well more than half an hour.

Tug's back there making the deal, I then thought. He's got to be.

And then I stayed put yet another half an hour beyond the first, and I knew so because the odds board said so.

And then, after gazing at the trees well beyond the odds board and even beyond the backside, I stood.

I wished I could run down to the ground level and out onto the concrete apron and hop the chain-link to take a shortcut across the homestretch and the infield, and maybe, with the track now fairly empty of patrons and workers and security, I could get away with this, especially if I jogged, but I thought: No.

You're an owner now.

Act like one.

And I walked up the concrete stairs that led out of the grandstand, past the betting windows now abandoned by bettors and tellers, the IRS window abandoned, too, and then I took the escalator down, walking quickly down it as I did.

And I walked quickly to the turnstiles as well, then past them, The *Form* Monger, of course, gone, pretty much everyone gone. Only the pockmarked guy who sold beer at the burger stand was there, just now getting into a rusted old Chevy parked several spots away from the familiar Corcoran family pickup, and the sight of the pickup assured me Tug was indeed on the backside, that, no, he had *not* taken my sixty-plus grand in winnings and skipped town, and my confidence in Tug as well as my humoring myself for having ever let a worry like that cross my mind helped me walk as gracefully as a young woman could along this unkempt side of the old steel blue grandstand. I was on the wide asphalt lane that hugged the far out- side of the clubhouse turn, headed for the backside, following Tug's recent footsteps, I was sure. And I again thought about jogging, but again thought no. Tug wouldn't have gone to the backside alone if it hadn't been for the best. Maybe he'd figured that, without me with him, he'd save us money on Equis Mini's haggled-over price, what with how obviously fond I was of Equis Mini and all that.

And again, I trusted Tug as I walked. If nothing else, I believed he was smart.

But when I reached the backside, I went up and down all the shedrows twice, but there was no sign of him. Worse, I came upon Equis Mini being given a hose bath by a hand in shade thrown by an oak, and I asked this hand if he'd seen Tug, and this hand shrugged, then ignored me more coldly than the hose water must have felt, making it clear he was resolved not to talk to me anytime soon. And Equis Mini wouldn't look over at me; he just kept shifting his weight from both left hoofs to his right, and trying to chomp the hose and letting his tail swat at a stubborn twitch in his hide. And then, after I left Equis Mini to keep asking around about Tug, I saw Arnie DeShields near the shedrow fifty feet away—not his own barn, curiously—at least as far as I knew—and he, too, ignored me and quickly ducked back inside, and then, when I stepped inside, neither Arnie nor Tug were anywhere, as if they had left through some back door or were hiding crouched in the feed bin, and no one in that barn would answer my questions about them. It was as if somehow neither Tug nor Arnie had been there all day, or they both had and no one wanted to think about that, let alone talk.

But this reticence wasn't like the one I'd endured there the day after Tom Corcoran had disappeared. This was something new, with its own kind of opaque sheen. Certainly it made me more queasy than the one about Tom had. Were the barn hands here today quiet because they knew I'd slept with Tug? But how would they have known—unless Tug had told them? And why would Tug have said anything about *that*? Why on earth? And if for some reason he had, what would this mean about his deepest true feelings for me?

Then all I could think was: Go home. I knew the Corcorans' house wasn't my home, never had been, really, but for me it now served as the next closest thing, and I felt compelled to be there. Tug could be sitting in the kitchen, or, at the very worst, napping on the couch. Maybe he was hiding the sixty grand in some cranny up in his room?

But even as I imagined Tug doing these things, I didn't feel good. I did *not*. If Tug had been worried when his father had told him he'd worried too much, I now had to admit that I, alone here on the backside, was worried, too.

And all I could do now to fight this worry was run, so then there I was, doing it, more or less jogging across the backside's gravel parking lot. And it wasn't long before, over the railroad ties, I was running undeniably. Again the ties challenged me but I didn't care; I tripped and fell once but kept on. And then, just after the first prick of perspiration through my scalp, it occurred to me that, now, this time, this evening, with today's sun still not quite gone from sight, the longer I ran the more I worried, to the point that it now seemed possible everything would turn out opposite of the way things were supposed to be. Tug and I, I realized, were supposed to be together. He, the responsible Corcoran, was supposed to return. And Equis Mini was meant to be ours to bathe, not some stupid, tongue-tied barn hand's.

And now I found my legs accelerating, maybe because worry was fueling me. I was acting like a Corcoran whether I'd end up being one or not: They, the Corcorans, had all been worriers, all of them second-guessers, too, but primarily worriers, with nothing ever right in their minds, and nothing good ever trusted in as being able to remain good. They were wrong. They were wrong. The Corcorans were wrong about that, but they were also just plain wrong in what they did, and in how they conducted themselves. After all, they argued. They argued a heck of a lot. And held grudges. They kept secrets and pursued familyhood in a business that thrived on greed. They treated love as if it were some privilege you needed to earn, or at least Tom and Colleen had.

And what about Tug, anyway?

Could he really love?

On the other hand, could he really have first assessed me as nervously as he had and not been as bonkers about me as I'd been about him? Could eyes as spontaneous as his lie? Could kisses like that? And the way he touched me, and the way he'd kept me awake talking long after he'd made sure I finished. What kind of guy *did* that? Who on earth did that with a woman like me unless there was out-and-out love?

But what I was really trying to ask myself was: Could he really have taken my winnings and run? Could he really, really have played me? I was now jogging so fast I wished he *had* taken my winnings, all sixty-plus thousand, and driven the pickup so far I could never find him, because that would have been easier, that would have been cake compared with what I feared now, and, yes, fear could be bad; fear nearly always *was* bad; no human body should ever need to fear, but sometimes there came the kind of fear animals felt, the necessary kind, the honest kind, the kind that's akin to survival, the kind that makes bees sting and hummingbirds quit humming to zip off into woods, the kind that makes fish, of any size, know when not to bite and instead dart and zigzag toward depth. And it was this kind of fear, my legs now told me, that I, Janette Price, the daughter of the renowned jockey Jamie Price, had inside of me, inside my legs certainly but also now up into the rest of me including my mind and soul and whatever else I was made of, maybe even inside any bits of Tug still carried by me, at least inside any cells of his skin still beneath my fingernails from when I'd squeezed his shoulders, back when his coming had made me come, too.

And when I reached the hedge of milkweeds, I wanted to sprint to the house as I always had, but such a sprint was pointless—because if he was now in the house, he wouldn't need me, not as direly as he might if he was where this fear in me sensed he was. And now, here, undeniably on the Corcorans' lawn, I took the right onto the trail he and his father had blazed, the narrow one into the woods, my shins and ankles tearing through the thickened berry canes, my feet dodging the fattest roots, and I didn't want to keep going but then there I was, needing only to duck under a birch log he'd probably cut, and then I was on the inside, letting go of the birch fence and sprinting again, this time over the horse farm, over turf that, dammit, was supposed to be his and mine, wanting to stop on it, needing to cross it, and after I cleared the August-narrowed creek, I was puffing all out, headed toward, yes, a forty-gallon drum, just as I had so many times back in June, except, face it, this wasn't that drum; this drum was orange, the same orange as that but this one rust-free, this one, you could say, Tug's and Tug's only, and everyone at the track knew why Tug had bought it and shown it around. And of course I knew why he'd made that move, too; I knew all about how assertion worked among men whether they gambled or not. And I now guessed what was inside this orange drum of Tug's, and now it was at most ten feet away, now fewer than four, and I hated how knowledge married you but forced you to keep running, and then I was up against it, this newer, rustproofed drum, my fingers needing to squeeze its rim to keep the rest of me up, because, yes, my fingers were fine and strong and not in the least trampled upon, but breathing was the problem, mine and his, he being this brand-new Tug now just beyond my fingertips, his eyes bulged and tongue swollen horrifically like his father's had been, and it was clear to me that this strangulation—this one smack in front of me now—was done by the same goons who'd strangled Tom Corcoran, maybe wiseguys connected to The Nickster, and now that this truth was obvious to me, the rush of thoughts flying through me like a herd scared by thunder included one of the last things Tug had told me: "If this Douglas Sharp is innocent, we both probably owe him an apology."

And I couldn't hide now from how I needed to make that apology on my own, how I alone needed to remind anyone who'd listen that accusation doesn't mean guilt, how one of Tug's last thoughts must have been that he was leaving a world where enmity was an odds-on favorite to defeat truth.

Because one glance at Tug assured me there'd be no saving his life, since those goons had not only used wire on his neck just like they had on Tom's, they'd also obviously snapped his spine while stuffing him completely in. He was a mess is what I'm saying—at first all I recognized were his lips and the uneven wear of the heels of his shoes—and what made the shock of it worse was I still felt this need to know if there was hope, if there was anything I, as the first one to find him, needed to do without pause. There was, when I saw his neck, this flash of compulsion in me to see if the wire had severed more than just skin, but I couldn't look inside him like that, not in my state then—I could barely get myself to reach toward him. But when I did I took hold of a hand and pulled, as if I had the strength to yank him all the way out and straighten him into standing again on that meadow. The fingers in mine felt cool and limp and careless all the way into the meat of his palm, and it was probably then that I stopped kidding myself about my belief that departed souls speak through starlight—I mean, it was hitting me squarely that everyone knows any star's light was sparked into being centuries ago, that maybe everything good I'd believed about my father had been lies piled up to protect me.

Even so, I kept holding Tug's hand and pulling, and something in me, the lover, I guess, must have kept clinging to the chance that your heart can stop beating yet your ears and brain can still work, because then there I was, whispering out loud, actually trying to communicate, but I screwed that up, too, since all I could manage was one word, and that word was *"Baby."* And just after I said it I remembered him asking me never to call him that, so then there I was, wishing he'd been dead and gone long enough not to have minded, which then had me cussing myself out, meanly, almost viciously, using words adopted by pretty much only the most callous of gamblers—probably because there was no way I was set to say anything like good-bye.

# Epilogue

"TEN MINUTES," the guard said, and now here was Jasir, quickly stepping inside this small bright space yet just as quickly gone still, well held together across the table from his father.

And here were those same skinny arms of Jasir's, not folded like they'd been on that sidewalk in Brooklyn, no longer protecting him as they had then, just poised in wait at his sides, his back parallel to the door, his right hand behind him even after the door had clicked shut, his left adjusting his purple baseball cap, which was too big on him anyway.

"That woman who just left—she your attorney?" he asked.

"She's an angel," Deesh said.

Jasir nodded. "I got eyes, man," he said. "I could see she was fine."

"Not what I'm saying. She just came here to help. I mean, help get me the hell out of here."

"Really."

"Uh-huh."

"How?"

"Gonna testify that no way did I kill the jockey. 'Cause the killer offed another dude while I was in here."

And Jasir loosened up enough to move his arms, but only to set his hands on his hips, wrists now flexed but again gone still, as if he needed to steel himself to reconsider his prospects as Deesh's son.

Finally, he said, "You need more angels than her."

"No doubt, man," Deesh said. "But it's a start. You know how it goes, man: People scared, but as soon as they see it's cool to step forward, they start stepping forward so much they form a line."

Jasir kept on standing, still like that.

"And then a crowd," Deesh said.

"Yeah, but on TV they're saying you're set to plead guilty to keep your ass off death row."

Deesh sighed with his cheeks puffed out, now sure, with no more thought needed, that he would definitely plead innocent until the day he took his last breath—and he'd keep pleading innocent whether they put him on death row or not.

He asked, "And you're gonna believe them without asking me first?"

And it was here, finally, that Jasir glared angrily, and, worse, he had turned pointedly away from Deesh, facing a corner of the small white ceiling.

"Okay," Deesh said. "Understandable."

And Jasir said nothing, just glared like that.

And while Jasir took his time doing this, letting them both feel the room's smallness and also its unrelenting brightness, Deesh tried to conjure things a father should discuss with a grown son, things like how, yeah, when you finally get down to it, you've got only yourself, so you might as well let yourself be your own best friend. Things like how fishing is just an excuse to miss the coziness of your home, but how, mostly, it's the people you miss, and how after the people are gone, it's the apologies you remember, theirs and yours both, and how maybe, more than anything, you shouldn't be shy about forgiveness. How a room as private as this wasn't a bad place at all for any abandoned son to let loose of his resentments.

And with these things and more at the ready inside him, Deesh said, "I'm sorry, Jasir."

And there were Jasir's fingertips, on his side of the small white table.

"For what?" he said.

"Jasir—"

"Don't call me that. Don't call me that stupid-ass name. Fucking *Courageous* One. That is just bullshit."

And now Jasir was yelling about all sorts of things, starting with his belief that fame as the son of a killer was worse than not knowing who your dad was at all, letting Deesh hear how his words sounded when his harshness burst out. He was yelling at Deesh loud enough that the guard could possibly hear, certainly loud enough that Deesh figured saying he was sorry a second time was pointless and probably even a bad idea, because any brother knew that saying it even once could be damned near impossible, and that hearing it more than once was not what a brother lived for—a brother just wanted to be heard.

So you had to just sit for a while, with your newly grown-up son who was this ticked off. Because sitting with him without saying a thing was gold. It was letting him know you were there to absorb his shit in case he still needed to get more off his chest, and that meant more than pretty words because it said, Yeah, yeah, right, I messed up, but I'm staying here to respect you if nothing else.

And Deesh's sitting like this with this brother who was also his son meant doing what his own father had failed to do. It meant saying, We're it—we're in the same thing, and it was a lot, Deesh thought, like being part of the knot of brothers at the end of a fast break stopped by a hard foul, where there was always then arguing and finger-pointing and cussing and shouting, where every mind focused on whether or not what happened broke the rules, on who initiated contact and who needed to get tough, on who needed to quit being a prick who was just out there trying to knock guys down, on what, really, the latest rules said—but then, Deesh remembered, they would get back to the actual game, with the fouler and the guy who'd taken the hit wordless and back out there, everyone again trying to win to hold the court, again zipping no-look passes on breaks as freakishly as they could, and as they'd run it all melted away—all the anger and hurt, all the shock there was in yet again learning that muscle and bone and ego and skin were far more tender than you'd thought. There was always, Deesh remembered, something uplifting about this resumption of play, about these two wounded brothers having abandoned argument to continue on.

And now, in this room, with Jasir's tirade mellowing, Deesh took heart in how the two wounded brothers could then forge a certain power: how as long as they kept pushing their pace over that sunbaked asphalt, their time together on earth would become more of a life in which only they, these lovers of this game with all of its well-felt dangers, could orchestrate so many unforeseen moves to create the next unstoppable drive.

# Acknowledgments

Grateful acknowledgment is made to Salman Rushdie and Heidi Pitlor for including the opening of Deesh's story in *Best American Short Stories 2008*, and to the editors and staffs of *Antioch Review*, *Virginia Quarterly Review*, and *The Idaho Review* for publishing material elsewhere in this book, and to Bill Henderson for mentioning excerpts in *Pushcart Prize* anthologies, and to Noah Ballard, my agent, for his valor, particularly early on, and his dogged belief, always, and to Liz Stein, my editor at Putnam (and, as far as I'm concerned, the best anywhere), for her stellar talent and kindness and tirelessness. Special thanks to Mitch Wieland and all who nominated excerpts for Pushcart Prizes, and to the Isherwood Foundation for the generous and timely fellowship, and to Ben Fountain, Tim Johnston, Ru Freeman, Christine Sneed, Anne Serling, and

Jonathan Lethem, all of whose camaraderie and expertise inspired me to persist when circumstances grew difficult.

Endless gratitude as well to Rebecca Makkai, Dan Chaon, Alethea Black, Lou Berney, Mark Ebner, Sandy Novack, Clarence Major, Jay Neugeboren, Pam Houston, John Edgar Wideman, Lee Martin, John Dufresne, Wendy Barker, Lynn Petrillo, Jack Smith, Kenneth C. Pellow, Bret Lott, Michael Griffith, Andy Mozina, Lisa Maulhardt, Georgette Dini, Jennifer Daddio, Joe Duraes, Elizabeth McKenzie, Daniel Woodrell, Jennifer Fields-Summer, Pete Peterson, Georges Lederman, Bob Conflitti, jacket designer Eric Fuentecilla, book designer Stephanie Huntwork, and Elizabeth Tallent, and to all of the residents of the town of Lake Peekskill, New York, and to my parents, Ted and Rita, and my siblings, John and Mary and my older brother, the late Dr. Thaddeus Wisniewski, who blazed just about every trail, then overcame immeasurable distance to make miracles involving me visible and commonplace.

Eager thanks to Captain Sean Jones of the New York City Department of Correction for assuring I knew what life's like behind bars on Rikers Island, and to Belmont Park thoroughbred owner Juan Fernandez and trainer Juan Ortiz for letting me hot-walk and feed those powerful, gentle animals, and to Dr. Patrick Thomas as well as Dr. Lars Svensson of the Cleveland Clinic for their enthusiasm and patience in teaching me all about aortic valves and thoracic surgeries, and for their skill in opening me up, repairing my heart, and keeping it beating.

And to my one and only wife, Elizabeth: Thanks for every bit of you, and the v.b. love to you—always.

# About the Author

Mark Wisniewski's widely acclaimed first novel, *Confessions of a Polish Used Car Salesman*, was likened to *Huckleberry Finn* by the *Los Angeles Times*. His work has appeared in *Best American Short Stories*, *The Sun*, *The Virginia Quarterly Review*, *New England Review*, *TriQuarterly*, *The Southern Review*, *The Georgia Review*, and *The Iowa Review*. The winner of a Pushcart Prize, a Tobias Wolff Award, and an Isherwood Fellowship in Fiction, he has taught writing nationwide and, as a book doctor and freelance editor, helped dozens if not hundreds of writers achieve publication. He lives in Manhattan with his wife, Elizabeth, and a gray Persian cat named Vern.